I Blame the Club

JADE EVERHART

Chapter 1

Mo

I hit my alarm before it goes off.

Moving slowly, dark hair slides from my chest as I slip away from the woman lying next to me. She doesn't stir as I grab my smart watch and cellphone from the nightstand before silently creeping toward my walk-in closet. Gently closing the door, I quickly change and grab my gym bag from one of the many racks lining the spacious closet.

Perfume lingers in my bedroom as I exit, the woman's sleeping form undisturbed and sprawled across my California king bed. I wouldn't have thought a woman that small could take up that much space, but Stephanie had proven me wrong multiple times last night.

God, I hate cuddlers.

I snag a protein bar from a bowl on my kitchen counter before leaving my apartment and taking the elevator down to the gym on the first floor. I chose this location specifically because of the fully equipped weight room conveniently located within the apartment building.

When I enter, there is only one other person lingering around the weight room, an attractive woman I recognize from other morning sessions. The 5AM regulars are few and far between, so we tend to see a lot of each other. The redhead gives me a nod of recognition before returning her attention to the squat rack.

I give her ass an appreciative glance as I walk by, the thin material of her shorts doing nothing to hide the sweat stain forming between her cheeks. If we didn't live in the same building, I would consider making a move.

Stopping at the pull-up bar, I drop my bag and grab my gym log to check how much weight to use today. There's no point in hitting the gym if you plan on lifting the same weight as last time. As my father would say, the only way to change yourself is to to challenge yourself.

So, either start the challenge or get the hell out of the gym.

Two hours later, the whirl of my blender finally awakens the sleeping beauty.

"I was wondering where you had disappeared to." A small body presses against my back as I carefully pour my protein shake into a to-go mug.

"I'm surprised you noticed I was gone."

I'm only half-focused on the conversation, my mind already running through the tasks I need to complete today.

"Mm, I was hoping for another round this morning." Stephanie runs her hands along my chest, clearly hoping to trigger some sort of a reaction.

"Afraid I'm on a tight schedule today. Maybe next time."

There won't be a next time. Her BJ skills were adequate but not worth the bed-hogging.

She pouts, "Will you at least stay for breakfast?"

"No. I need to shower and then head to the office."

Her face brightens, "Sounds like an invitation."

"It's not."

The teasing smile falls from Stephanie's face and an annoyed line pinches her brows together, "So, that's it then? I should just pack up and leave?"

I reach around her and grab my drink.

"Your Uber is already on the way. You have ten minutes to get dressed."

I take a sip of my shake to hide the irritation on my face. I thought Stephanie understood the rules when she came over last night.

She huffs, "God, you really are a dick."

"You didn't have any complaints last night."

This is the part I hate. You set up a mutually beneficial arrangement, a one-time sexual transaction, and suddenly you're the bad guy for sticking to the original plan.

"Yeah, well, I was faking it."

I knew Stephanie was on the younger side, but I didn't expect her to be this immature. Her phone number is getting blocked the second she walks out my front door.

"Is that right?" I lean in, closing the distance between us. She licks her lips, her eyes dropping to my mouth.

As if I would want to kiss a child.

"If I remember correctly, you screamed my name no less than five times last night. Which happens to be the same number of orgasms I gave you." Her face flushes but I continue before she can respond, "I'm sure the DNA you left on my bed could attest to that fact. So, unless you are willing to be sued for slander, I suggest you make yourself presentable and leave this apartment before I get out of the shower."

Anger flashes in her eyes, but she keeps her mouth shut.

I force my lips into a smile, "Last night was fun, but that's all it was. Feel free to take a protein bar on your way out."

Turning on my heel, I walk from the kitchen without giving her a second glance.

Nico

I've almost made it out the door when he wakes up.

"Going somewhere?" My steps halt and I snatch my hand away from the door handle.

Damn it. Freedom had been so close.

"I was just going to get breakfast." I wince as the lie slips out of my mouth.

Glancing over my shoulder, I see Dhillon sit up in bed, the sheets tumbling down his naked waist. I fight back a shudder when my eyes drop to the dark mass of hair covering every inch of his chest. Drunk me must have wanted an ape to play with.

"You were taking your backpack to get breakfast?"

I nod, pasting a bright smile on my face, "Better to be prepared than not prepared."

"Uh-huh." Dhillon studies me for a moment, his Mediterranean complexion almost making up for the lack of manscaping. The thick hair was not just on his chest, let me tell you.

"Give me two minutes to get dressed and I'll join you."

"I don't mind going by myself." I inch closer to the door, hoping I can make a break for it before the gorilla puts some pants on.

"I have a feeling I won't ever see you again if I let you go by yourself." Dhillon grins at me, and I curse my drunken self for choosing a smart one.

"You got me. I don't like to overstay my welcome."

He goes to swing his legs out of bed, but I hold up a hand to stop him.

"Look, I had a really great time last night, but I don't see this going anywhere." Honestly, I can barely see anything from all the hair assaulting my vision.

He frowns, "I thought we were going to get to know each other."

God, I hate this part. You have a drunken, unmemorable one-night stand, and suddenly you're the bad guy for hightailing it out.

"We got to know each other multiple times last night."

"So, that's it then? You're just going to leave?"

I do my best to look disappointed, "It was great, Dhillon. But now I have to go."

Hiking up my backpack, I yank the door open.

"Nico, wait!"

Despite my better judgement, I pause to look back at my drunken hookup.

"My name is Devon."

Taking that as my cue, I bolt out the door.

"How many times do I have to tell you I can't be trusted to make good decisions when I'm drunk?"

I give my best friend the evil eye as I bite into my breakfast sandwich. We are at my favourite coffee house in Taber, a cute mom-pop shop that's only five minutes from the university.

"And how many times do I have to tell you, you are impossible to argue with when drunk?" Wes shrugs, looking annoyingly cheerful this early on a Sunday, "Besides, Devon seemed like a good guy. He bought the whole team a round."

"You knew his name was Devon?"

"You didn't?"

"I could have sworn he told me his name was Dhillon." I take another bite and chew thoughtfully, "Honest mistake. They are pretty much the same."

"You got at least 3 of the same letters."

"Exactly."

Wes laughs, his eyes crinkling at the corners. We've been best friends since second grade, but that doesn't stop me from admiring the man's good looks. It's a good thing I see him as a brother because otherwise the dark hair, green eyes, and dimples would be a seriously dangerous combo.

"Did you have fun at least?"

I shrug, "Same old, same old. Nothing exceptional broke through my drunken haze."

"You know, if you actually allowed emotional attachments to form-

"Just because you're whipped doesn't mean I want to be."

-you might find the sex gets better if you commit to more than one night."

I glare at him, my raging hangover doing nothing to improve my mood.

Wes holds up his hands in surrender, "Just think about it. Wouldn't hurt to shake things up."

"Whatever."

Wes grins, "Are you excited for Monday?"

"Hell yeah." I grin back at him, my moodiness momentarily forgotten.

Our newfound status as co-captains for Taber University's lacrosse team still feels like a dream come true. Our old captain, Cody Ellsworth, stepped down last year to spend more time with his girlfriend, so the responsibility of team captain has fallen to us.

Wes snorts, "I wonder if Mighty Mo has gotten over your failed seduction yet."

I scoff, waving away his comment, "I was barely flirting that night."

"Dude. You offered to service him."

I grin, "Like I said, barely flirting. I'm sure our assistant coach has forgotten all about it by now."

Honestly, I barely remember that night. Everything after the championship dinner is pretty hazy, the endless rounds of tequila shots sufficiently blurring my memories of last year's lacrosse banquet. I vaguely remember approaching our new assistant coach with his delectable physique in mind, but I would be hard pressed to say what went down after that.

Something pokes at my gums, and I drop my breakfast sandwich with a frown.

Wes shoots me a concerned look, "Are you okay?"

Reaching into my mouth, I pull out a strand of thick black hair and stare at it in horror. Wes makes a gagging motion across the table.

"Please tell me that's yours."

My face crumples, "It's Dhillon's."

I throw the offending piece of hair on the table and Wes jumps up, knocking his chair over.

"Don't let it touch me!" He backs up, trying to increase the space between himself and the table, "And his name is Devon, man. Say it with me."

"Fuck that. I'm going to be sick."

Smothering another gag, Wes covers his face with his hands, "I can't even look at it. Please, for the love of God, go floss your teeth."

I cross my arms, glaring at the hair that was trapped between my molars.

"I'm never touching another man again."

My best friend snorts, keeping his distance, "Doubt it. But maybe go for someone with less body hair next time. Or buy a razor to have on hand."

I poke at my breakfast sandwich with disgust, "I hate drunk Nico."

"You know what they say. Don't hate the game, hate the player."

"I *am* the player, you idiot."

Wes grins, "Then maybe it's time you played a different game."

Flipping him off, I abandon my breakfast and follow him out the door. The familiar ache of a hangover has my body feeling bruised and dehydrated, but it's nothing new. My weekly routine is well established by now and suffering Sunday morning is all part of the schedule.

Tequila shots. Tabletop dancing. A man or two to play with. Eat, sleep, repeat.

Despite my recent complaints, I live for being the player. The alcohol, the chase, the fleeting satisfaction of one night. It's a shallow game, but it's the only game I have ever wanted to play.

At least it was until I met him.

Chapter 2

Mo

"That's a terrible idea."

I paste a smile on my face as Steven Andrews, the newest prick at MacNeil Incorporated, shoots down yet another one of my ideas. We are in the main boardroom, half of our team filling the leather seats surrounding the conference table while the rest of them have joined online from our Toronto office.

Steven rambles on, listing all the reasons why our company is better suited to Canadian markets rather American ones. I listen half-heartedly, too amused by Steven's surface-level answers and ill-fitted suit to consider his opposition as any sort of threat.

"...not to mention, we have no idea how to cater to Americans. The investment to do a consumer analysis alone would outweigh any profit we could hope to achieve for at least five to ten years."

He adjusts the red tie hanging from his cheap black suit as if the colour might distract from the fact he's put on at least ten pounds since our last meeting.

It doesn't.

Steven finally sits down, and I let his idiotic words sink in before rising from my own chair. I feel my father's gaze as I walk to the front of the room, but I don't glance in his direction as I plug in my laptop and pull up my presentation.

My father may own the company, but I had to work my way up the corporate ladder like everyone else. Doing physical labour for six months was not the most productive use of my time, but I am grateful for the insight it gave me into our operations and what opportunities lie within them.

Steven, on the other hand, was brought in as a Strategic Development Manager two years ago, and besides challenging my every decision, has yet to make any sort of impact.

Hence why he always leaves these meetings looking like a fool.

"Thank you for your insight, Steven. As you pointed out, there are many risks associated with an international expansion, especially one where we do not know the consumers well." I pause, sweeping my gaze around the room, making eye contact with every team member present.

"However, I took it upon myself to connect with American companies who align with our consumers and products. From there, I reached out to numerous market specialists who walked me through the best strategies in approaching new markets."

I switch my slide with a click of a button, pulling up the data I spent the last two months accumulating.

"Here are the estimates of the net profit these companies are currently making as well as the percentage of consumers that relay back to our own criteria. The state of California alone has a larger population than Canada does as a nation, meaning even if we sold half of what we do here, it would be substantial to anything we could make in Canada."

In my peripheral, I see my father studying the numbers closely.

"But Steven is right, a complete market analysis is a costly investment." I turn and nod at Steven, who smirks back at me. I maintain eye contact, not wanting to miss his reaction.

"So, I ran a rough cost analysis, using our lowest sales month as a predictor for how the market analysis would affect our bottom line." I flick the screen again, not bothering to look at the numbers I memorized last night.

Murmurs go around the room as the numbers pop up on the screen.

"Less than ten percent. On the assumption that we get minimal sales for the first month of our expansion and that our Canadian sector plummets, our bottom line would drop less than ten percent."

Steven's face starts to turn an ugly shade of beetroot as I continue to explain the metrics of offsetting the costs and finish my presentation with a sales forecast on what MacNeil Incorporated could achieve with the expansion.

The room falls silent as I walk back to my seat, everyone's eyes glued to the number of zeros projected on the screen. There's a glint in my father's eye as he stands up, quickly capturing everyone's attention.

"That settles it. Maria, start recruiting candidates for the market analysis, I want some on both sides of the border. Maurice, forward these numbers to Stuart so he can run more tests and lock down realistic predictions. Any questions about the expansion can be sent to Maurice. Meeting adjourned."

Everyone stands up and starts to file out, my co-workers giving me warm smiles as they walk by. Steven sneers as he passes me, his flushed skin tone a perfect match for his hideous tie. I can barely hold back my smirk as he leaves the room.

"You know he does it on purpose."

My father pushes back from his chair and stands up, his strong build showing no signs of weight gain over the years.

"I know. He can't stand the fact I work for my father." I pull my shoulders back as Jonathan approaches, his height a couple inches shorter than mine but not any less intimidating.

"That's why I made sure you earned every position you worked in." Cold blue eyes sweep down my body, looking for an imperfection to critique.

A nod of approval tells me he found none.

"It's good for you to have challenging co-workers. Helps keep you sharp."

"I swear you only keep Steven around to antagonize me."

"I do enjoy your little showdowns, I'll admit." There's a hint of a smile, but it does nothing to soften the coldness in his eyes, "Though it really is for your own benefit. If you don't push yourself-

"You don't change yourself. I know, Jonathan." I cut him off, the motivational pep talks long since ingrained in me.

"Good. Don't forget to send Stuart those numbers." My father turns and heads for the door.

"Oh, and Maurice? Make your intro more concise next time. It felt sloppy."

I grit my teeth as the door swings shut behind him.

"Do you have to leave? Who else is going to carry the team?" Corey, the co-worker I tolerate the most, follows me into the elevator.

"It's only for two weeks. Then I'll be virtual for the next six months. Back in the office by February."

"But who is going to destroy Steven while you're away?"

I chuckle, "You'll have to carry on the tradition for me."

He groans, "Not the same. No one puts that man in his place like you do."

"As long as you do the proper research and collect legitimate data, you'll do just fine."

The elevator dings and we head for the parking garage. Corey sighs, running a hand through his dark hair, "You're kind of a dick ninety percent of the time but I'll miss you."

"Wish I could say the same."

He laughs, "Ouch."

Our steps echo off the pavement as we walk towards our cars, our respective rides side-by-side. I don't consider my co-workers my friends, the fact that their pay checks come from my father is reason enough, but if I were to have a favourite, it would be Corey.

"I will miss watching you try and park every morning." Amusement seeps into my voice as I look at the tiny Honda Civic parked next to my black Cadillac.

"I genuinely don't know how you drive that behemoth. My parking anxiety is bad enough in a car." He shakes his head, stealing a sideways glance at me, "Are you excited about the transition? Most people would say taking time off to be an assistant coach is a step backward career-wise."

I shrug, "It's only temporary and I felt like a change in scenery."

"Couldn't be me. A small town in Southern Alberta sounds way too limiting, never mind a small university town."

"Taber University has its charms. I'll get to see my sister and catch up with some old friends while I'm there."

"Like I said, couldn't be me. Bring me back some corn though, eh?" Corey laughs and slaps me on the back, "Guess I'll see you around, Mo. Take care of yourself."

I smile, "You too."

Corey climbs into his car and I give him one last wave before climbing into mine. As I pull out of my father's office building, I take my first breath of fresh air.

Freedom at last.

Nico

"He's probably uglier than I remember."

Wes is helping me set up the lacrosse nets as we prepare for the first practice of the season. We're officially sophomores, but the 5AM wake-up call still hurts like a bitch.

"I thought we agreed never to speak of Devon again."

Wes lets out a curse as his side of the net falls to the ground. I wander over to give him a hand.

"Oh God, not that man. I'm talking about Mighty Mo." I roll my eyes at the nickname, one that Wes has fangirled over more than once.

The guy was an outstanding forward player. We get it.

Wes grins, "He's big and a douche. Totally your type."

Well, then.

"I don't go for douchebags. Look at Devon."

We both groan at the name, one that resulted in the local grocery store selling out of their floss section.

"Face it, Nico. If there's alcohol in your system, *everyone* is your type."

He's not wrong. Beer goggles are a beautiful thing.

I sigh, "You're right. Let's go check out the new recruits."

A group has formed by the benches lining the field, the tired faces and nervous energy giving away the rookies immediately. Crazy to think that was Wes and me a year ago.

"Welcome to the first practice of the season!" Hyping up the early risers, I let out a whoop of excitement as Wes introduces the newest members.

"André and Preston will be supporting our defensive line this year and Millard will be supporting the forwards." The two defensive men grin at each other while the new forward shuffles his feet nervously.

"Welcome to the Tigers, boys."

One of our teammates steps forward and I do a double take, "Holy shit, Hunter, did you cut your hair?"

Hunter grins, running his hand along his buzz cut, "The new Mrs. didn't like my flow, so I had to change it up."

Thank God someone told him to cut off that mop. It had started giving me nightmares by the end of last semester.

"Looking good, man." Wes nods before turning back to the rest of the team, "Our assistant coach hasn't arrived yet, but why don't we start warm up. Five laps around the field... and go!"

We all take off, the rookies making a point to sprint ahead of everyone else.

"Should we tell them we're doing sprints in today's practice?"

Wes laughs, his easy gait keeping pace with mine, "Nah. Let them burn off some nervous energy. Going too hard during warm-up can be their first lesson."

I grin, "Someone's already feeling his captain status."

"You know it."

We finish our last lap just as someone walks onto the lacrosse field. The rookies already look winded by the time they grab their water bottles and the rest of the team forms a huddle around the newcomer.

"Mo must have arrived." Wes shoots me a look, "Best behaviour, Nico."

"I'm always on my best behaviour."

He gives me a pointed look, "It's too early to seduce him, okay? Save that for later."

Please. Without my trusty beer goggles, I am sure this man is nowhere above...

Holy shit.

Perfectly styled brown hair, piercing blue eyes, broad shoulders, and a body that Greek Gods would envy hits me as I eye-fuck the shit out of our new assistant coach. His athletic t-shirt is thin enough to show muscles that go on for days, and a quick glance at his legs tells me this man believes in equal proportions.

I wonder if *all* of him is equal proportion.

My mouth starts to water as those pale blue eyes lock on mine. Any thought of fooling around immediately vanishes when I see the distaste shining back at me.

Damn it, Wes was right. I do like douchebags.

Tamping down my lust, I give him a big grin and swagger over to where he's standing. Wes is already explaining today's practice when I slide up next to the man I would happily call Zeus in or out of the bedroom.

"Was your ride in okay?" I'm trying to be civil while I drool over his side profile, but the gorgeous man doesn't spare me a glance.

"It was fine. You guys started practice early."

"We started five minutes early. Wes and I were here fifteen before that."

Mo turns towards me, his expression carefully neutral, "I would have been here sooner, but you failed to inform me that practices are half an hour earlier this year."

My grin grows wider, "Did I? Must have slipped my mind."

"I don't appreciate being undermined, Montez. Especially by a captain who thinks it's appropriate to hit on his teammates."

I blink, momentarily speechless by the fact he not only remembered my promiscuous advances but also my name.

I must have been drunker than I remember.

"Babe, I meant no harm by the service comment. Just wanted to test the waters."

He visibly stiffens at my use of the endearment and I can't help but smirk. It's just too easy.

"Don't ever call me that again. Moving forward, I expect professionalism from you and your co-captain, or I will figure out a way to get you both removed from this team."

"Don't worry about me, Coach. Your attitude and overall presence on this lacrosse field has taken you from a ten to a seven, and I'm not one to go for sevens." I throw him a wink,

"As long as that unflattering scowl is on your face, rest assured I won't approach you for anything other than lacrosse drills."

I turn and walk away feeling his glare on my back the entire time.

Feels like a victory to me.

Chapter 3

Mo

Nico Montez is a pain in the ass.

The two-week training camp at the end of August is supposed to be difficult. It's supposed to catch you up on the missed months of training and get you prepped for the season. The fatigue and pain level should be so high, you are crawling from the field by the end of each day, wishing like hell you didn't have to come back and do it all over again the next morning.

And yet, no matter how much endurance the team does, one of the co-captains manages to look fresh as a daisy every time he steps off the field.

It pisses me right off.

"Montez!" Nico looks over at me from his position in goal. I've watched him play these last few days and was surprised to learn he actually has decent talent.

If only he didn't have such a big mouth on him.

"A word, please."

Nodding for a sub to take his place, Nico runs off the field, taking off his helmet as he approaches me.

"Why is it that all the other players out there, including your co-captain, look like they've been giving it their all these last four days while you look like you just took a vacation at the spa."

A growl seeps into my voice and Nico smirks at me, "I must have better stamina than the rest of them."

I glare at him, his dark hair slightly damp from his helmet but nowhere near the drenched state it should be.

"Or maybe you aren't putting in substantial effort."

My accusation only makes his smug smile grow wider.

"I'm sorry, have I not been performing up to your standard?" His gaze trails down my face to my chest, sending a jolt of irritation through me.

"It's not about how you're currently performing it's about how you could be." I can see my father's look of disapproval as I echo the words of my childhood.

"Nah."

I feel my nostrils flare as I force myself not to react, "I'm sorry?"

"Nothing to be sorry for, Maurice. I forgive you."

I take a deep breath and count to three.

"I don't think you understand me."

Nico grins, the dark scruff along his jaw making his teeth look like a set of veneers, "I understand you perfectly. You're pissed that I don't look as tired as the other players and are about to tell me how much of a terrible role model I am for the new recruits."

I narrow my eyes as he continues, "But you see, unlike the diehard players here, I play lacrosse because I enjoy it. I perform to the best of my abilities, but I will not kill myself trying to be the best goalie to ever walk this Earth. That's for people like you and Wes who feel the need to be the best."

He shrugs, "So unless my performance is negatively affecting the team, don't bother with the pep talks."

I'm speechless when he turns and walks away, unable to remember the last time someone spoke to me like that. Even Steven wouldn't dare turn his back on me during an argument.

Glaring at the orange and black jersey swaggering back to his position, I refuse to acknowledge the tanned calves flexing with every step.

Nico's legs are built for running, goddamn it. He should be out chasing the ball, not just standing around a crease.

Let it go.

I suck in a breath, wishing it didn't still smell like Nico's cologne. The spicy scent lingers throughout the next play where Nico manages to save every shot that comes his way.

This is going to be the longest training camp of my life.

"He puts in fifty percent less effort than everyone else but still manages to catch every fucking ball." I spit out the words as I push the barbell above my chest.

Last year's lacrosse captain grins down at me, "Maybe he's just doing it to rile you up. Nico loves making waves."

Cody goes to take the bar as I hit my last rep, but I shake my head and push for five more.

"I don't get riled up." I finally let him re-stack the barbell and sigh, "Normally. But it's bullshit when people don't use their full potential."

Cody watches me silently as I sit up on the bench. Using my shirt to wipe the sweat off my face, I give him a look, "Spit it out, Ellsworth. Your thoughts aren't worth anything unspoken."

"Not everyone was raised like you and Stella." Tilting his head to the side, his spiked blonde ends follow suit, "You're both extremely driven and you love being the best. But not everyone is like that. Some people are happy just hitting their goals and not pushing beyond that."

"Why would anyone be happy with the bare minimum?" I force my brows out of the scowl they seem determined to be stuck in.

Cody laughs, "Everyone has a different minimum, Mo. Some are higher than others, it's impossible to compare."

We switch places and as Cody readies himself under the barbell, I glance around the university gym.

"That's ridiculous."

A familiar sight greets me, the lower floor of Taber's gym exactly how it was back when I was a student. The upper floor is dedicated to cardio machines and fitness courses while the bottom floor is split in two: one side for free-range activities with yoga mats and a climbing cage while the other side makes up the weight room.

Normally, varsity athletes use the high-performance gym, which is where I spent most of my time as a student, but given my friend is no longer a varsity athlete, we are back with the general public in the main one.

Even the desk attendant, the guy with the crazy curly hair and permanent smile looks exactly as I remember.

It's nostalgic in a claustrophobic way.

"Maybe, but that's what makes life interesting." Cody gives me the signal and I help him lift the barbell off the rack, "How's the training camp going otherwise?"

"Fine. Wes has star potential. One of the rookies needs a confidence boast and the others need less confidence. All in all, fine."

"Are you glad to be back?" Cody pants as he pushes the bar back up for his final rep. I smirk at his trembling arms, making no move to take the barbell.

He knows the drill by now.

"I am. Boardroom meetings were getting dull, so the change in pace is welcome."

I watch the bar hover dangerously above Cody's chest, the veins running down his arms bulging impressively. He's about two seconds from breaking, so I relent, reaching down to help him re-stack the bar.

"Asshole."

Watching Cody rub his arms, I smirk, "Just making sure you don't do the bare minimum."

Nico

"He hates me."

Wes doesn't bother looking up from his phone, "Probably."

"Dude. You're supposed to take my side."

He looks up with a grin, "I did. I agreed with you."

"Dick."

Wes blows me a kiss and goes back to texting. I sigh, throwing myself on the patchy dorm couch across from him.

"Quit texting Trip and sympathize with me. Better yet, let's hit the town tonight."

Wes sighs, putting his phone down, "I haven't talked to her all day. What are you moping about now?"

"Our assistant coach. Why does he have to be so attractive?" I groan, grabbing a nearby pillow and covering my face.

"Told you he was your type." He sounds smug but I can't even be mad about it.

"We need to change my type. Let's hit *Lifestyle* tonight."

Southern Alberta is pretty limited in the homosexual department, so we have to make an hour's drive to the nearest city so I can keep my reputation going strong.

When in doubt, hit a gay club. That's my life motto.

"You know, that's not a bad idea." Wes snatches his phone, "It's about the same drive for Trip, so maybe she could meet us there."

"You know what? Why don't you go back to Trip's place after, so you guys can spend the weekend together. I'll cover tomorrow's practice."

Wes pauses his furious texting, "You sure? It's still the first week of training, I don't want to put that pressure on you."

Tossing the pillow back on the coach, I sit up with a smile, "Hell yeah, it'll be great. I'm still on probation from last weekend so I'll stay sober and drive home."

Wes grins, excitement sparkling in his eyes, "You're the best."

"I know."

I feel the beat before I hear it. Wes climbs out of the passenger side and lets out a whistle when he sees the line snaking along the outside of the nightclub.

"We might not get in before it closes."

I grin, "Have a little more faith. Once your girl arrives, I'll work my magic."

Wes groans, leaning against my car, "Try not to get us arrested this time."

"Low blow, man. That only happened once."

"Twice."

My jaw drops, "When was the second time?"

"When you failed to be my lookout for skinny dipping?"

Oh shit. He's right.

I laugh, remembering teenage Wes and his hookup being pulled from the community lake we'd broken into.

"It was 4AM. How was I supposed to know there was a guard making his rounds?"

Wes groans, "That's the whole point of having a lookout. To look out for guards."

"Hey, did I or did I not bail you out?"

Headlights flash our way as Trip pulls into an empty spot.

"You did, but not before the guard saw my junk."

I smirk, watching Wes visibly melt as his girlfriend climbs out of the car.

And that, my friends, is the definition of being pussy whipped.

"If that's all the guard saw, he didn't have much to remember you by."

Wes flips me off as he walks over and scoops Trip up off the ground. She laughs when he swings her around, her converse nearly giving me a concussion before we even get inside. The display of affection tugs my heartstrings, but it's more about my friend finding his person than me wishing I had my own.

Let's be honest: women don't align with my particular tastes and the thought of dating a man makes me want to poke my eyes out. I live for thrills and terrible decisions. First dates and weekend cuddles do not fall into either category.

"Enough being cute. It's time to find me a man."

Trip turns to me with a smile, "Good to see you, Nico. What's the criteria for tonight?"

I give Wes a pointed look, "Did you hear the lack of judgement in her tone? That's what being supportive looks like."

He laughs, burying his face in Trip's golden-brown curls, "She doesn't have to put up with your moaning all day. Did I mention Nico's got a thing for our assistant coach?"

I shoot Wes a glare but he's too busy sniffing his girlfriend's hair to notice.

"Mo?" At my nod, Trip throws her head back and laughs, "Stella is going to die when she hears this."

I groan, "Don't tell Stella. The worst thing a man can do is admit their attracted to someone's older brother."

"You know I can't keep anything from my roommate."

Trip is still laughing when we approach the bouncer at the front of the ridiculously long line. Snips of lyrics drift out the open door.

"But I'll do my best to keep quiet. Can't say I'm surprised, though. Mo fits your type."

My body starts to sway to the beat pulsing through the sidewalk. One of the many things I love about *Lifestyle* is the Latin playlist they always have on hand.

"Why does everyone think I'm into douchebags? Just because I like tall men doesn't mean I like them mean."

Trip bites her lip, "I wouldn't say you like douchebags, Nico. You just tend to go for confident men with big egos."

"Which is a nice way of saying you like douchebags." Wes cheerfully interjects just as we reach the big, burly bouncer.

I smile at him, the neck tattoos and face piercings adding to the intimidation factor.

"Raphael, babe, it's been too long."

A pierced eyebrow lifts as the man who may or may not be part of a motorcycle gang rakes his gaze down my body. The red silk shirt I'm wearing tonight is one of my favourites and I made sure to leave the top three buttons undone to show off my tan, and dare I say it, hairless chest.

Raphael's eyes gleam as he brings them back up to mine, and I already know what he's going to say before he says it.

"Depends on your definition of long."

This is why I love hookups. You get the chase, the challenge, and the satisfaction all in one night. The after-effects aren't always pretty, but that's why I normally go for guys with the same morals as me.

That is to say, none.

I smile and lean in, "Pretty sure you still owe me that BJ from that last game of pool we played, remember?"

Pulling back, I catch the flinch he tries to hide.

"But I'm not really in the mood tonight, so why don't you let my friends and I skip the line and we'll call it even."

Stepping aside, Raphael doesn't look at me as he unhooks the rope and beckons us inside.

"Can we rewind to when you were telling us about your type?" Wes cracks the joke as we enter the nightclub, but I don't crack a smile.

Being a gay man in a conservative small town has its minefield of downfalls but the moments that suck the most are when closeted gays would rather bend over backwards pretending the slip-up never happened than accept their sexuality.

"What is this place?" Trip looks around the room in wonder and I smile, forcing myself out of my sullen thoughts.

"Welcome to *Lifestyle*. Otherwise known as my religious temple of choice."

Chapter 4

Mo

The fork creeps closer to my plate and I smack it away.

The blonde sitting across the table grins, retracting the utensil that almost stole my last fry.

"One of these days I'm going to get you."

Scooping up the fry, I throw it into my mouth with a smirk, "You've been saying that for years."

My sister leans back against her seat with a huff, "One day soon it's going to be true."

"We'll see."

We grin at each other, and for the first time since I drove into Taber, it finally feels like home.

"What are you doing back in Taber so early, anyways?"

"Figured I'd come down and visit my big brother." Stella grins, "And I wanted an excuse to have Cody all to myself before school starts again."

I grimace, "You don't need to go into detail."

She laughs, "I don't remember you being a prude the last time I had a boyfriend."

"That's because I was too wrapped up in my own world to think about what was going on in your bedroom. Not to mention, I actually know the guy this time around."

"That should make it better, not worse." Stella wiggles her eyebrows, "You've seen Cody in the change room. You should be applauding me for tapping that ass."

I shake my head, "You're hopeless. How was your trip to Banff this summer?"

She beams, her smile almost as bright as the sparkly makeup lining her dark blue eyes. We both got my father's recessive genes in that department, but whereas mine are cold and impersonal, Stella's are always bursting with emotion.

"It was amazing. We stayed at this chateau and hit the hot springs." She laughs, "Cody almost got into a fight with some B-list celebrity who tried to hit on me."

"Couldn't imagine that going over well even if the guy wasn't a celebrity." If there's one thing my friend and old teammate does well, it's looking out for my sister.

Stella grins, "It's kind of hot when he gets jealous."

I watch her take a sip of water, the all-too familiar tug of concern rising to the surface. Reaching across the table, I grab her hand, "It's okay to let yourself drink occasionally. It won't change what happened to mom."

She sighs, squeezing my hand gently, "I know. My therapist is helping me work through it. Cody has been my rock through this whole thing."

Our mother got run off the road by a drunk driver back in my freshman year. My sister was in the car at the time, and while our mother died of internal bleeding, Stella survived with a few broken ribs and eighteen stitches up her right side. She underwent physiotherapy for months after the accident, but it wasn't until she started dating Cody that she realized she needed help dealing with the emotional stuff as well.

"I'm glad to hear it." Giving her hand one last squeeze, I release it with a wink, "If you and Ellsworth ever need a DD, you know where to find me."

Stella laughs, "I'll keep that in mind. How are you doing being back in Taber?"

"Better now that you're here." She rolls her eyes and I smile, "It's been good. MacNeil Incorporated was getting a little suffocating, so it's been nice to branch out."

"By suffocating you mean..."

"Jonathan."

She winces, "Jonathan. Have you talked to him about changing departments?"

I shake my head, reaching for my whiskey, "Not yet. Things have been busy lately, so I haven't broached the subject."

An eyebrow raises, "Sounds like you're making excuses."

"O'Briens don't make excuses." Taking a long sip, I savour the burn the whiskey leaves in its wake. If there's one man who can lead me to drink, it's my father.

Stella watches me closely, "You don't have to live up to his expectations, Mo."

I shrug, "I'm used to them by now. You can't be the man of the house without bearing the weight that comes with it."

My sister frowns, toying with the ends of her long braid, "Maybe you should join one of my sessions with Karen. It's not healthy trying to be perfect all the time."

I smirk, "Guess it's a good thing I don't have to try."

"You're unbearable."

Stella sticks her tongue out and I smile, pushing down the pressure in my chest that has been there since I was twelve-years-old.

"Do you see this?"

My father wipes the tear from my cheek, holding his finger up to the light, "This a sign of weakness and that is something I never want to see."

I sniff, rubbing my eyes, "But what about when I'm sad? Mom says everyone is allowed to be weak when they're sad."

"Your mother is wrong." He kneels in front of me, his cold gaze locking on mine, "To be weak is to be average, and you my boy, are not average."

I frown, "But why is Stella allowed to cry when she's sad?"

"Your sister won't be the man of the house when she grows older, that responsibility will fall to you." My father wipes my cheek

again, disappointment shining in his eyes, "But only if you're strong enough to take my place. Are you strong enough, Maurice?"

I nod, hastily wiping away the rest of my tears, "I am strong, Father."

"Good. I don't ever want to see your cheeks damp again. Do you understand me?" He stands up, blocking the light behind him and casting me in shadow.

"I understand."

Cheer explodes from the bar, and I turn my head to see the TV playing the hockey highlights of tonight's game.

"See anyone you like?" Stella grins, tilting her head towards the excited crowd.

I shrug and grab my coat from the back of the chair, "No one worth fighting for. Come on, let's get out of here."

Nico

"That's going to hurt in the morning."

Trip winces as her boyfriend drops to the floor and tries to do the worm in the middle of the dance circle. This is the third time tonight he's tried this move and it looks just as terrible as the last two tries. I could blame the lack of coordination on the four shots of tequila he's had, but I know for a fact that Wes has been practicing this move since we were teenagers.

Spoiler alert: It's never gotten better.

"Dude! You need to find a new move." I crack up as Wes rejoins us, his white t-shirt stained with God knows what substances were on the floor.

"And a new shirt." Trip steps away from him and earns herself drunk puppy dog eyes.

"But wasn't that better than the last try?"

Trip shoots me a panicked look, so I step in, "It was worse. So much worse."

"Awe man." Wes looks genuinely disappointed, so Trip accepts the risk of an infectious disease and wraps him in a hug.

I laugh, "Cheer up, man. Now you've got room for improvement."

Wes grins, his dimples making an appearance, "That's true."

Lights flash around us as the opening notes to a Pitbull song comes on. A new wave of energy hits the crowd as the well-known lyrics are screamed from every corner of the nightclub.

I laugh, throwing up my arms and letting myself be swept away with the music. Sweat drips down my back as I jump and dance with the strangers around me. Vertical strands of lights hang down from the arched ceiling, the bulbs changing colour with each new song. A red haze hits the room when the song fades into the next, triggering another bout of energy to wash over the room.

A winding staircase occupies the back corner of the nightclub, a section catered only to the super rich or the super famous. The railing has strands of leaves woven throughout, blending in with the nature theme that *Lifestyle* is known for. Even the drinks come with some sort of leaf or flower addition, each one stamped with the club's logo.

Trip was so excited when her Dark & Stormy cocktail came with a daisy, she snapped a picture and immediately put it on her social media.

Ah, heterosexuals.

I'm in the middle of a terrible Mr. Brightside rendition with an incredibly handsome black man when someone calls for my attention.

"NICO!"

The shout drags my attention from the glistening dark skin begging for a taste. I turn to see Wes gesturing towards the exit.

"Trip and I are going to head out. Do you want us to call you a ride?"

I wave him off, "I had two shots in the last four hours. Even if I wasn't a river of sweat, it would have worn off by now."

He nods, throwing an arm around Trip. She gives me a knowing look, "Be careful, Nico. Text us when you get home."

I shimmy over and plant a big kiss on her forehead, "You're the sweetest. I'll jam out to a couple more songs then head home. Go take care of our boy."

She nods and leads Wes through the crowd. I turn back and find my dance partner lip locked with an equally attractive blonde. I watch them go at it, getting hornier by the second before turning away with a sigh.

I really should be getting home.

Groaning at my sudden ability to be responsible, I head for the exit. I spy Raphael pushing someone out the door and quickly swerve for the side door to avoid unnecessary contact.

Cold air hits my sweat-soaked body when I push through the door, raising goosebumps on every inch of exposed skin. I sigh happily as I make my way towards the car, the cool breeze blowing through my damp hair.

Nothing beats the rush of *Lifestyle*.

I turn off the music as I make my way home, the ringing in my ears and leftover adrenalin giving me more than enough fuel to stay awake. My stomach lets out a growl about halfway through the drive, and a quick glance at my fuel tells me I'm running low.

Gas up, grab a snack, and then crash in bed. Sounds like the tamest Friday night I've had in a while.

I pull into the next gas station I see, parking at the fuel station next to a massive, souped-up Cadillac. Groaning, I quickly register the BC plates and the warrior-sized shadow moving past the convenience store windows.

Out of all the gas stations I could have stopped at, I ended up at the same one as Maurice O'Brien. Typical.

What's he doing out this late, anyways?

I frown, glancing at the clock above the gas station. Almost 2AM. Seems a little late for an assistant coach to be grabbing a snack.

Humming to myself, I make the mature decision to bypass the snack and get the hell out of here before the grumpy O'Brien comes back outside.

A huge Ford truck pulls up behind my car, its headlights momentarily blinding me. Rowdy laughter explodes from the back as a group of guys stumble out of the truck, the loose jeans and flannel shirts leaving no question as to what group they belong to.

My neck pricks with unease as I watch the numbers on my fuel station slowly tick by. A beer can gets thrown my way and I flinch, making one of the guys laugh.

"Fellas, would ya look at that. We found ourselves a queer all dressed up on the outskirts of town."

Ignoring them, I reach for my phone in my pant pocket. The fabric presses against my leg, empty.

Shit. I left my phone in the car.

"Hey pretty boy! Were you out getting some dick tonight?"

I make a show of looking around before turning to the idiot stumbling towards me.

"Looks like the only dick here is you, Johnny boy."

The pump in my hand clicks and I yank it out and screw on my gas cap.

"What the fuck? He knew your name, man."

Someone hops out of the driver seat, and I quickly make my way to the safety of my own door.

"Wasn't hard to guess given that most men from incestuous families are named Johnny. Tell your daddy I say hi."

I hop in my car and turn the ignition just as something smashes through my windshield.

I throw my hands up and jerk back, trying to shield my eyes from the glass shards falling around me. My palms burn as glass slices through my skin, the exposed column of my neck and upper chest just barely missing the impact. My door gets ripped open and I lunge for the phone lying on the passenger seat. I let out a curse as the device slips through my bloody fingers and suddenly I'm being dragged from the car by rough hands.

My body hits the concrete with a loud thud, the jarring impact vacuuming the air from my lungs. I twist and turn on the ground, feeling my shirt start to tear as I frantically scramble back onto my feet.

"Look guys, I think we may have gotten off on the wrong foot-

A punch to the stomach has me hunching over with a groan. The four guys have surrounded me now, the sneers on their faces not putting the odds in my favour.

Let's face it: I'm a lover not a fighter.

The one with the hideous mullet steps forward, the greasy strands of hair putting a bad taste in my mouth before he shoves me backwards.

"Shut your fucking mouth. We don't like queers around here."

I stumble back and another guy shoves me forward. The momentum throws me off balance and I go crashing down, skin burning as gravel scrapes the cuts in my hands. I make an attempt to crawl to my knees but a well-placed kick has me sprawling face down on the blood stained concrete.

Fuck this shit.

Spitting the blood and grit out of my mouth, I flop onto my back and make blurry eye contact with the leader.

"I'm flattered babe, but you really aren't my type."

He looks down at me with a sneer, "You're fucking disgusting."

A boot comes down and then everything goes black.

Chapter 5

Mo

"Fucking gays."

I pause, the sports magazine in my hands flipped open to the bodybuilding section. A snort sounds behind me, and I turn, finding the old shopkeeper watching his security feed with a shake of his head.

"Is something the matter?"

Bushy grey eyebrows frown at me, the wrinkles around his eyes deep and bitter.

"I was gonna take my baseball bat to the fella' but it looks like the local boys took care of 'em. Look." He points to a grainy image on the monitor above the counter.

I frown, stepping towards the counter to peer at the screen. A group of guys have surrounded someone and are pummelling away.

"What the fuck?"

I look out the window and sure enough, a bunch of guys look like they are having the time of their life beating the shit out of some poor soul on the ground.

"Fella' got out of his car wearing a shirt no man should be found dead in." The shopkeeper chuckles, watching the carnage continue on-screen.

"Did you call the cops?" A quick scan of the security feed tells me its four to one.

"Hell, by the time the sheriff gets here, the gay man will be dead." The old man grins, showing brittle and yellow teeth.

"So you're just going to stand there and watch?"

"There ain't nothing wrong with letting the local boys do the Lord's good work." He makes the sign of the cross over his chest. I stare him down, feeling rage simmer beneath my skin as Jonathan's voice sweeps through me.

You don't fight other people's battles, Maurice. You only fight your own.

But at what cost?

Clenching my jaw, I reach into my pocket and throw a twenty on the counter, "I need to borrow your baseball bat."

"Son, if you 'bout to join the boys, there's no need to pay me. Hell, you can keep it for free."

The shopkeeper pushes the cash back before walking over and grabbing a wooden bat from the storage closet. I leave the bill on the counter and snatch the bat out of his hands.

"Happy hunting!" The old man cheerfully calls after me as I walk out the door.

Taking a quick scan of the situation, I assess the group of men mercilessly kicking the victim on the pavement and the jacked-up pickup truck sitting empty. I make a snap decision and stalk towards the truck before lifting the bat over my shoulder. A glance to the left tells me the group hasn't noticed me yet so I go in for the kill.

One swing takes out the left headlight. Another swing finishes the right one.

My carefully contained anger starts to boil over as I keep swinging, the ever-present voice of my father taunting me with every window I smash.

Are you strong enough to take my place?

I'm just getting started on the windshield when I hear a shout behind me.

"Fuck, he's hitting your truck!"

Turning, I lower the bat and watch the four men stagger towards me. I roll my shoulders and stand up to my full height, towering a good five inches over the tallest of them.

"What the fuck man?" The biggest one of them stumbles towards me, his greasy hair tickling the collar of his stained shirt, "We were just havin' some fun."

I tilt my head, watching him sway closer, "The fun is over. Pack up your runts and go home."

"There's no need to be bitchy about it." The drunk ambles closer, the confidence in his step starting to falter when he realizes the size difference between us.

"Ya man, we were just havin' a bit of fun. Chill the fuck out."

The one wearing a baseball hat flashes me a grin and that's when I snap.

Grabbing the one closest to me, I lift him up by the collar and slam him against the side of the truck. He whimpers when his back makes contact with the broken window, but I don't give him a chance to scream. I lean in closer, his pockmarked face blurring into something cold and disdainful.

Something that looks a lot like my father.

"Touch another person again and I will ruin you. Not kill you, ruin you. I will drain your family's measly income and destroy every acre you grew up on. Do you understand me?"

Bloodstained eyes blink a few times before he gives me a shaky nod.

"Good. Now get out of my sight."

I throw him to the ground and he shrieks when he lands on broken glass. Stepping over him, I hold my bat steady as I approach the rest of the group. They scurry like rabbits, running over to pick up their friend and pushing each other into the truck.

"Fuck! There's glass everywhere."

"Just go!"

The headlights flicker as they rev the engine, shards of glass littering the concrete as they peel out of the gas station.

Good riddance.

Taking a calming breath, I take a moment to shove my emotions back under lock and key. Carefully rearranging my expression back to neutral, I turn to see the shopkeeper staring at me in horror.

I meet his gaze with a slight tilt of my head, "You can keep the change."

Not bothering to wait for a response, I walk over to the man lying on the ground. The guy's dark hair is caked with blood, his red shirt torn so thoroughly that I can see the dark bruises blooming all over his unconscious body. I swallow the nausea rising in my throat and kneel next to him to search his pockets for a wallet. Finding it in his back pocket, I flip it open and stare at the face smirking back at me.

It's Nico Montez.

Nico

A cool washcloth presses against my forehead.

I blink, my vision blurry as a ball of fury pounds its way through my brain. Groaning, I try to sit up only to lie back down.

Fuck. Friday nights are the worst.

Shutting my eyes again, I lean into the washcloth pressed against my hot skin, "Wes, you bastard. How many times do I have to tell you I'm not allowed to crowd surf anymore? I'm too old for that shit."

My voice is hoarse and my chest feels like it got trampled. No one must have been in a catching mood tonight.

"You're too old for a lot of the shit you pull, Montez."

I blink, tilting my head to look up at the pale blue eyes watching me.

I scream.

Mo raises a brow, tossing the washcloth on my lap, "Do that again and I'll duct tape your mouth shut."

My mouth snaps shut and my panicked gaze skitters down to my bare chest.

Oh my God. I slept with our assistant coach.

I watch in horror as Mo crouches down to face me, "Do you remember what happened tonight?"

His gaze is calm and collected, the exact opposite of what I'm feeling. I glance around the room and spy bloodstained bandages covering an otherwise gorgeous apartment.

Is that a curved TV I see?

"I asked you a question." The brooding man regains my attention and I widen my eyes.

"Did we... fuck?"

The only change in his expression is the slight twitch of his upper lip. I narrow my eyes, daring him to laugh at me.

"No, we didn't fuck." Mo's deep voice sends a chill down my spine.

God, I love a good baritone.

"Did we reenact *The Shining*?"

A deep chuckle escapes his throat, and it's all the motivation I need to try and sit up again. A large hand pushes me back down.

"No, we didn't. You were beaten by a group of farmers at the gas station just outside of Taber." He delivers the news in a monotone, as if he's reporting facts instead of recalling a traumatic experience.

I frown, "Did someone call you?"

Mo shakes his head, "I found you."

"You found me?"

He nods, "Half-dead next to the gas pump. Not the most comfortable place to stop for a rest."

My mouth drops open, "Did you just tell a joke?"

A smirk tugs at his ridiculously full lips, "Very observant of you."

I raise my finger to flip him off only to catch sight of the torn skin hanging off my fingers. Memories come flooding back as I look down at my bare chest and notice the boot-shaped bruises.

My throat starts to close as I struggle to push myself into an upright position.

"I need to leave."

Mo sighs, making no move to help me, "You're in no shape to leave this apartment. Stay here tonight and I'll drive you home in the morning."

"Thanks, but I'd rather not sleep on your couch."

I bite back a scream when my feet hit the floor. My body feels like it got run over by a freight train.

Or a group of homophobic rednecks.

Taking a shaky step forward, I collapse against Mo when my knees give out.

"Montez." Mo exhales, his strong arms the only reason I'm not a heap on the floor, "You've been through a lot tonight. You're staying here. End of discussion."

"Always so bossy."

Ignoring me, he bends down and sweeps my legs out from under me, carefully lifting me off the ground. My head spins with the sudden movement, so I squeeze my eyes shut and focus on not puking all over my assistant coach.

"You should not be able to lift me this easily. We're the same height."

I can barely lift my head as Mo carries me from the room. He chuckles, and if I could move my body, I would put my hand on his throat to feel it.

"Different builds, Montez."

"Not everyone likes big, buff guys you know."

His scruff brushes my cheek as he gently lowers me onto the bed, "But you do."

"Hell yeah, I do." Sinking into the mattress, I watch the man who can't stand me carefully pull the comforter over me.

"Get some sleep, Montez."

"I'll do my best." I watch him walk across the room, his stride just as confident as the rest of him. He pauses at the door, and for a moment, I think he might say something else. My eyes start to close as Mo shakes his head and turns off the lights.

And for the second time tonight, I let the darkness take me.

Chapter 6

Mo

"Understood."

I hang up the phone as soon as I see Nico limping towards the kitchen. Holding back a wince, I take note of the purple bruises covering every bare inch of his torso and legs.

"If you're done checking me out, could you point me in the direction of some food?"

Nico limps closer and I smirk, raising my brows at the maple leaves decorating his underwear.

"How patriotic of you. Breakfast is in the blender."

He winks, "Just being a good citizen, babe."

Ignoring the taunt, I look back at my phone when Nico groans loud enough to wake my neighbours.

"Are you trying to kill me, Maurice? This shit is green." He holds up my state-of-the-art blender where I'd thoughtfully left half of my protein shake inside.

I frown, "There's spinach in it. Of course it's green."

Nico takes a cautious sniff and pretends to gag, "I wouldn't give this to a dog."

Tamping down the urge to roll my eyes, I walk over and take it from him, "Then don't drink it. Make yourself something back home."

"Don't you have pancake mix or something?" His dark eyes flick to my chest, "What about eggs? You look like you eat a lot of eggs."

I open my mouth to snap back, but then Nico turns and my words disappear. Massive welts run down his spine, the tender skin bruised and ripped all the way down to the black elastic band of his briefs. The same horrible bruising runs down his arms and legs, fading only around Nico's face. His nose looks a little more crooked than normal and I had to stitch up the deep cut above his left eyebrow last night, but overall, his body took the worst of the beating last night.

Guilt hits me unexpectedly, and I find myself biting back an apology. The closest hospital is over in Lethbridge, and given that I'm CPR certified, it only made sense to bring him back to my place last night. But looking at Nico now, I'm wondering if there wasn't a way I could have stepped in sooner...

"Earth to Maurice."

A swollen finger snaps in front of my eyes and any feeling of remorse vanishes as his signature smirk blocks my line of vision.

"Thought I'd lost you there. Listen, this green sludge-

"Shake. It's a protein shake." I interrupt him, but Nico doesn't pause to take a breath.

-isn't going to work for me. So, how about we swing by McD's on our way to morning practice?"

I cross my arms, leaning against the granite countertop, "You aren't going to morning practice."

He mimics my position on the opposing counter, "I am."

"No, you're not."

"But I am."

"No, you're..." I close my eyes, pausing to take a breath before Nico sucks me into another one of his juvenile games. Opening my eyes, I find him grinning at me.

"The only thing practice will give you is more bruises." I pointedly look up and down his lean frame, "And that's something you have enough of."

Nico shrugs, "What's another bruise for the collection? The assistant coach already gets on my ass for not putting in enough effort."

For the love of...

"That's different."

I feel my left eye start to twitch and will myself not to explode. If Nico wasn't already a walking corpse, I'd be sorely tempted to knock his front teeth out.

"Is it?" A stitched eyebrow goes up and something flashes in his eyes, "You seem to have forgotten your place on this team, Maurice. You aren't the captain anymore. You don't get the final say on what goes down on the field. That's on me and Wes. You're just here to support us."

Nico steps forward, closing the distance between us. His breath hits my cheek, but I don't back away. His irises are almost black up this close and I can see his upper lip is still slightly swollen.

"I am going to morning practice even if I have to walk there. I may not give it my all in every practice, but when it comes to being a leader for those boys, I will give one hundred and ten percent every single time."

His gaze flicks to my lips, as if he finally realized how close we are. Stepping away, Nico turns and grabs the car keys lying on the counter.

"What's it going to be, Maurice? Are you giving me a ride, or should I start walking?"

I study him, watching the way his eyes dart around my apartment as he waits for my verdict. There's a skittishness in him that wasn't there before and it doesn't take a genius to figure out why there's fear still running through Nico's system.

Sighing, I walk over to my pantry and grab a protein bar. Tossing it to him, I nod towards my bedroom, "If we don't want to be late, you're going to have to borrow some of my clothes."

Surprise lights up his eyes and the smile that spreads over his face pulls at something deep in my chest.

"McD's after then?"

"Don't push it, Montez."

Nico

Maurice O'Brien has stained my skin.

It's no joke. I slept in the man's bed and now I am wearing his clothes. It's one thing to enjoy another man's aftershave, it's another thing to live and breathe it for twelve hours straight.

I am horny as fuck.

Turns out, my dick wasn't injured in the smackdown last night because little Nico is up and moving this morning. The only saving grace is Mo's athletic shorts are a lot bigger than what I normally wear, so it's easier to hide my excitement on this fine smelling morning.

Subtlety doing my best to adjust myself, I yell out encouragement from the sidelines.

"That's it, Millard! Take the shot!"

Our new forward races towards the net, where my sub is currently playing, and lines up his shot. Before he can take it though, Taber's legendary all-star comes out of nowhere and sends the poor kid flying.

I blow my whistle, "Maurice! What did we say about taking it easy on the rookies?"

He turns to me, sweat glistening beneath his helmet and I have to refrain from fanning myself with my clipboard.

Mo walks over, his powerful stride eating up the field in no time. He stops in front of me and I take the moment to appreciate the thick leg muscles outlined beneath his shorts.

"If they want a chance to play first string, they have to be treated like they are good enough to play on the field." Mo grabs the water bottle from my lawn chair and sprays it into his mouth.

"True, but if you kill them before our first tournament, I'm not sure it's going to matter." I smirk, "Those boys aren't used to someone your size."

Mo shrugs, "Vin is basically my size. And he's a lot more aggressive."

I wince, remembering the injuries Silverwood's leading forward gave our old captain.

"Bad example. As your coach, I'm telling you to lay off the rookies. Got it?"

He lifts a brow, "I think you're enjoying this a little too much."

"Hey, a deal's a deal." I blow my whistle, "Now get your ass back on the field!"

Mo grunts and runs back over to resume drills.

Upon arrival, it quickly became clear that I was in no shape to play lacrosse today. I made one epic save during warm-up and Mo almost had to carry me off the field because I was in so much pain. After that, I accepted I would coach from the sidelines and Mo would take my place on the field.

Had I known this is what he looked like in lacrosse gear, I would have suggested the switch much sooner.

My phone buzzes in my pocket and I pull it out with a wince. Those boots did a number on me, and I am not ashamed to say there will be an Epsom salt bath in the near future.

"NICO!"

Jerking the phone away from my ear, my face breaks into a grin.

"Mi amor! I've been dying to hear from you." I drop my voice into a whisper, "You know you're my favourite Williams sibling."

Lacey laughs and I swear the world becomes a brighter place. Wes' younger sister is the light of my life, and had my sexuality not gotten in the way, she would have been the love of my life as well.

"Wes must be within hearing range if you're dropping that line."

Quickly signalling for the team to take a timeout, I struggle out of my lawn chair and hobble a couple feet away.

"You know I only speak the truth." She giggles and the pain in my body seems to fade.

There was a time when Lacey's ex-boyfriend had stopped her joy of life altogether. Those were dark days, and I will do everything in my power to make sure it never happens again.

"You need to learn how not to flirt, Nico. You break too many hearts with your charm."

"Where's the fun in that?"

I watch the team assemble for a water break, all of them laughing and joking except for Mo, who is standing off to the side, furiously typing into his phone.

"I'm scared." Lacey sighs and steals back my full attention.

"Scared of what? Starting university?"

"Yeah." She goes quiet and I wait for her to continue, "Wes made it look so easy, you know? He makes friends like it's the most natural thing in the world."

Distress leaks through her voice and it rips at my heartstrings.

"You can't compare yourself to Wes, or anyone else for that matter. Everyone experiences university differently and it will all come down to what you make of it." I pause, "Plus, let's be honest. Your brother has always been a freak of nature when it comes to making friends."

Lacey laughs, "You're right. I guess I'm just nervous about leaving home for the first time. I'm excited to have a fresh start after, you know..."

She trails off and I know what we're both thinking. She's ready to leave the town and the people who led her to almost taking her own life.

"... but it's still nerve racking. What if my roommate hates me? What if I fail all my classes and have to dropout?"

I shake my head even though she can't see me, "There's no point in worrying about things you can't control. Except for the school part, you could probably put in some effort on that end."

She sighs, "You're right, I'm just being ridiculous."

I cluck my tongue, "You are not being ridiculous. Everyone feels this way, trust me."

Turning around to check on the team, I spy half of them running laps while the other half start the next passing drill. I squint, trying to pick out Mo among the orange and black jerseys.

"And remember, you've got a whole support system behind you. I'll be taking you out every weekend and Wes will be making sure only the good guys put their eyes on you. And if you get really desperate, I'm sure Wes' girlfriend would be more than happy to hangout as well. She didn't have many friends starting university, either."

"Trip is the best. We hung out a lot when she came over last Christmas." Lacey blows out a breath, "I don't think I'm ready for another boyfriend. Not yet anyway."

Vulnerability seeps down the line, making me wish that I was rich enough to hire a hitman to take out the prick who did this to her.

"Hey, as long as you have me, you don't need another man in your life. Right?"

"Damn right." I can hear the smile in her voice.

"Good. Now, I'll see you in a few days and we will tackle any potential roommate problems then. I'm thinking glitter glue should be our first weapon of choice."

Lacey laughs, "Sounds like a plan. Thanks, Nico."

"Anytime, mi amor. Love you."

"Love you too." She blows a loud raspberry through the phone, and I hang up with a smile.

Turning to rejoin the group, I crash into a brick wall. Letting out a string of expletives, I hunch over as the brick wall crosses his arms.

"If you're done talking to your boyfriend, practice has resumed."

A cold gaze meets mine and I stare back at Mo, confused.

My boyfriend?

Tossing the thought aside, I stand up and start limping back to my lawn chair with no offer of an explanation.

Chapter 7

Mo

Anytime, mi amor. Love you.

My grip on the steering wheel tightens as the tail end of Nico's phone call plays on my mind. I can't remember the last time I said those words to someone who wasn't my sister.

Seeing Nico's face light up when he answered the phone triggered something inside of me. The full-fledged grin and crinkled eyes showed every emotion passing through his body as he spoke to whoever was on the other end of that call.

Happiness. Excitement. Love.

God. Does he have to be so expressive?

Annoyance seeps through me as I turn my attention to the other aggravating issue on hand: Nico Montez won't get out of my car.

Engine rumbling beneath us, I make a show of looking at my watch.

"In case you hadn't noticed, we've arrived."

Nico ignores me and continues to stare out the window. I grit my teeth and survey the nondescript varsity residence building. The front lawn is perfectly maintained, offering a vibrant green to the dull backdrop of the beige building.

Tapping my fingers impatiently, I clear my throat, "Do us both a favour and don't strip in my car. You can keep the clothes."

He looks like he is drowning in those shorts, but I decide not to vocalize that comment.

Nico stays silent, his body completely still. If I couldn't see the tension in his shoulders, I would think he had fallen asleep.

"Montez." I wait until he turns to look at me. "You can go home now. I'll make sure your car is taken care of."

"Right." Shaking his head, Nico blinks as if he had forgotten where he was, "Guess I owe you a thank you for that, huh?"

"Don't worry about it." I let my eyes drift over his shoulder to the door, hoping he'll take the hint and leave. Nico nods and reaches for the door handle.

Finally.

Pausing just as his hand reaches the latch, Nico turns and looks at me, "What are you doing for the rest of the day?"

I frown, seeing where this conversation is going, "We aren't spending the day together, Montez. Twelve hours was more than enough."

He gives me a smile that doesn't quite reach his eyes, "Babe, I was just making conversation. No need to read into it."

Grinding my teeth together, I can't stop the growl that leaks out, "I told you not to call me that."

"Did you?"

"Numerous times." Counting to ten in my head, I think of all the reasons Uber was invented.

"Bad habit I guess." He turns and looks back out the window, making no move to exit the vehicle.

"The bad habit is over-staying your welcome."

He flinches at my harsh tone, but I can't bring myself to feel bad about it.

"Roger that, Coach. See you next practice."

Finally extracting himself from the passenger side, I wait until Nico shuts the door to hit the gas. The Cadillac roars to life as I punch it, ready to clear my head and get on with my day.

I've almost made it out of the parking lot when I give my rearview mirror one last glance. My foot eases off the gas pedal when I see Nico standing exactly where I left him, staring mindlessly at the visitor lot. Craning my neck, I follow his gaze and suck in a breath.

Fuck.

A pickup truck idles next to the doors of the varsity residence, casually waiting to pick someone up. It's not the location that's the problem, it's the truck itself.

A black F-150. The exact make and model as the one from last night.

The lack of broken windows tells me it's not actually the same one, but Nico wouldn't know that. Cursing under my breath, I whip around the parking lot back to where Taber's lacrosse goalie is still standing. He glances over just as I roll down my window.

"Get in."

Relief washes over Nico's features as he plants his ass back in my passenger seat. I hit the accelerator before he can buckle up.

"Where are we going?"

I sigh, "The police station."

Nico hoots as we pull out of the parking lot and I can't help but notice this time his smile reaches his eyes.

"I see."

Officer Duncan looks at us with suspicious eyes, his thick black brows creeping towards his hairline. I glance at Nico and find an encouraging thumbs up waiting for me.

Amateur.

"I don't believe in words, sir. I believe in data." Pulling out my phone, I open up the email my family lawyer forwarded me this morning. Turning my screen sideways I place my phone in front of the officer.

"You realize any evidence you present will convict you of vandalism." He leans forward, looking me dead in the eye, "And as of right now there are no charges pressed against you."

"I understand." I gesture towards the phone, "This is the security footage from the gas station just outside of Taber. You should be able to pull the license plate from the video."

"The license plate of the truck you damaged." Shaking his head, Duncan looks between Nico and me before taking my phone.

"The license plate of the men who beat up an innocent bystander."

Nico opens his mouth to say something, but a sharp look quickly changes his mind.

There is no sound on the video but it's pretty easy to guess what is playing out on the screen based on the queasy look on the officer's face. By the time he puts my phone back on the table, Duncan's eyes have started to glisten.

"You know, my boy came out to us a few months ago." Looking away, he clears his throat, "Got into makeup and all that stuff. I've seen him wear similar outfits when he goes to that club on the outskirts of town."

Nico grins, "*Lifestyle* always brings out fashionistas."

Duncan gives him a nod, "Henry moved to a big city as soon as he could. Guess the people there are a lot more open than country folk."

"Glad to hear your son found a safe place to land." Interrupting the history lesson, I lean forward and open the other email my lawyer sent this morning, "Based on the amount of damage caused my lawyer has drafted a bail agreement and sent it over for you to sign. All you have to do is approve it and we can be on our way."

Duncan's brows pull into a frown as he reviews the document, "In case the vandalism charges are pressed against you, this covers your bases?"

"That's correct."

Nico shifts uneasily beside me but I don't spare him a glance. Lawrence MacLaren has been representing my father's family for decades and there is no way in hell he would let something as simple as property damage be his first slip up.

"May I ask why you decided to turn yourself in?" Duncan slides my phone back towards me but I make no move to take it.

"I always take accountability for my actions. There's no point in waiting for the storm to hit if you can stop the storm before it begins."

"I see." Nodding his head, Duncan pushes back his chair and rounds the desk, "Thank you for taking the time to stop by Mr. O'Brien and Mr. Montez. I appreciate you looking out for Taber's citizens."

"Oh, I'm actually just a university student. I'm not from here." Nico shudders, "Too many corn fields for my liking."

Jesus Christ.

Duncan laughs, holding out his hand for Nico to shake, "Can't argue with you there. Pleasure meeting you both."

He turns to me with a smile, "I'm assuming that fancy lawyer of yours sent a copy of that footage to the investigation office?"

"Should already be in your inbox."

"In that case, you are free to go."

I frown, "Sir, about the bail agreement-

Duncan waves a hand, "I ain't seen no sign of vandalism on that video. The old camera must have cut out right when you walked out looking mean with a baseball bat." He winks, "Henry would have been proud of what you did."

I'm momentarily speechless, "Officer, the law really isn't up for debate. I would feel better if you took the agreement."

Duncan grins, clapping a hand on my back, "Don't worry son, the law around here is in good hands. I'll make sure those boys are fined with assault charges. You worry about getting good grades in school."

My frown deepens, "This isn't protocol. And I'm not a student."

"He's my assistant coach." Nico cheerful interjects the comment and I shoot him a glare, "Which is why he's not used to the way things work around here. Thank you so much Officer Duncan, we will leave take our leave now so you can get on with your day."

Grabbing my arm, Nico pulls me towards the door. I sigh, giving Duncan one last look over my shoulder, "The agreement is in your inbox as well if you change your mind."

"Like I said, nothing to change my mind about. Have a good day, son!"

Nico

"Babe, we've got to go celebrate."

Pulling down Mo's expensive vanity mirror, I grin at my own reflection, "We just got off scot free and took down a group of homophobic rednecks. Time to get drunk."

Keeping his attention carefully focused on the road, I see a tiny smirk pull at Mo's lips.

"I'm not sure alcohol is what your system needs right now."

"Alcohol is exactly what my system needs right now." Snapping the mirror shut, I adjust the oversized collar of Mo's shirt, "I'm thinking a round of tequila. Maybe a vodka cranberry to wash it down."

"It's 2PM."

"And the problem is?"

Mo gives me a wry glance, "Happy hour hasn't even started."

I smirk, "When you're with me, Maurice, every hour is happy hour."

He chuckles and the sound has little Nico stirring back to life. Shifting to get a better look at Mo's side profile, I have to hold back a sigh when I take in his chiseled features. The cold blue eyes are framed by dark lashes that somehow look intimidating rather than pretty. My eyes trail down the high cheekbones and I have to grab my seatbelt to stop myself from leaning over and planting myself on those full lips right here, right now.

God, and don't get me started on the hair. The perfectly styled strands of brown hair are just long enough to run my fingers through but short enough to maintain the professional business persona Mo has got going on.

"Incoming phone call from Jonathan O'Brien."

Jumping back against my seat, I stare at the navigation system in horror, "Did your car just talk to us?"

"Yes because my car isn't from the 1970s." Mo glances at me, "Pretty sure that bumper I saw yesterday was older than my father."

Cheeky. I like it.

I open my mouth to respond but he cuts me off with a serious look, "I need to take this. Please don't say a word."

Shocked he asked nicely, I nod and make a show of zipping my lips closed. He rolls his eyes and presses answer.

"I just got off the phone with MacLaren." A harsh silence fills the car and I see Mo grit his teeth beside me.

"There was a situation that required his services."

"Do I need to remind you what's at stake here?"

I feel my eyebrows raise as I try and figure out Mo's relationship with the faceless speaker.

"No. I made a mistake and now it's been fixed."

"Thanks to MacLaren." Teeth clenching, Mo grips the steering wheel tighter and falls silent.

"You took two weeks worth of vacation so you could re-live your glory days before taking your corporate position to the next level. I allowed it because I thought it would help straighten out your priorities." My mouth falls open but the cold voice continues, "And now I find out that you are spending your time getting into bar fights in the middle of nowhere and putting the O'Brien name to shame."

Slowing to a stop for a red light, I try to make eye contact with Mo but his gaze doesn't leave the road.

"They were going to kill him, father."

Father?

My mouth snaps shut as I glance at the navigation screen. The name Jonathan O'Brien screams back at me and I want to slap myself for not putting it together sooner.

"Then you should have called the police. What did I teach you about fighting other people's battles?"

"You only fight your own."

"That's right."

Silence ensues and I shift uncomfortably in my seat. I am a sucker for family drama, but this shit is above my pay grade.

The light turns green and Mo calmly presses the accelerator. His entire posture screams tense but it hasn't affected his driving in the slightest. It's as though he's been trained to stay on autopilot.

Sadness hits me and for once it's not about the fact that a smouldering man is within touching distance but off-limits. I'm finally starting to understand where Mo's intensity comes from and it's not from a happy family life.

Mo clears his throat, breaking my train of thought, "It won't happen again."

"See that it doesn't." Jonathan hangs up without another word and I wince.

"Guess your family isn't big on *I love you*, hey?"

It's a pathetic attempt to lighten the mood but I'm desperate.

"You could say that."

Mo doesn't crack a smile as he flicks the indicator for the university exit. A twinge of disappointment hits my chest at the thought of our day together ending so soon. The car doesn't slow down until we drive past the university and I heave a sigh at the sight of my residence building.

"Thanks for letting me tag along today. It was... interesting."

Mo glances over with a frown, "Who said anything about it being over?"

My heart stutters when we roll by the exit for my building. A massive smile takes over my face when I see what's coming up ahead.

"Just wanted to get the words out sober."

A smirk pulls at his mouth, "Sure. You ready to get drunk, Montez?"

"The answer to that question will always be yes."

"You and me. Pool. Now."

Stumbling off my barstool, I hiss in pain when my battered body hits the counter.

"Didn't realize you enjoyed losing so much." Mo grins, his face slightly flushed from the six rounds of tequila shots we did.

Was it six or eight rounds? I can't really remember.

Steadying me with his arm, Mo helps me wobble over to the pool table tucked in the corner of the dim sports bar. Purposefully leaning in closer, I shamelessly inhale the expensive cologne wafting off his skin. Smelling the scent on the man himself is one hundred times better than walking around in his clothes.

"Babe, you smell fucking delicious. What cologne do you use?"

He smirks, "Obsession by Calvin Klein. You can order it from Amazon."

"I'm ordering a bucket when I get home."

Mo laughs and leaves my side to round up the cue stick.

"You know how to play 8-ball?"

He grabs the rubber rectangle from the wall and puts everything in position. His shirt stretches across his broad back when he leans over the pool table and my level of intoxication skyrockets.

Who the fuck needs tequila when you have an assistant coach who looks like this.

"Hell yeah, I do."

"Good. You can break." Passing me the cue stick, Mo gives me a devilish grin, "Figure you could use the head start."

Lust and tequila race through my system as I snatch the cue stick from him.

"That was your first mistake, Maurice. The name Nico Montez causes fear in pool players everywhere."

Mo lets out another laugh and I all but swoon. This is the most carefree I have ever seen him and to say I am loving it would be an understatement.

"We'll see about that."

Chapter 8

Mo

The eight ball sails smoothly into the corner pocket.

"Shall we play another one?" Smirking, I turn to the fuming Latino who just lost his third straight round.

"You broke my streak!" Nico glares at me, his dark eyes glazed and more than a little unfocused. We've been drinking at the same rate, but just like the pool game, I came out on top.

If there's one thing my father did well, it was teaching his children how to be the best.

My smile slips at the thought of Jonathan and the painful car ride home. I don't get embarrassed, but based on Nico's reaction, I could tell lesser men would have found the situation embarrassing.

Lesser men? God, I am becoming more like him every day.

A bitter taste fills my mouth and my buzz starts to fade. Taking the cue stick, I walk over to the wall and carefully put it back in place. Closing my eyes, I tune out the bar and take a second to breathe.

"No, no!" Fingers snap in front of my face, "You aren't allowed to do that." The words are slurred and the hint of an accent seeps through.

I blink my eyes open, "Do what?"

"Get all serious. You get an ugly line right there." Nico grins, reaching out to touch the scowl line etched between my brows. His thumb strokes the spot gently, a futile attempt to erase the permanent mark.

"Are you calling me ugly?"

I feel my lips start to twitch, the combination of alcohol and Nico Montez making my emotions run dangerously close to the surface.

He gasps, smacking a hand against his chest loudly, "Mi madre would slap me if she heard such a blatant lie come out of my mouth."

The smile breaks loose from my lips, "Starting to lose me with the Spanish there, Montez."

Nico makes a show of looking around before bringing his finger to his lips, "It's my deepest, darkest secret, Maurice. My grandparents are first generation Canadians."

Taking in his tanned skin and dark complexion, I shake my head, deadpan, "You're kidding."

A finger jabs my chest, "Your kind of funny when you're drunk. I think I like it."

His eyes darken as he sways closer to me and I can't tell if he wants to fuck me or eat me.

Nico's spicy cologne is close enough to taste, so I don't think before I lick my lips. His eyes drop to track the movement and I lean in closer.

"Wait. We can't do this."

Pausing my trek, I blink at the man who has been eye-fucking me all evening.

"What?"

"We can't do this." Nico repeats it slowly and takes a step back.

My eyes narrow, "Not sure we have the same read on the situation here, care to explain?"

Nico's signature smirk disappears as he takes another step back and runs his hand through his hair.

"Shit, I can't believe this is happening."

I cross my arms, watching the Tigers' goalie pace back and forth in front of the pool table. Half the shit he's muttering to himself is in Spanish, but even the English bits are so slurred it's hard to interpret.

"Montez." Pausing his pacing, Nico turns to look at me, "Do us both a favour and calm the fuck down."

"You're right."

"I know."

"But you weren't the one who almost kissed the heterosexual assistant coach!" Nico shrieks the last part and a couple of bar patrons look our way.

"If you don't keep it down, the whole bar will chase us out with whatever bat they have on hand." Sighing, I pull out my phone and open the Uber app.

Nico pauses his pacing, "What are you doing? Why aren't you freaking out right now?"

"I am getting us a ride because I am too drunk to drive and even if you weren't three sheets to the wind, you are too unstable to be behind the wheel. And I am not freaking out because it is a waste of time and energy. Learn to control your emotions, Montez, and you might find life gets a whole lot simpler."

One click later and our ride is paid for and on its way.

If only people were so easy to handle.

"Fuck that, I'd rather be a drama queen than an emotionless robot like you."

The slurred words hit home but I don't so much as flinch.

"Let's wait for our driver outside." Taking Nico's arm, I carefully guide him through the bar and out into the safety of the night.

"You do realize you almost kissed a guy, right? This is me waving the rainbow flag." I watch, unamused, as Nico waves his arms back and forth in the air.

"You've made your point."

"Have I? You're acting like nothing almost happened tonight."

Leaning against the wall, I pull out my phone to countdown the minutes until I can escape.

"Seriously, Maurice, look at me." I look up and find Nico spinning in a circle.

This driver can't come fast enough.

"No tits. No vagina. No bueno." Running a hand over his face, he groans, "I would have given you a beard burn."

Despite the growing desire to duct tape Nico's mouth shut, I find myself laughing. His head whips around, the shock on his face making me laugh harder.

"This isn't funny."

"Your right, it isn't." Giving myself one last chuckle, I pull myself together just as the driver pulls into the visitor lot.

"O'Brien?" The driver peeks his head out the window.

"That's us."

Walking over and opening the back door, I motion for Nico to climb in. He stumbles his way inside and I pause just before closing the door.

"My skin isn't that soft, Montez. It takes a lot to leave a mark."

Swinging it shut before Nico can say another word, I walk around to the passenger side and climb in.

Nico

It takes a lot to leave a mark.

The words rattle around my alcohol infused brain as the Uber driver's terrible taste in music fills the silence of the car. It smells faintly of cheese but I guess it's better than the concrete ground of a gas station.

Shit, was that only twelve hours ago?

The tequila shots helped numb the aches and pains of my body but I can feel them start to creep back in. I'm nowhere close to sober but suddenly I feel a lot less drunk than I was thirty minutes ago.

Re: When I tried to kiss Taber's all-star lacrosse legend.

I groan as the memory resurfaces, the blurry image of a pool table and Mo's smiling face weakening my resolve to the point of making a move. Because I was the one who made the move, wasn't I?

I frown, my thoughts flying past me like the corn fields outside. The last twelve hours dug up so many questions that now I want answers.

Glancing at the man occupying the passenger seat, I let his rigid features soften my thoughts until they start to drift off. My eyes grow heavy as I take in the white-knuckled state of Mo's hands gripping the armrest.

See? My homosexual tendencies must have turned him off to the point of being ill. Speaking of being sick, he really does look like he's about to...

"Pull over. Now."

The driver jerks the wheel and I'm thrown against the door as the car comes to a shuddering stop. Mo jerks out of the passenger seat and flings himself out the door. Rubbing my screaming shoulder, a flush of embarrassment hits my cheeks when the sound of retching echoes from the fields outside.

I've really done it now.

Cursing myself and the driver's terrible shift work, I yank my own door open and hobble out into the night. It takes my eyes a few moments to adjust to the darkness, but it doesn't take long to spot the man spewing chunks all over the ground.

Breathing through my mouth as I draw closer, I awkwardly bend down to pat his heaving back.

"That's it. Get it all out."

Mo smacks my hand away, "You are not helping."

So physical touch is not his love language. Noted.

Tucking my hands in my pockets, I do my best to look useful, "Anything I can do to help?"

"You've done enough."

My shoulders hunch as another round of heaving takes over Mo's body. I wait until the convulsions stop before bringing up the elephant puking in the room.

"I'm sorry, Maurice. I crossed a line tonight and that's unacceptable." Mo spits on the ground while I shuffle nervously, "I will never make another move on you again. I promise."

Using his hand to wipe his mouth, Mo sits back on his knees and looks at me. His hair is completely disheveled and his mouth glistens with the leftovers of his vomiting session. For the first time since I've met Maurice O'Brien, he doesn't look perfect.

He looks human.

"What the fuck are you talking about?" Mo stares at me, seeming unbothered by the fact his stomach contents are on the ground next to us.

I grimace, motioning towards the mess he just made, "I was just saying sorry for going gay on you and making you do... this."

Mo brushes off his knees and climbs to his feet, "You drink too much, Montez. I didn't throw up because you hit on me. I threw up because I get motion sick."

My brain screeches to a halt.

"You get car sick?"

He nods and I burst out laughing. Shoulders shaking, I hunch over to catch my breath as Mo glares in my direction.

"It hasn't happened in a long time."

I keep laughing and the death glare continues.

"I'm normally the driver so it doesn't affect me."

"Sure."

"I'm serious."

Still chucking, I give him a friendly pat on the back, "Oh, I know Maurice."

His eyes narrow into slits, and just for a moment, I get a glimpse of all the emotions bubbling beneath the surface.

Anger. Frustration. Disappointment.

The last one catches me by surprise because as far as I could tell, the disappointment isn't directed at me. It's directed at himself.

"You are the most aggravating person I have ever met."

"Babe, we've already established that."

Mo's jaw clenches and I feel my smirk turn into a real smile. The hardest ones to crack are always the most satisfying.

"But now I know why you drive that big ass Caddy with the tinted windows. It's so no one can see the puke bags stashed everywhere, right?"

"I hate you."

"That too, has already been established."

Giving me one last glare, Mo turns and starts walking back to the car. I watch him walk away, the desire to ask severely personal questions on the tip of my tongue.

"You know, there are wrist bands and ear patches that are supposed to help. Maybe I could buy us a matching pair so I could be your emotional and physical support system."

Mo sighs, "Get back in the car, Montez."

"Yes, Coach."

I pretended not to notice the fact Mo didn't let the driver leave until I was safely inside my residence building, but half an hour later I'm still obsessing over it.

I've never had someone idle for me before.

Humming to myself, I reach for my phone lying on the nightstand next to the sad single mattress I'm lounging on. Residence life has a lot of things going for it, but a comfortable living space is not one of them.

My feet dangle off the bed as I make myself semi-comfortable, my alcohol buzz all but gone by this point. I click my best friend's name and quickly type out a message.

ME: You'll never guess who I hung out with today.

I start strolling through my TikTok feed as I wait for his answer. It's just after midnight, but knowing Wes, he's probably forced Trip to watch some sort of movie marathon with him.

Sure enough, my phone pings five minutes later.

WES: If you say Devon, I'm blocking you.

ME: Who?

WES: The ape.

I groan, remembering that beautiful, hairy man.

ME: I still think his name was Dhillon.

WES: I'm blocking you.

ME: Fine. Maybe the ape's name was Devon but that's not who I hung out with.

WES: ... unblocked. Was it Mark Chen?

Shit, I forgot about Chen. We met at the bar on campus and ended up exploring the erotic magic of blindfolds. It was a good night.

ME: Wrong.

WES: Lucas from economics?

ME: Why are you listing all my hookups?

WES: You told me to guess!

ME: Slut shamer.

WES: I'm going back to my movie now. Trip says hi.

I grin, reading his message. Ten bucks says it's a trilogy.

ME: Nico says hi back. What movie?

WES: Back to the Future.

Knew it.

ME: Classic. It was Maurice O'Brien.

WES: ...

WES: You mean our assistant coach? The one who hates you?

ME: The one and only.

Typing bubbles appear then disappear on my screen. There is definitely an off-screen conversation going on over there.

WES: Why?

ME: I was bored.

My fingers hesitate over the keyboard, the desire to share every detail suddenly disappearing.

WES: I have no words. Did you keep it in your pants?

ME: Remember my comment about slut shaming?

WES: It's not slut shaming if it's a valid question.

ME: My pants stayed zipped the entire time.

Glancing at my open closet, I see Mo's borrowed clothes hanging next to my own. Even after a full day of wear, his cologne still lingers on the fabric.

I don't plan on ever washing them.

WES: Proud of you.

ME: Thanks. Sad to report he broke my pool streak and whooped my ass tonight.

WES: So much to unpack. Fill me in at practice tomorrow.

ME: Deal. Give Trip a kiss for me.

WES: Already did.

Putting my phone down, my thoughts jump back to the disappointment etched across Mo's face tonight. In that brief slip of control, I'd gotten a peek behind Mo's stone cold exterior and found a minefield of explosive emotions.

The only problem is now I want to see more.

Chapter 9

Mo

Nico's mouth is around my cock.

He puts that infuriating mouth to good use, drawing me in deep before sucking his way back to the tip. His tongue presses against the head of my cock, drawing a moan out of my mouth. The sound echoes around the room, my hands fisting his dark locks as he swallows me back down his throat.

Fuck.

The word rings in my ears and I jerk awake. My sheets are tangled between my legs and my hands are gripping the top sheet like there's no tomorrow.

Forcing my grip to loosen, I ignore my throbbing dick and glance at the clock. 3:17 AM.

Fuck.

A growl escapes my throat as I rip off the covers, my rock-hard shaft springing up to greet me. I glare at it, feeling betrayed by my own body.

Pushing off my bed, I stalk over to the bathroom and turn on the shower. I hop in without giving it a chance to warm up, hissing out a breath when the cold water hits my back. Numbness takes over and I close my eyes, letting the fleeting moment of peace tether me back to the ground.

Only once I feel a headache coming on, I finally reach down and turn off the tap. Exiting the shower, I don't bother grabbing a towel before walking to my closet and pulling on some gym gear. The cold droplets running down my back serve as a welcome reminder as to why you don't fool around with teammates.

By the time I get to the lacrosse field, my foul mood has only gotten worse. My protein shake tasted less than satisfactory this morning and the drive to the university was painfully slow. Not because everyone suddenly decided to leave for work before dawn but because I managed to hit every goddamn red light on the way here.

There's only five traffic lights in Taber and I managed to hit all five.

Taking note of the two rookies setting up the lacrosse nets, I do a quick scan of the field and note the absent captains. Giving the rookies a nod, I head to the locker room to drop off my gym bag for a post training gym session. I don't use caffeine to stimulate my body, so the extra endorphins will be a much needed push to get me through the day.

Low murmurs float down the rows of lockers as I turn and head down the farthest one on the end. A tanned, lean body catches my eye as Nico pulls his shorts over his legs. I pause, my unknown arrival giving me the chance to assess the bruised skin covering Nico's torso. His movements are a lot less stiff than they were yesterday but far from normal.

"You'll sit this week out and reassess your condition next weekend."

Nico starts at the sound of my voice, making no effort to put on a shirt before turning to face me.

"And here I thought you might be less bossy on Sundays." He smirks and my mind flashes back to this morning when those same lips were featured in my R-rated dream.

A bolt of lust shoots through me but I shut it down quickly.

"I'm surprised you were able to get up this morning. I almost had to carry you home. Again." Ignoring the angry marks etched along Nico's otherwise smooth chest, I turn and open my locker.

"Training while hungover is one of my greatest superpowers." He grins in my peripheral, "Although I'm not surprised you're looking well, we had a bit of a pit stop on the way home."

Do not rise to the bait.

"We all have our moments." Tamping down my annoyance, I slowly click the locker closed and turn to find Nico studying me.

"How are you feeling this morning? Any... regrets?"

I resist the urge to roll my eyes. He has the subtlety of a toddler throwing a tantrum.

Staring back at him coolly, I reply, "My only regret is not beating you in a fourth round of pool. See you on the field, Montez."

He doesn't say another word as I leave, my footsteps echoing through the suddenly empty locker room.

Nico

Why does he have to be so *hot*?

Even if you took away the sculpted body, that face would sell magazines around the world. And let's not forget the dominant and untouchable façade he marches around with. One look at Maurice O'Brien and you get the mouth-watering basics: disciplined, rich, and used to getting what he wants.

But then you throw in the assault charge he almost got for smashing in some guy's truck, the condescending father, the dark groves under his eyes, and suddenly there's a lot more to Mo than meets the eye.

It's safe to say that I am addicted.

"There's my favourite co-captain!"

Wes comes barreling around the corner like the overexcited golden retriever he is and wraps me in a hug.

I barely hold back a groan when he picks me up off the ground. "It's good to see you too, Wes. How was your weekend with Trip?"

Wes grins, his green eyes sparkling more than usual, "Too good to be true. I could go into the dirty details, but I would much rather hear about your rendezvous with a certain assistant coach."

I laugh, hugging my best friend tightly, "There is too much to tell. Where would I begin?"

"The beginning would be a safe bet."

Wes flashes me his dimples before pulling his shirt over his head. I turn away to give him some privacy – not that I haven't seen it all before – and reach for my water bottle sitting on the top shelf.

"What is that?"

I peek over my shoulder to see Wes frowning at my exposed lower back.

"Oh, that's nothing. Wait until you see the rest."

Shaking my head, I pull up my shirt to give him a front row seat to the Nico-got-his-ass-kicked show. Wes' eyes go wide as they take in the tragic state of my normally spotless skin.

"Nico, what the hell did you do?" His brows pull together as he stares at my back, "Are those... boot prints?"

I laugh darkly, "It's not about what I did, it's about what Maurice did. You should have seen-

"Mo did this to you?" Wes' eyes harden as he glances between my face and the boot-sized bruises gracing my body.

"What? No, Maurice didn't... Wes, wait!" I run after Wes as he storms from the locker room and breaks into a sprint towards our assistant coach.

Shit, shit, shit.

I scurry after him, cursing myself for not telling him about the gas station situation earlier. I'm halfway across the field when Wes reaches Mo. Willing my legs to speed up, I run as fast as I can to stop my best friend from making an ass of himself.

Damn it. I should have tried harder during sprints.

Thankfully, Mo had the foresight to initiate warm-up, so the rest of the team is busy running laps when I finally reach the men facing off. It's comical seeing Wes square off with Mo, the latter towers over him with at least forty pounds of extra muscle.

What is not comical, however, is the furious look on Wes' face. The last time he looked this mad, it took me and half the soccer team to drag him off Lacey's ex-boyfriend.

"What the fuck is your problem, O'Brien? You show up in Taber as an assistant coach and the next thing I know you're beating the shit out of my co-captain." Wes is practically spitting while Mo stares at him coldly.

"Not sure I understand your allegations."

I throw myself between them, forming a human barrier between the snarling golden retriever and Iceman.

"Wes, this is a misunderstanding. It wasn't Maurice who-

"Step aside, Nico. I'm not going to let a condescending asshole think he can put his hands on you." Wes glares at Mo over my shoulder, "Is it because he hit on you? Are you not strong enough to handle a man flirting with you?"

The last blow lands, and I watch Mo's eyes light up with a cold fire.

"The next time you go around accusing people of assault, you should check to make sure you have the right facts."

He doesn't so much as glance in my direction before turning and stalking off the field.

I turn to Wes with a groan, "Dude. Maurice saved me. A group of farmers ganged up on me and he beat the shit out of their truck until they left me alone."

"What?" Wes blinks at me, the attack dog already retreating.

"Maurice. Saved. Me." I repeat the words slowly, making sure they have time to sink in, "He literally carried me back to his place, patched me up, and then took care of me for the rest of the weekend."

Well, he took me to a police station and got me drunk but that was close enough.

"Oh fuck." Realization dawns until Wes looks physically ill, "Why didn't you say something?"

I groan, "I tried but you were out for blood. Which I appreciate from the bottom of my heart, but in this instance, it was very much misplaced."

"Shit." Raking a hand through his hair, Wes looks at me with panicked eyes, "Why didn't you call me? We have a protocol for this type of thing."

I sigh, "I'm sorry, Wes. By the time I could have called you, Maurice had already taken care of everything."

"This is so messed up." He pinches the bridge of his nose, "I need to go apologize. I feel like such an asshole."

I pat his arm, "You are an asshole, but a loyal one. You stay with the team, I'll go talk to him. We're kind of friends after this weekend."

I pause, "Well, we were until you blew up at him."

"Oh God."

I give Wes one last supportive pat before taking off after Mo. This is the most cardio I have done all year, but somehow, I can't bring myself to feel bitter about it.

Chapter 10

Mo

Are you not strong enough?

I rip my gym bag from my locker and throw it on the bench. It may have been Wes who said the words, but the voice was all my father.

Grinding my teeth together, I yank my shirt over my head and hurl it to the ground. My mind is stuck on the same loop it's been stuck on since the day Jonathan pulled me aside to scold me for crying, the never-ending crash and fall of disappointment landing on my shoulders.

I made sure you earned every position you worked in.

My chest starts to heave as the walls close in. I can feel the emotions bubbling just beneath the surface, waiting for a chance to explode. Forcing myself to breathe through the pressure, I close my eyes and lean my forehead against the locker, letting the cold metal ground me.

"Maurice?" Nico's voice is soft and tentative but it's enough to break through my father's.

"Not now, Montez."

Keeping my eyes closed, I exhale and count down from ten. Once I reach zero, I feel composed enough to push away from the locker. I find Nico staring at me with his mouth open.

"You don't have a shirt on."

I frown, "If you plan on being Captain Obvious, you might as well leave."

He ignores the insult and wanders closer, "Did an artist sculpt you? There's no way these things are real."

To my utter disbelief, he pokes my left pec.

I grab his hand before he can touch me again, "Most artists charge for their work. And trust me when I say you couldn't afford me."

Nico grins, "Name a price and I will rob a bank."

Staring at the impossible man in front of me, a chuckle escapes my lips.

Nico's eyes lit up at the sound, "Now that I have you in a good mood, I want to formerly apologize for my co-captain. There was a misunderstanding, and he took it out on you. That was wrong and I'm sorry."

I frown, "Communication is important, especially as a captain."

"Extenuating circumstances aside, that is something I promise to work on." He winks, "It's not every day I get saved by a lacrosse legend."

"You're ridiculous." I try to keep a straight face, but a smirk tugs at my lips.

"You love it."

Nico's eyes drop to my mouth and the tension from last night resurfaces. My sleepless night must be taking its toll because just like moments before, I feel my control start to slip.

"I really don't." I realize I'm still holding his hand, but instead of letting go, I use it to pull him closer.

"I don't believe you."

"I don't care."

His tongue peeks out as he licks his lips, his gaze dropping to my bare chest. Grabbing his chin, I tilt his head until his eyes are back on mine.

"Tell me one thing, Montez. How serious are you and the boyfriend?"

He frowns, staring back at me, "I don't have a boyfriend."

Now it's my turn to frown, "Who were you talking to the other day?"

"Huh?" Scrunching up his face, Nico suddenly laughs, "Oh! You mean Lacey, Wes' younger sister – we go way back."

"Good to know."

He doesn't have time to respond before I crash my mouth on his.

Nico

I have died and gone to heaven.

It's the only explanation for what is happening right now.

Mo's lips land on mine, and I don't even hesitate. I take what I've wanted since Taber's lacrosse legend arrived back in Taber.

Pulling that sinful body closer, I press every inch of us together as Mo snakes his tongue into my mouth. Hard muscle meets my torso as I push him against the locker, my hands tangling through that perfect hair as he claims my mouth. We fight for control, biting and pulling at each other until finally Mo snaps.

Letting out a growl, he spins us around so I'm the one with my back pressed against the locker, completely at his mercy.

"Always in control. Typical." I pant the words against his mouth, letting my hands roam the bare chest in front of me.

Mo smirks, "Why would I let someone else take the lead when I know I can do it better?"

Shoving his knee between my legs, he pins me against the lockers and reclaims my mouth. I hike my leg over his hip and grind against him, my dick getting harder by the minute.

"Your arrogance knows no bounds."

Mo pushes back against me, his own erection digging into my hip as I lick a path down his neck.

"It's not arrogance if it's true."

Reaching the sensitive spot under his ear, I suck hard enough to leave a mark. He jerks back, glaring at me with hazy eyes.

"What the hell was that?"

I give him a lazy grin, "Just exploring the territory, babe."

The door to the locker room bangs open, and I look at Mo in panic. His expression remains eerily calm as he untangles himself from my body, and my eyes drop to the tent he's sporting in his shorts.

Ladies and gentlemen, let it be confirmed that Maurice O'Brien is completely proportionate.

Mo pulls a shirt out of his gym bag just as Millard peeks around the corner, "Hey guys. Wes sent me to retrieve you, Nico."

Making sure my boner is out of sight, I smile at the rookie over my shoulder, "I'll be right out, thanks Mill."

"No problem." Sneaking a glance at Mo's impressive back muscles, Millard nods and walks away.

As soon as I hear the door close behind him, I turn and find Mo bent over, lacing up his runners. Any thoughts of hiding my hard-on fly out the window as my dick soaks in the view from behind.

"Are you not returning to the field?"

I'm still staring at Mo's ass when he puts his foot down, his own boner significantly reduced.

This man's willpower is unbelievable.

"No. I need to burn off some energy." He shoots me a look, "Alone."

I hold up my hands in surrender, "I've got captain duties to return to. Just wanted to make sure you were feeling better."

A smirk makes its way onto my face as I spot the red mark forming beneath his ear.

"Right."

He falls silent, and I wait for the inevitable *let's pretend this never happened* speech.

I watch in shock as Mo picks up his gym bag and heads for the door.

"Wait. That's it?"

He pauses, "I don't fool around with teammates, Montez. It makes things messy."

I feel my jaw drop, "You're worried about messing around with a *teammate*? Am I missing something here?"

I can count on one hand the number of hookups who claimed to be bisexual the night before and who remained to be bisexual the morning of. The bicurious folk enjoy venturing on the gay side, but when it comes time to face their actions, it's usually an abort situation.

Mo shakes his head, "One make-out doesn't change the fact I despise you. And even if I didn't find your inability to keep your mouth shut intolerable, I still wouldn't pursue things because of your position on the team."

I'm stunned speechless, as he continues, "This was a one-off, Montez. I won't let it happen again."

It takes a moment for my tongue to remember how to function.

"Maurice, wait."

He sighs impatiently as I struggle to put the pieces together.

"Don't you like women?"

The tiniest smirk crosses Mo's face, "Not always."

And with that bombshell, he turns and walks away.

Chapter 11

5 years ago...

Mo

"Just do it."

My teammate gives me a shrug before turning his attention back to the naked girls. The blonde watches us with her hands on her voluptuous hips while the redhead smiles at us coyly.

"Come on, boys. You know the deal: If you make out, we make out."

The alcohol buzzing through my veins is so strong at this point, I can't remember either of their names.

Not that they seem to mind.

Brett, another freshman on the lacrosse team, takes a step towards me and I hold up a hand to stop him.

"Take another step and I'll deck you."

This isn't our first foursome together, so he knows the rules by now. Brett comes off straight as an arrow, but rumour has it he enjoys hitting up the gay club outside of Taber during his spare time.

And that is something I want no part of.

I shudder, thinking about what my father would have to say if he heard I made out with another man. Even if it was for the sake of watching two attractive women get each other off, Jonathan would pop an ulcer if he ever caught wind of this.

Hell, he might even cut me off.

The thought sobers me enough to give Brett another glare before turning to the girls, "Sorry ladies, that's not on the table."

"What a shame. We were just starting to have some fun."

The redhead leans down and plants a kiss on the blonde's neck. The blonde moans, reaching out to stroke the other girl's pointed nipples. I chuckle, watching Brett start to drool. I'm just getting into it myself when the redhead pulls back with a wink.

"The real fun begins after you kiss."

Brett whips his head in my direction but I stand firm, "Not going to happen."

"Dude, stop being a pussy."

The blonde smirks, "What's wrong big boy? Is the almighty Mo not confident enough to kiss his teammate on the lips?"

O'Briens don't run from our problems. We face them head on.

The loop pounds through my drunken haze as I narrow my eyes at her. My father taught me to never back down from a challenge, but he sure as hell didn't tell me that it was normal to kiss another man.

Grinding my teeth together, I march over and grab Brett by the back of the neck. He stumbles as I yank him closer, his large hands grabbing ahold of my shoulders as I bring our lips together. Brett's scruff rubs my cheek and I grimace, waiting for the disgust to hit me.

But it never does.

His hand snakes its way up to my jaw, roughly tilting my head for a better angle. I let him, not because I enjoy being submissive but because I am too shocked by the lust exploding through my body to do anything but kiss him back.

Brett eventually breaks the kiss and turns his attention back to the girls. With a happy squeal, the blonde latches herself onto her friend and they pick up right where they left off. I'm left standing off to the side, shaking, as Brett joins the girls in a sloppy threesome.

The room spins with alcohol and fear, my desire to join the lacrosse bunnies completely gone. I watch as my teammate sinks himself into the redhead, her exaggerated moan making me cringe. The blonde is busy getting herself off as she watches them, but even that doesn't stir the slightest interest in me.

Because for the first time ever, it's not the girls I'm watching.

It's my male teammate.

1 year ago...

"What brings you to town?"

The blonde Adonis grins at me, his sharp cheekbones and full lips ensuring my attention stays entirely on him.

"Picking up my sister for winter break."

I throw back the shot, savouring the burn it leaves behind. It's been a while since I've been to *Lifestyle*, but nothing has changed. The base is still loud enough to cause permanent hearing damage and the VIP section is still dark enough to find fleeting pleasure.

Which is exactly what I'm here for.

"How long are you in town?"

Interest gleams in those gorgeous brown eyes as Carter does an unsubtle scan of my body. It doesn't bother me in the slightest considering I did the same thing to him a few minutes ago.

"Just one night." His grin widens and I feel my own lips pull into a smirk, "So you better make it count."

"Good thing I'm more of a show than a tell kind of guy."

I snort at the terrible pickup line and look out over the railing to the drunken mass moving on the dance floor. The urge to join them creeps in but I force myself to turn back to the hard body beside me.

"I hope your moves are better than your lines. Otherwise we will both be disappointed."

Carter laughs and the low sound heightens my buzz. My freshman year was spent fucking every girl I came across, but it wasn't until that night with Brett that I realized there was so much more satisfaction to be had with men.

My father taught me raw masculinity was the greatest power a man could have. Turns out, that remains true in the bedroom as well.

A large hand trails down my back and my dick thickens in response.

"Why don't we test out that theory?" His breath is warm in my ear and I grin, motioning towards the overpriced rooms kept especially for this reason.

"After you."

Grinning, Carter turns and heads over to the bouncer while I take one last scan of the dance floor below. The blasting music tugs at my consciousness, a memory slipping past the carefully constructed barriers.

"Mom! Look, I think I'm dancing."

Flailing my arms in the air, I do my best to follow the graceful rhythm of my mother's body. My baby sister is strapped to her chest, her tiny blue eyes filled with joy as mother twirls around the room.

"Dancing isn't about thinking, Mo. It's about feeling."

I let out a shriek of laughter when she takes my hand and spins me around.

"What do you feel when you're dancing, mom?" Swaying my hips, I stumble a couple steps before my mother helps me rebalance.

She smiles, "Dancing has always been where I find peace. Whether it's been a good day or a bad day, everything is better when I'm dancing."

I frown, coming to a stop, "I don't understand."

Mother laughs, taking my hands and pulling me close, "There are some things in life you will never understand, Mo. Just remember to make time for the things that bring you peace. Whether that's dancing or skiing or something else completely – find that thing that helps you escape and hold on to it."

Wrapping my arms around her legs, I bury my face in mother's flowing dress.

"But how will I know when I've found it?"

Mother bends down and plants a kiss on my cheek, "You'll know because you won't think. You'll feel."

I blink back to present when the room flashes purple and a Latin beat kicks in. Shrieks rise up from the crowd below and I feel the energy seep into my bones.

A tall, lean Latino catches my eye and I turn to see him hop up on the bar and begin to move. The cheers grow louder as his hips twist and turn without any hint of hesitation. I watch him with interest, my earlier arousal growing with the fluidity of his movements.

Feeling my stare, the handsome man glances up and meets my eyes. He grins, blowing me a kiss before hopping off the bar and disappearing into the pulsing crowd.

I squint, trying to find him again, but it's no use.

"Cold feet already?"

Carter's voice fills my ear and the spark of lust returns.

"Just making sure you were ready to give me a show."

Feeling lighter than I have in weeks, I turn and give him a genuine smile, "Lead the way."

Chapter 12

Present day...

Mo

"Another one."

Hunter squats in front of me, his knees shaking to the point of concern. Sweat drips down his forehead as he pushes the barbell back up to standing.

We make eye contact in the mirror and I can see the desperation in his eyes.

"Another one."

Hunter grunts but does as he's told, lowering himself back down like a man on the verge of death. I can see some of his teammates watching through the mirror, each of them wincing as Hunter's knees bow inward.

Stepping forward, I calmly help Hunter re-stack the barbell and as soon as the weight is off his shoulders, the sophomore collapses to the ground in front of me.

I glance down at the sweaty body heaving on the ground, "That was enough for today. Go stretch and then you can hit the showers."

"Yes Coach." Hunter barely lifts his head as I walk away.

The rest of the team is huddled around the bench press, watching one of the new defensemen push the barbell above his chest.

"C'mon, Preston! You can do it!"

Nico cheers as the rookie does another rep and Wes helps him re-stack the barbell. I watch, unimpressed, as the co-captains hand out back claps and high fives to everyone around.

"Great job, guys. Remember to drink lots of water on your rest day tomorrow."

Wes gives the group a dimpled smile while Nico mimes taking shots behind him. Chuckles go around the room and I feel a smirk tug the corner of my mouth.

"And don't forget to help out with move-in this week. It will go towards your volunteer hours."

Nico steps forward and whispers something in Wes' ear. The co-captain laughs and the smirk falls from my lips.

"Practice dismissed. Keep your eyes peeled for any struggling freshmen!"

Wes gives everyone one last wave before he grabs a cleaning rag and starts wiping down the equipment. I let the team funnel out of the performance room before walking over to Nico and snatching the cloth out of his hands.

"Captains are supposed to be the leaders of the team. Not the cheerleaders." Crossing my arms, I give him a pointed look, "And you should be home resting. Not wasting your energy on rookies who can barely bench two plates."

"Concerned for my well-being, Maurice? I'm touched."

"It's not your well-being I'm concerned about."

Nico's dark eyes dance with amusement, "You sure about that?"

My brows furrow as annoyance pounds through me, "Positive. The only reason you're on this team is because you are a somewhat decent goalie. If your body is out of commission, there's no point in even competing for the championship banner this season."

The words are harsh but Nico's grin remains solidly in place.

"Last time I checked, my body was in working order. But I'd be happy to let you take a closer look." His gaze flicks to my lips and my irritation spikes.

"Do you not take anything seriously?"

"Only serious things." Nico grins, giving me an obvious once-over, "You on the other hand, don't have that problem."

"What's that supposed to mean?"

He raises an eyebrow, the scruff on his jaw noticeably thinner than it was a few days ago.

He must have shaved since we made out.

For some reason, the thought irritates me.

"To put it bluntly, you walk around with a stick up your ass. The only time I have seen you loosen up is when you are either drunk or horny." He smirks, "Both of which were thanks to yours truly."

Closing the distance between us, I lean forward until our noses are almost touching. Nico's eyes go wide, his eyes darting between my face to the few stragglers still roaming around the performance room.

"Don't get the mistaken impression you're something special, Montez. You aren't the first guy to get me drunk and you certainly aren't the last. And as for that kiss in the locker room the other day?"

Letting my eyes drop to his lips, I watch the grin slide off his face, "It was unmemorable. Which is exactly how your reign as team captain is going to be."

I regret the words the second they leave my mouth, but I'm sure as hell not taking them back. Dropping the cleaning rag into the bin, I turn and walk away before I see the hurt cross Nico's face.

"I thought it was you!"

A small body tackles me from behind, the familiar squeal immediately easing the tension from my shoulders.

I laugh, wrapping my arms around Stella, "I would have thought you sleep in now that Ellsworth doesn't have to train at this hour."

Hearing a deep chuckle, I look up and find Cody watching us with a smile.

"Your sister has a problem with sharing gym equipment so we have to go before the morning rush."

Stella pulls away and gives me an exasperated look, "Why would anyone think they can use the pull-up bar when I'm in the middle of the circuit?"

I tilt my head, "Did they know you were using it?"

She huffs, "How could they not? I had used it during the last four rounds."

Cody coughs, "Stel, most people only do four rounds."

Turning to her boyfriend, my sister narrows her gaze, "Whose side are you taking, Ellsworth?"

He grins, "Yours, of course."

"That's what I thought." Adjusting her topknot, Stella turns her attention back to me, "Want to join us for breakfast? We were just headed to the cafeteria."

I smile, "If they have protein shakes, lead the way."

Falling in step beside them, I take the chance to look around my old university. Not much has changed, Taber's limited budget was never anything impressive, so the overall structure and classroom layout appear to be the same. The only difference I can see are the event dates printed on the colourful posters hanging from the wall.

"You know, I heard a rumour the other day."

Tearing my gaze from the Punk Rockers banner hanging off the music hall's doorframe, I turn to see Stella grinning at me.

Cody snorts, "It's all she's been talking about for the last two days."

Stella ignores him and gives me a bright smile, "I heard that a certain lacrosse goalie might be into you."

"Really."

She slaps my arm, "I get enough sarcasm from Lou, I don't need it from you too."

Cody looks at me quizzically, "You don't seem surprised."

My mind flashes back to the groping session that went down in the locker room the other day. I lied when I told Nico our make out was unmemorable. The memory of his hands running down my bare chest and his tongue in my mouth is something that's been hovering over my head like a persistent storm cloud.

Always in control. Typical.

Clearing my throat, I shove the memory and Nico's words to the back of my mind.

"Montez has made it very clear what he wants from me."

Stella gives me a sly look, "Maybe you should go for it. Nico has quite a bit of experience under his belt."

I ignore her as we hop in line behind a group of girls also waiting to order, the short spandex shorts and team t-shirts making it easy to guess they came from the university's volleyball court. A few of them cut glances my way, giggles rising up from the group when I give the tallest one a wink.

Stella rolls her eyes, "They are way too young for you."

I give her a pointed look, "They are probably the same age as Montez."

She waves away my comment, "Nico is mature for his age."

Cody laughs, "Not sure about that one, Stel."

I give my friend a nod, "Exactly."

The line shuffles forward and we place our orders. Reaching for the largest protein shake on the counter, I find a receipt with a number waiting for me.

Cody grins, "Good to see some things don't change."

Stella shakes her head with a sigh, "And here I was hoping some things would."

I don't say anything as we make our way over to a table, leaving the receipt untouched on the counter.

You and me both.

Nico

I fucking jinxed it.

Hiding my grimace behind the stack of moving boxes in my arms, I try to keep my voice as upbeat as possible, "It could be worse, Lace. You could have your brother as your roommate."

"I guess."

Lacey looks sullen as we place the last of her stuff on the Styrofoam mattress this university calls a bed. Thankfully, I'd thought ahead and purchased the necessary 4-inch mattress topper so my favourite girl wouldn't wake up crippled tomorrow.

Not that her sleeping arrangements are the biggest concern right now.

Pulling up my dance party playlist, I hit play and start pulling random items out of the boxes.

"Seriously though, you need to tell Wes the shower karaoke has to stop. I haven't been able to nap since we moved back in."

Lacey giggles and starts to sway to the music, her willowy body becoming more relaxed with each Latin beat.

"I'll remember that the next time we get into an argument."

I grin, taking her hand and twirling her around the room until more laughter eases the ache in my chest.

"I'm always happy to provide blackmail material."

We keep dancing until the song fades into the next one. Lacey sighs, slowing to a stop and tucking her head under my chin.

"She hates me, Nico."

I wince, "Hate is a strong word. Dislike might be more fitting."

"Trip always talks about how amazing her roommate Stella is. How am I supposed to have a good university experience if I'm trying to hide from my roommate the whole time?"

She blinks up at me, those beautiful green eyes identical to those of her brother.

"You've only had one interaction. There's lots of time for roommate bonding." I flinch when a bang hits the wall separating the two dorm rooms.

"TURN DOWN THE MUSIC OR I'M CALLING HOUSING SERVICES!"

Lacey looks at me in panic and I give her a weak smile, "Roommates are overrated. Ditch this depressing dorm and move in with Wes and me."

"I'M CALLING THEM RIGHT NOW!"

Marching over to the adjoining wall, I bang my fists as hard as I can.

"This is Enrique, you tasteless snob!"

Silence ensues and I hear Lacey stifle a laugh behind me. Giving her a victorious grin, I pump my fist just as the door swings open.

Oh shit.

Green hair and piercings occupy the doorway of Lacey's new bedroom and it takes all my willpower not to throw myself out the window. The girl's leather jacket screams *fight me* and the amount of eyeliner she's got smudged under her eyes probably costs more than my monthly food budget.

"What did you say to me?"

Narrowing her eyes, Lacey's new roommate looks like she's about two seconds away from pummelling me. And if her septum ring is anything to go by, this freshman has a much higher pain tolerance than I've ever had.

"Babe, you were disrespecting Enrique Iglesias."

"Who?" Cecelia's brows furrow as if she thinks I'm still the problem. Just as I'm about to launch into a lecture on culture appreciation, a loud gasp echoes from the dorm's living room.

"Have you never heard Hero before? Or Bailando?"

Cecelia frowns as Wes comes walking in, his timing as impeccable as always.

"That's not even English."

He grins, popping those dimples for all their worth, "That's what we call culture. My good friend Nico here actually speaks Spanish fluently." Wes throws me a wink, "He'd be happy to teach you. Just say the word."

My best friend is a cruel man.

I smile painfully at the Enrique hater, "Translator and part-time linguistics instructor at your service."

She ignores me, studying Wes with curiosity. If I didn't know better, I would say there was even a spark of interest in those blue eyes...

"Are you single?"

I choke on my tongue, coughing and laughing to the point of needing an ambulance.

Lacey grimaces, "That's my brother."

Cecelia cocks out a hip, "So?"

Wes looks at me in panic but I'm already on fire control.

"I'm afraid that fine man over there is happily cuffed. Should that status change however, you will be the first to know."

I give her a big grin, ignoring the death glare Wes is sending my way.

What can I say? Karma is a bitch.

"Deal."

Cecelia nods, her eyes lingering on Wes before heading back to her room. The second we hear her door close Lacey lets out a snort.

"Thanks for being the peace treaty, Wesley."

Wes groans, covering his face with his hands, "That was wrong on so many levels."

I grin, "But now Lacey has a conversation starter *and* incentive for good roommate behaviour."

She smiles, walking over to flick her brother on the nose, "We all know Trip isn't going anywhere anytime soon. Stop being a drama queen and help me unpack."

"Yes ma'am."

Picking up the closest box, Wes rips off the top and starts stacking books on Lacey's desk. I follow suit, returning my attention to the box in front of me. I smile as I pull photographs out of the box, clips from Lacey's childhood and our teenage adventures filling me with warm memories.

"Do you want to hang or fold your shirts?"

Lacey sighs dramatically, "Always hang, Wesley. That way they don't get wrinkled."

"You know, there is this wonderful invention called an iron."

I grin, listening to the familiar sibling banter as I empty out Lacey's stash of memories. A flash of orange catches my eyes and I feel my grin falter as my fingers wrap around the pill bottle rolling around the otherwise empty box.

Chapter 13

Mo

I curse as Nico lets another ball sail into the net.

The players lining the bench shoot me a look at my swearing but I don't care. We are one week away from our first tournament and suddenly Nico has become the worst lacrosse goalie I have ever seen in my life. Every single shot that has been taken this practice has gone in.

Even fucking Millard managed to make it past Nico's guard.

Clenching my clipboard until my knuckles turn white, I jerk my head towards the sub sitting on the bench.

"Out on the field. Now."

"But Coach, Nico isn't-

My glare sends him scrambling to his feet and running out onto the field. I watch the interaction go down, Nico taking off his helmet and giving the player a supportive pat on the back before jogging towards the sidelines. He runs right past me without a glance or promiscuous comment and I feel my teeth clench for an entirely different reason.

He's giving me the fucking silent treatment.

The shooting drill resumes and to my relief, the sub does a semi-decent job of keeping the forwards on edge. His technical skills leave a lot to be desired, but the quick reaction time behind each save shows promise.

Despite the improvement in the drill performance, I can't shake off the nagging feeling that there's something more to Nico's behaviour. As immature as he is, radio silence really isn't Nico's signature – hell, he wasn't even silent after that group of farmers lay a beating on him.

The unease itching beneath my skin grows until I finally march over to the bench.

"Montez. I'd like a word."

He doesn't look at me, simply nods and follows me away from the field. As soon as we are out of earshot, I turn to face him and cross my arms.

"What's your problem?"

Nico glances away, "I don't have a problem."

"Then explain to me how a sloth took over your body in the last forty-eight hours because that is the only explanation for your performance today."

A smirk tugs his lips, "Can't say I've ever been compared to a sloth before."

Tilting my head, I wait until those dark eyes meet mine, "Tell me what's going on, Montez."

He sighs but doesn't say another word.

"If this is about what I said the other day…"

Don't you dare apologize.

"…you shouldn't let it mess with your head. I was angry and spoke out of line."

Fuck.

Nico quirks an eyebrow at me, "Was that an apology, Maurice?"

"No." *Liar.*

He grins, "Are you sure?"

"Yes, I'm sure." Snapping my teeth, I glare at him, "I'm just making sure we won't have to forfeit this weekend's game because our goalie decided to get hung up on his emotions."

"Babe, there were no hard feelings on my end. Your persistence in denying the attraction between us only makes the flames grow stronger." He winks, "As do your sad attempts at pretending you don't care."

I hate him.

"Cut the bullshit, Montez, and tell my what's wrong."

Nico sighs, running a hand through his hair, "Fine. I recently made a discovery about a loved one and I don't know what to do about it."

I frown, "A little more context would be nice."

He blows out a breath, "Do you remember Lacey, the girl I was on the phone with the other day?"

I nod and he continues, "There was a situation with her ex-boyfriend that led to her trying to commit suicide. It was rough for a long time, but eventually she started seeing a therapist and things got better."

"Is she going to be seeing someone while she's here?"

Nico nods, "She's booked in with a therapist over in Silverwood but the sessions don't start until next week."

He looks off into the distance and I wait for him to continue.

"Wes and I helped her move in this week and while we were unpacking I found a pill bottle with the same prescription she tried to use the first time."

"Have you told Wes?"

Nico shakes his head, "No. That's part of the problem. I panicked and took the bottle but now I don't know what to do."

I pause, taking a moment to think about the situation and the data on hand.

"Were there any pills in the bottle?"

Nico frowns, "Does it matter?"

I pull out my phone and do a quick google search.

"The risk of another suicide attempt is much higher if there are pills in that bottle. If it's just an empty pill bottle then we have a whole bunch of different scenarios that could be at play here."

"Did you seriously just google suicide stats?"

Ignoring him, I put away my phone, "First step, find out if there are any pills in that bottle. Then you would either broach the topic with the subject or consult a loved one to plan the best course of action."

Nico stares at me like I've suddenly grown three heads.

"That was... actually helpful."

I shrug, "Solutions are easiest when you have all the variables present."

He blinks, a slow smile spreading across his face, "You almost sound like a nerd there, Maurice. Any chance you have a pair of glasses stashed away somewhere?'

"I keep them locked away with the puke bags saved for long car rides."

Nico throws his head back and laughs. Shaking my head, I start walking back to the field, fighting a smile every step of the way.

Nico

"What do you think of this one?"

Wes holds up another graphic t-shirt and I pull a face.

"I don't even know what I'm looking at."

"Dude. It's an album cover." He raises an eyebrow, pointing to the band name scrawled along the top, "Fall Out Boy. You've heard their music before."

I sniff, turning away from the offensive piece of clothing, "Not by choice."

Wes grins, "Pretty sure I remember someone screaming the words to Uma Thurman just last week."

"Must have been someone else."

"Mmhmm."

Throwing the shirt over his arm, Wes leads me to the other side of the fan mania store. I've counted five different Anime tattoos on the employees wandering around the store, and I'm not even going to talk about the array of graphic t-shirts decorating the walls.

Hot Culture is every emo's fantasy.

And my worst nightmare.

"Who the hell watches anime anyway?" I shudder as I make eye contact with one of the life-sized dolls standing near the checkout counter.

Wes shoots me a sideways look, reaching for another punk rock t-shirt, "Have you ever watched it before?"

"Well... no." My eyes narrow, "Have you?"

He smiles, popping out a dimple, "Trip introduced me to it. It's surprisingly good."

"You're pathetic."

Wes ignores me, tilting his head as he holds up another t-shirt. Not bothering to hold back my sigh, I look at the nonexistent watch on my wrist.

"It should not take you this long to pick out a t-shirt."

"Shut up. I'm just making sure it'll be one Trip likes." He frowns, looking from the one in his hands to the one on his arm, "Do these look the same to you?"

I sigh, pointing at the dark material in his hands, "That one has the vintage sticker on it, the other doesn't. Isn't her birthday in October?"

Wes nods, "October 17th."

"It's September 2nd."

Broad shoulders lift in a shrug, "It's going to creep up before we know it."

And that, ladies and gentlemen, is what a relationship does to a man.

I let out another exasperated sigh and Wes shoots me a look, "What is your problem? You love shopping."

It's true. There's nothing I love more than an excuse to voice my opinion.

"Sorry, man. I'm just... tired."

Turning so my back is facing him, I hide my pained expression by flipping through a stack of CDs.

Since discovering Lacey's pill bottle, I have done my best to avoid my childhood friend. Wes always knows when something is bothering me, so the fact he hasn't caught on yet is almost as big of a shock as finding the pills was.

Almost.

"I know what you're doing." Wes ambles beside me, his indecision with the t-shirts weighing down both his arms.

"Hmm?" Refusing to look at him, I pick up the closest CD and flip it over.

"You're trying not to tell me something. But it's not going to work, do you want to know why?" He studies me, his usual charming smile nowhere to be found, "Because I already know what you're not telling me."

My fingers freeze, "You do?"

Wes nods, "I was waiting for you to say something."

Relief and guilt fill my system as I carefully put the CD back in its place.

"I didn't know how to bring it up, Wes. I was worried it would be breaking her trust if I told you before I confronted her."

Wes blinks, "What are you talking about?"

My heart plummets at the confused look on his face.

"What do you think this was about?"

He frowns, "The crush you have on our assistant coach."

"Er, right. That's what I was talking about too."

Swerving my gaze, I make eye contact with the creepy doll again. Her painted smile mocks me as my best friend waves for my attention.

"You're lying." The dimples are long gone as Wes stares me down.

"Am I?"

I go to walk around him but he shuffles to the left and blocks my path. A guy dressed up as Darth Vader glances in our direction.

I give him a cheerful wave, "Luke is your son!"

Vader holds up his hands as if to air choke me, so I drop the wave.

"Nico, stop being a dipshit. Tell me what's going on."

Turning to look at Wes, I can see the disappointment written across his face. The sight hits me straight in the gut.

"I…" Clearing my throat, I force my gaze to meet his, "I found something in Lacey's room that I need to talk to her about."

Wes looks at me in concern, "Is it bad?"

"That's what I need to talk to her about. To make sure it isn't." Biting my lip, I feel the guilt surge to the surface, "Lacey's trust has been broken so many times, she needs to know she has someone besides you in her corner."

"You're right." He nods, grabbing a Green Day CD from the stack, "She needs someone she can trust. And there's no one I trust more for that role that you."

Emotion cracks his voice and my own throat thickens dangerously.

"You know I will always protect her. She's my sister as much as she is yours."

Wes grins, his eyes glistening, "Lucky for her, she got my hair."

I laugh, poking at the t-shirts bundled in his arms, "Your midnight locks might be pretty but we both know she got my charm."

He snorts, "More like your dramatics."

"Hell, I'll take it."

We smile at each other and the uncertainty I've been carrying around finally lifts from my shoulders. My mind flashes to the heart-to-heart I had with Mo earlier this week and I feel a warm flush work its way through my body.

"Have you ever heard any rumours about Maurice being gay?"

Wes groans, finally putting one of the band t-shirts back on the rack, "Dude, you need to leave that man alone. He already hates everything we do."

I raise my hands in surrender, "It's an innocent question."

"From what I've heard, Mo was a notorious ladies' man. He always celebrated his win with whatever lacrosse bunny was nearby. Sometimes there was more than one."

The image puts a bad taste in my mouth.

"He was into threesomes?"

Wes nods, "Threesomes, foursomes, whatever was convenient and available. The nickname Mighty Mo didn't originate from the lacrosse field if you know what I mean."

Well, fuck me. The man's hookup resume is more impressive than mine.

"So, there was never any rumours of him going to *Lifestyle* to blow off some steam?"

Wes laughs, "A lot of guys go to that nightclub to blow off some steam. Even Trip came with us last time. *Lifestyle* is an awesome nightclub whether you're gay or not."

I sigh, feeling oddly disappointed, "Good point."

He gives me a friendly bump on the arm, "Let it go, Nico. When it comes to Maurice O'Brien, you can look but you can't touch."

That's what I thought until Maurice made the first move.

"You're right." Giving my head a shake, I shove the jumbled thoughts aside, "Hurry up and pay so we can find your girl some spicy birthday lingerie."

"Now we're talking."

Chapter 14

Mo

My sister stole my car.

Yanking out my phone, I jab her phone number.

"Stella speaking!"

"I stepped outside my apartment this morning and do you know what I saw?"

Her laughter flows through my phone, "I thought the handwritten note was a nice touch! Ellsworth and I just need to borrow it for the weekend, my jeep is currently out of commission."

"And you didn't think to ask if you could borrow my Cadillac?" Pinching my brows together, I stare at the hastily scrawled note I found tapped to my front door this morning.

"That's what the note is for! To explain the situation and send some sibling love in your direction."

A low murmur echoes through the phone, telling me Cody is nearby.

"Why didn't you take Cody's car?"

"It's in the shop right now."

My left eye starts to twitch so I squeeze my eyes shut.

"I need my car today. The team is hitting the road in an hour."

Background noise cuts through before Stella's upbeat tone hops back on.

"Take the bus with the team. Problem solved."

Gripping my phone tighter, I let out a growl, "You know damn well why I can't take the bus with the team. Turn around now."

"It'll be good for you. Father always tells us the only way to grow-

-is to push past your comfort zone, I know."

I finish her sentence and she falls silent. I soften my voice and try for a different approach, "Stella. Do me this one favour and bring back my car. You can borrow it any other time."

She hums, "Take the bus, Mo. I have a good feeling about this."

My frustration unleashes and I snap, "This isn't funny. Get your ass back here right now or I'll call the cops."

"And they would arrest me for what? Having the spare key?" She laughs and I resist the urge to smash my phone against the kitchen wall.

"Sorry, Mo. Take some motion medicine and hope for the best."

"Stella, I swear to God-

"See you soon!" She blows me a kiss and hangs up the phone.

Taking a deep breath, I put my phone back on the table. I can feel my anger threatening to unleash itself, but I lock it down with a few deep breaths.

Think, Mo. Don't let the emotions rule you.

Shaking the lingering turmoil from my body, I glance at my watch and quickly formulate a new plan.

Thirty minutes to get my things in order. Ten minutes to get my ass over to the university and onto the team bus. Because thanks to my sister, driving to the away game is no longer an option.

I wait until the last possible second to board the bus. Climbing the narrow stairs, recycled air immediately fills my nose and I make a beeline for the seat directly behind the driver.

"Coach Mo! Come back and chill with us. We're playing cards against humanity." André waves at me from the last row but I ignore him and plop down in the first row.

Shifting uncomfortably, I curse my sister for the umpteenth time as my legs press into the ripped leather in front of me. Taber University lives and breathes on a tight budget, so it came as no surprise that the team bus was a regular, ugly, yellow school bus.

Laughter rings out behind me but I don't bother turning around. My shoulders are almost as wide as the seat itself and I can barely move from the claustrophobia already pressing down on me. Reaching for the window next to me, I pry the rusty metal frame open as far as it will go, but it doesn't offer the faintest breeze.

Sweat coats my forehead as panic sinks in, the nausea already rising in the back of my throat. I'm going to be stuck in this airtight cylinder for over two hours with no fresh oxygen to think of.

Forcing myself to swallow, I quickly grab my air pods out of my bag and jam them into my ears. Restarting the podcast I was listening to this morning, I try and focus on the narrator's voice as the bus pulls out of the parking lot.

Our Tiger chant breaks through my podcast and I risk a glance over my shoulder to see Nico and Wes walking up and down the aisle, hyping up the boys. My eyes linger on Nico's snug jeans as he walks by the group of rookies, the ripped material hugging his lower body perfectly.

The bus jerks forward and my eyes snap back to the front, my stomach contents swirling from the rocky motion. Grabbing my bag again, I pop two pills into my mouth and swallow them dry.

Don't feel, just think.

The opposite use of my mother's wisdom puts a smile on my face, the memory of her soft features and bright smile flashing through my mind. She was the light to my father's dark, the warmth to his chill.

For my mother, it was dancing that made everything better.

For me, it was my mother.

My thoughts drift away as we hit the highway, the smoother roads easing my body as my mind takes me back to a time when my mother was alive.

"I got you something." My mother's eyes sparkle with excitement, her hands tucked behind her back, "Close your eyes."

I shake my head with a sigh, "Aren't I a little old for surprises?"

She smiles, "No one is ever too old for surprises."

"Pretty sure father would disagree."

Her smile only brightens, "Your father loves my surprises. Now, quit being stubborn and close your eyes."

I groan, making a show of closing my eyes, "Happy?"

She taps my nose, "Just because you're off to university doesn't mean you get to be cheeky. Okay, open them."

I slowly open my eyes, seeing my mother's unbridled excitement radiating from every pore in her body. The sight has me smiling before I see anything else.

"You're going to love it." She claps her hands, barely able to contain herself.

I look around the room, letting out a confused laugh, "Mom, there's nothing here."

She smiles coyly, "Check your pockets."

"You know, most people put the surprise out in front of them."

Chuckling, I reach into my pocket and find a piece of paper. She waits patiently as I read it, the warmth in my chest expanding with each box on the list.

"Do you understand what those names are?"

I nod, my throat painfully thick, "You found all the dance clubs near Taber University."

She nods, motioning for me to flip the paper over, "Dance clubs, bars, and other areas I thought were worth noting. Now you have something to do when you aren't busy training or studying."

Swallowing the emotions clogging my throat, I pull her in for a hug, "Thank you, mom. It's perfect."

She squeezes me tightly, "You can scope out the dance floors for when Stella and I come to visit."

"I can't wait."

The drone of my podcast fades away and it takes me a moment to realize that one of my air pods is gone.

"You're missing out on team bonding."

Turning, I see Nico holding the stolen item with a smirk. I hold out my hand, turning my gaze back to the road ahead.

"I'm too old for team bonding. Hand it over."

"What you listening to?" Nico inspects the earbud, letting out a low whistle, "You've got the latest Apple tech. Nice."

"Comes with the job."

He slides into the seat across from mine, making himself comfortable, "You work for your dad, right?"

"Yes."

"What's that like?"

My brows furrow, "It's fine. Can I have my air pod back?"

"Please."

"Excuse me?"

He grins, "You didn't say please."

I stare at him, "Give me that air pod right now or I will come over there and get it myself."

Nico's grin grows wider, "Promise?"

Before he has the chance to think, I lunge across the aisle, throwing myself on top of him. Using my bodyweight to pin him against the worn leather seat, our chests are completely flushed together as I look at him with narrowed eyes.

"Never present a challenge you can't win, Montez."

He stares back at me, those dark eyes studying my face as I slowly extract myself from his body. The bus jerks around a corner just as I go to standup and I have to grab the back of Nico's seat to steady myself. It's only when I make eye contact with Hunter do I realize I'm facing the wrong way.

My stomach lurches as the bus takes another corner and only one thought races through my head.

I'm going to kill my sister.

Nico

Mo drops into my seat like a man possessed.

His immaculate skin has turned a ghastly shade of white and the sheen of perspiration on his forehead is making my own stomach cramp up.

"You okay, Maurice?"

I press myself into the window, trying to give him more breathing space. These bus seats were made for children, not two grown men.

Mo doesn't respond, just stares ahead as if the open road might be the divine answer he's looking for. I sneak a glance to the back of the bus to call for help, only to find my co-captain slumped awkwardly in his seat, mouth open, fast-asleep.

Useless, I tell you.

Grimacing against the uncomfortable position, I offer Mo his stolen air pod with a weak smile.

"You won. Fair and square."

His lips remain clamped shut so I do what any desperate man would do in this situation: I grab his hand.

Mo looks at me in surprise, "What the hell are you doing?"

Intertwining our fingers, I start rubbing soothing circles on the back of his hand.

"I'm distracting you."

"It's weird. Stop it."

Ignoring him, I continue tracing gentle circles with my thumb, "You just took my hand holding virginity. Congratulations."

His lips twitch, "You've never held hands before?"

I shrug, "I prefer more explicit displays of affection."

"You could give me a blowjob if that would make you feel better."

I burst out laughing, "How considerate of you."

Mo flashes me a grin and I swear I've never wanted to give road head more in my life.

Leaning closer, I whisper softly in his ear, "Babe, if these seats had an inch more space, I would already be on my knees."

"Be careful there, Montez. You don't know who you're dealing with."

Grinning, I release his hand and let my fingers run up his thigh teasingly.

"I know exactly who I'm dealing with, Maurice. Give me a time and place and I'll be on my knees, waiting for you." Reaching the bulge in his jeans, I give him a firm squeeze.

Mo is quick to grab my hand, "Unless you want me to bend you over and fuck you against that window in front of all your teammates, I suggest you don't touch me again."

My balls tighten at the thought, "Promise?"

"I already told you, Montez. Never present a challenge you can't win."

Mo doesn't spare me another glance as he stands up and walks back to his seat. I stand up to follow suit but he calls my name before I can make it past his seat.

"Montez."

I pause, turning back to look at him.

"Don't get in your head tomorrow. We will need you present on the field if we have any hope of beating the Dinos." He pauses, weighing his next words carefully, "Just remember you are playing for more than just yourself out there."

The complete one-eighty leaves me at a loss for words, so I simply nod and head back to my seat at the back of the bus. I stare at the back of Mo's perfectly styled hair for the rest of the drive, wondering why our assistant coach had to be my perfect type.

"We're already here?" Wes blinks at me sleepily, his dark hair matted from where he was slumped against the window.

"Welcome to Calgary, Sleeping Beauty."

The bus rolls to a stop and a collective sigh of relief sounds along the team. This road trip was tame compared to some of the ones we will have to do later this season, but that doesn't stop us from complaining.

"Taber needs to invest in a bigger bus." Hunter grumbles as he stretches his legs, his lacrosse bag precariously balancing atop Wes' seat.

Wes grins and pokes the bag so it falls onto the stretching forward.

"You need to invest in a better attitude."

"Dick."

I laugh, grabbing my bag from the floor and joining the line filing out the door. Our bright orange team sweaters are a shock to the grey backdrop of the hotel parking lot as we all assemble outside the bus for a quick debrief.

Wes takes the lead, reminding everyone to be respectful and to save the hotel bar for after our game tomorrow night. I tune him out as he goes over the check-in time for warm-up tomorrow, letting my eyes drift to the man standing off to the side.

He's typing away on his phone, the aviators perched on his nose giving him the bored expression of a movie star. At 6'2,

I'm used to being one of the tallest guys in the room, but Mo is a whole different level. Height-wise, we're the same, but the bodybuilding physique and commanding presence instantly makes him the most eye-catching person in the room.

He lifts his head and stares in my direction. The reflective sunglasses make it hard to tell who he's looking at, but based on the way my skin is burning, I'd bet my life savings his eyes are on me.

"Anything you want to add, Nico?" Wes glances over, jolting me out of my lustful thoughts.

"Nope, you covered it all. Let's kick some ass tomorrow!"

Pumping my fist in the air like a girl at a rock concert, the team rewards my efforts with a cheer. The group breaks to grab their respective gear and we all funnel into the hotel lobby. Mo disappears almost immediately while the rest of us are left to sort out our key cards.

"Dude, I'm supposed to be with Preston."

"Hunter, you're on the third floor with Millard."

"Why does Millard get to be on the third floor?"

I groan, listening to the chaos that is Taber's varsity team. Wes is in the middle of the mess trying to appease everyone when I walk over to the woman manning the front desk.

"Hey…" Sneaking a glance at her name tag, I paste a bright smile on my face, "Darlene. Could you do me a favour and help my friend out? He's a rookie captain and needs some help."

The middle-aged woman looks at me, her eyes narrowed behind wire-rimmed glasses.

"What team do y'all play for?"

I glance down at my jersey, the snarling tiger mascot hard to miss, "Taber Tigers, ma'am."

"Who?"

"Taber University. Down south?" I gesture towards my sweater in hope her eyesight is better than her hearing.

She sniffs, "Never heard of them."

I force my smile to stay bright, "Have you ever eaten corn?"

A hand claps my shoulder, moving me aside. I stare, aghast, as Mo easily slides into my position and gives the woman a wink.

"Hi Darlene, I need a printed list of all the accommodations booked under Taber University please."

The woman blushes, giving him an eager nod, "Of course, how many nights are the reservations for?"

"Two."

She starts typing away on her computer while I turn and stare at the man beside me.

"Since when are you charming?"

He smirks, tucking his aviators into the collar of his shirt, "I'm always charming. Just not to those who annoy me."

And here I thought this man couldn't get any hotter.

Darlene slaps a piece of paper down on the table, all but throwing herself across the counter.

"Here you go."

Mo grabs the sheet and gives her a warm smile, "Thanks Darlene. Have a lovely evening."

She beams like she just won the lottery, "You as well."

My jaw is still on the floor when Mo marches over to the rowdy group of boys and starts calling out the sleeping arrangements.

"Hunter, you're on the third floor with Millard."

André pouts, but keeps his mouth shut when Mo shoots him a look.

"André and Preston are on the first floor."

The two rookies pull a face at each other but take the card Wes holds out to them. Mo continues down the list, his tone leaving no room for argument as each player gets assigned a room and a roommate.

"And lastly, Nico and Wes are on the second floor." He puts the list down, giving everyone a glacial stare, "I trust everyone is capable of making it to their rooms on their own."

Echoes of *yes coach* go around and Mo gives everyone a nod.

"Good. In that case, I will see you bright and early on the field tomorrow. Don't be late."

The team dissembles and heads for the elevators. Wes falls in step beside me.

"How is he so good at that?"

I give the poor man a pat on the back, "He's a control freak who was raised to bark orders. You didn't stand a chance."

Wes groans and follows me into the elevator, "I used to be organized before I started university. Then it all went to shit."

I laugh, "First year really kicks you in the ass, hey?"

"First year and all the ones after."

Chapter 15

Mo

Game day.

The Calgary Dinos have already begun warm-up by the time our team files out of the bus, the McMahon Stadium bustling with excited university students. Nervous energy fills the air as the boys run out onto the field, the familiar buzz of adrenalin running through my body.

I expected to feel a sense of longing watching the players run onto the field, but all I feel is anticipation for the game ahead. The team has worked hard up to this point, so I'm curious to see how we hold up against one of our toughest competitors.

A shout catches my attention, and I turn to see none other than my sister and Cody waving at me from the bleachers. Shaking my head, a smile takes over my face as I walk over to the concrete barrier.

"You stole my car to drive to Wes and Nico's first game?"

Stella grins, leaning over the railing separating us, "We are here to support you as well, silly. Mom would never have missed your first game as a coach."

A flood of emotions crashes through me and I have to grind my teeth to stop them from breaching the surface. Carefully arranging my features, I give nothing away as I reach up and flick her nose.

"You get to sit in the back on the way home."

"TRIP!"

Orange lacrosse gear comes flying by me as Wes jumps up onto the concrete barrier and swings his leg over the railing. I watch, unimpressed, as the team captain risks life and limb to scoop up his girlfriend in a hug.

"You didn't tell me you were coming!"

Before she can answer, Wes sweeps her into the air and plants his lips on hers. Nearby spectators start to cheer while I observe the scene with pinched brows.

Stella slaps my arm, "Enough with the judgmental looks. He's happy to see her."

"I'm more concerned about my captain using up his stamina before the game even starts."

Cody snorts and I shoot him a look, "Don't think you're off the hook, Ellsworth. I'm still pissed about the bus situation."

Stella huffs, crossing her arms, "You'll get over it. We needed a big car to transport everyone. I wasn't planning on squishing everyone in the back of my Jeep."

I raise a brow, "I'm finding it hard to believe three people broke your vehicle's capacity."

She mimics my expression, "There were four people. Lacey joined the road trip as well."

I frown, "Who the hell is-

"Mi amor?" Nico materializes beside me, scrutinizing the crowd, "Where's my girl at?"

"Surprise!" Fair skin and dark curly hair appear beside Stella, the girl's youthful beauty causing fellow spectators to glance our way. Nico's face breaks into a huge grin as he jumps up to plant a kiss on her cheek.

"Best surprise ever."

The display of affection has my skin itching, so I give Stella and Cody one last wave before I turn and walk back to the field.

"Shoot Hunter!"

My shout disappears among the rowdy crowd, the frantic cheering growing more intense as the stadium clock counts down the last few minutes of the game.

Hunter ducks, dodging the defensemen blocking his path, and hurls the ball toward the net – making a perfect arch over the goalie's outstretched hand. The crowd explodes, orange and black banners waving excitedly while a few groans echo from the Dino section.

The scoreboard flashes, bringing the Tigers up to 12 points and tying up the game. There's only two minutes left on the clock, and both teams look beat. I signal to the ref, calling for a quick timeout to give these boys a much-needed pep talk.

"Alright Tigers, there's only two minutes left in this game, so now is the time for all that training to pay off. Tell me, have you been waking up at 5AM every morning just to lose 120 seconds from the end?"

I scan the group huddled around me, their sweat-streaked faces looking back at me with weary determination.

"No, you didn't. Just like you haven't been working your asses off just to go home and tell your friends and family you choked during the last two minutes."

Making eye contact with each player wearing an orange jersey, I give them a moment to let my words sink in.

"Now, get back on that field and score one more goddamn goal. Tigers on three." I initiate the count down and the team lets out a convincing roar before running back onto the field.

On the other side of the field, the Dinos let out a similar chant and fall back into their positions. At this stage in the game, it comes down to which shot the goalie saves and which one he misses.

Glancing at our net, I watch Nico saunter confidently towards the crease, the ease in his posture a complete contrast to every other player on the field. He positions himself at the net, his stance relaxed yet ready.

I hold my breath as the whistle blows, orange and red players darting around the field in a fight for the ball. One of the Calgary forwards intercepts a pass and darts forward, deking out both our defensemen and making a beautiful shot at the net. Nico throws his body to the side, stick raised as the ball goes hurtling towards the net.

A collective sigh goes through the stadium as he catches it and tosses it back to Preston running up the side.

"Pass to Wes!" I shout, watching the rookie execute a smooth pass to Wes who is sprinting up the centre field quickly. He catches it and swivels, his stick aimed at the Dino's net when two defensemen close in on him.

Wes glances around, adjusting his trajectory to pass the ball off to Millard, who just became open thanks to the defence's focus on the captain.

"Ten! Nine! Eight!"

The crowd chants the countdown as Wes passes Millard the ball, the flash of panic on the rookie's face making me groan.

"Four! Three!"

Adrenalin pumps through my body as I watch Millard turn and throw the ball towards the net, the awkward angle making it drop low just as the Dino goalie lunges for it. The ball bounces into the net as the buzzer sounds, ending the game with a goal.

We won.

Nico

I am ready to let *loose.*

Lifting the tray high above my head, I weave through the crowded bar stools and tables to reach the exuberant group occupying the back half of the hotel bar. What started as a team celebration quickly morphed into an open invitation when Wes insisted his girlfriend, sister, Cody, and Stella were allowed to join.

I spot a few Calgary players lingering near the edge of the group, their collared shirts a vast contrast to the casual wear the rest of our team is sporting.

"Tequila coming in hot!"

Everyone cheers as I place the tray on the table and the shots disappear immediately. Quickly grabbing the last two, I wander over to my co-captain, who looks like he's having the time of his life nuzzling the fuck out of his girlfriend's neck.

"You know there's a bed back at the hotel." Grinning, I make myself comfortable on the barstool across from them.

Trip blushes, "We're probably going to head out soon."

Wes lifts his head and gives me a dimpled grin, "We're leaving now."

"If you're abandoning me, I'm keeping the tequila." Tossing back a shot, I hold up the other one in salute, "Get out of here, lovebirds. Cody and Stella left to fuck hours ago."

Trip's cheeks redden while Wes laughs, "I'm surprised Mo wasn't right behind them. He's been talking up that brunette all evening."

Discomfort settles on me as I whip around, scanning the bar for Mo's distinguishable build.

"Now, this I have to see."

Wes clears his throat, "Red tank top next to the pool table."

Turning my head, it takes less than ten seconds for me to zero in on the perpetrator. The woman's low-cut tank top makes her breasts look ginormous as they bulge against the cheap material of her top. She's rocking bright red lipstick and jeans so tight I'm surprised she was able to get them on in the first place.

She's a total babe but I hate her.

Turning my attention to the alpha lurking in the corner, I sigh with content. Now there's a man who knows how to dress for a night out.

Blue polo shirt. Cashmere dress pants. Muscles outlined at every corner.

He's my personal charcuterie board.

"Lace made it back to the hotel okay." Interrupting my spiralling thoughts, Wes glances at his phone and quickly types out a response.

"She should have come out tonight. We could have found her a boy to play with."

I'm so busy checking out the man I'd very much like to play with that I almost miss the frown flickering across Wes' face.

"I don't think she's ready for that."

I sigh, turning to look at him, "You don't always have to be her big brother, you know. Sometimes you can just be her friend. She needs more friends right now."

"I know." He sighs, raking a hand through his hair, "But it's not something I can just turn off. My job as an older brother is to protect her."

Trip takes his hand and whispers something in his ear. He smiles, the tension melting from his features.

"But I guess Lacey is lucky enough to have two brothers looking out for her."

I grin, "Damn right. And one of them can give her the best BJ tips."

Wes looks at me in horror, "Tell me you're joking."

"I've been told my skills are exceptional."

Trip laughs, "Maybe you should give me some pointers."

"No. Nope. Not okay." Wes splutters, his whole body shuddering, "Both of you. Stop it."

Trip giggles, her grey eyes glowing in the bar's dim lighting, "Don't worry, Wes, we'll keep it on the down low. I'll text Nico for the details later."

I throw her a wink, "Hit me up anytime."

Wes groans, "That's it. I'm leaving."

Trip rolls her eyes and gives her boyfriend a kiss before pushing off her chair.

"Always so dramatic."

He grins, catching her hand and pulling her back in for another kiss. As always, their innocent kiss soon turns raunchy, so I clear my throat with a grimace.

"Leave and go be nasty elsewhere."

They break apart, breathing heavily. Wes turns and flashes me a grin.

"What are you going to do once we're gone?"

I toss back the second shot, savouring the burn as my eyes find their way back to the pool table.

"Find myself a man to play with."

Chapter 16

Mo

"Where are you staying tonight?"

Tanya trails her index finger down my arm, her heavily made-up eyes undressing me with each word. She's attractive in a one-night-stand kind of way, but far from beautiful.

"Nearby."

A satisfied gleam hits her face and I resist the urge to roll my eyes. I'm too old to be going after lacrosse bunnies, but the rack on this one intrigued me.

She smiles, "Maybe you could show me."

And there it is. The invitation I've been half-heartedly waiting for tonight.

"Maybe."

A flash of irritation crosses her face, identical to the one cursing through me. There's no reason for me not to take up Tanya's offer, so why the hell am I pissing around?

Laughter drags my attention to the makeshift dance floor where couples sway clumsily against each other. A tall, lean body catches my eye, and I feel my brows start to pinch.

What the fuck is he doing?

Tanya runs her nails down my chest, but I don't spare her a glance. My attention is too taken by the team goalie grinding all over a lacrosse bunny on the dance floor.

My gaze narrows as the girl throws her head back and laughs, tugging Nico's body flush against hers. He grinds against her, whispering in her ear to make her laugh again. Irritation flares beneath my skin as I take in the scene, my teeth clenching harder with every beat.

"He's hot." Tanya smirks, tilting her head in Nico's direction, "He yours?"

"No."

"Too bad. The three of us could have had some fun."

She grins, and I have to look away to hide the disgust on my face. I wouldn't let this tramp touch Nico with a ten-foot pole.

Why do you care? He doesn't even like girls.

Gritting my teeth, I sneak another glance at the dance floor and find Nico watching me with a grin. He bends his partner over, grinding against her ass while staring me down.

He's fucking with me.

The realization has the anger slowly dissipating from my body. If Montez wants to put on a show then he'll have to do better than that.

"Let's dance." I hold out my hand, and Tanya looks at me in surprise.

"You don't seem like the dancing type."

She takes my hand hesitantly, and I lead us over to Nico and the blonde.

"Let's test that theory, shall we?"

Spinning her around so her back is facing me, I trail my fingers down her waist and latch onto her hips. She immediately moves backward, rubbing her ass against my dick in time to the music.

Nico grins, spinning the blonde so she's facing him.

"Babe, we've got some competition."

She tosses me a glance over her shoulder and laughs, "Competition over. He's out of my league."

I smirk, rolling my hips in time to the music, "You should take notes, Montez."

He groans, "Don't encourage the ego. It's already unbearable."

The blonde purrs, running her hands up Nico's chest, "Guess we've got some work to do, Tiger."

She winds her hands around his neck, leaning in to whisper in his ear. Nico watches my reaction the entire time, his eyes never leaving my face as her hands roam his body.

Irritation and lust spike my blood and I have to clamp my teeth together to keep my expression neutral. Tanya digs her nails into my torso, but I don't feel the pain. My attention is solely on the man dry humping his partner into oblivion.

"Want to show me that hotel room now?" Tanya breathes the question into my ear, and I bite back a grimace.

"No."

She frowns but continues grinding, my fluid movements making it easy to stay on time with the music. Tanya's not a bad dancer by any means, but watching Nico guide his partner around the awkward beats has me wanting more.

I watch Nico for a while longer, the delight on the blonde's face making me feel uneasy. Shoving the feeling down, I do my best to focus on Tanya, but it doesn't take long for the feeling to return. Nico bends his partner over for a second time, making her shriek with laughter, and the turbulence inside me surges to the surface.

Untangling myself from Tanya, I don't spare Nico and his partner another glance.

"It's time for me to go."

She opens her mouth to say something, but I've already turned away, the bar's stifling heat pressing down on me as I push my way through the crowd.

The exit door bangs open as I stumble my way through, hastily gulping down a breath of fresh air. Leaning against the brick exterior of the building, I close my eyes as my stomach starts to churn, the queasiness identical to what I experienced earlier today on the bus.

Fucking Nico Montez.

Taking one last deep breath, I push off the wall and start walking in the direction of my hotel, counting with every step all the things I hate about Taber's lacrosse goalie.

Nico

"What the fuck are you doing here?"

Mo gives me a full-blown scowl, a deep crease forming between his brows. Lifting my head from its resting place, I give him a regal wave.

"Just passing through."

His scowl doesn't waver, "And you thought the floor in front of my hotel room was the best place to stop for a rest?"

"It's more comfortable than it looks." I grin, patting the disgusting carpet beneath my ass, "Feel free to join me."

"I'll pass." Mo steps over me and swipes his key card, "Go back to your room, Montez. I don't want you here."

Most people would be insulted by the clear dismissal, but it only adds to my incentive. Jumping to my feet, I throw myself in front of his door.

"You do want me here."

"No, I really don't." He reaches around me and pushes the door open, "Move."

"If you say so." Grinning, I walk backward into his room. He glares at me from the doorway.

"I'm only going to say this once. Get out of my room, Montez."

I cross my arms, "Not until you explain to me what happened tonight. Where did you run off to?"

He shrugs, "There's nothing to explain. I danced. I got tired. I left."

I raise a brow, "Without your dance partner?"

Mo steps inside and lets the door swing shut behind him. His muscular frame is washed in shadow, the sight raising goose-bumps along my flesh.

"I lost interest."

He stalks closer, the movements calm and calculated like a predator on the hunt. He stops inches from me, those pale blue eyes piercing mine.

"Doesn't look like your dance partner passed the test either."

My eyes dance over Mo's flawless face, his impeccable features tainted only by a weariness that never seems to go away.

"She was never a contender." I smile, lifting a hand to smooth out the crease between his brows, "But you knew that."

"Why were you dancing with her in the first place?"

There's an angry undertone to his voice but I ignore it, focusing instead on erasing the frown marking his skin.

"Because I knew you wouldn't like it." A grin splits my lips, "And your alpha side needed to come out so you could finally claim what's yours."

Mo tilts his head, "And what's that?"

"Me." I swallow, tracing the hard lines all the way down to his lips, "You needed to claim me."

My fingers press against his lips and he smiles, a genuine smile that reaches those devastating eyes.

"Right here, right now." He nips my finger before grabbing my waist and hauling me against him, "That's my time and place."

I don't get a chance to respond before his mouth crashes on mine and my heart goes soaring upward. Shoving his tongue deep in my throat, I meet him stroke for stroke as he grips my ass and grinds against me. He backs me up until the back of my knees hit the edge of the bed and we go toppling on it, both of us wrestling for control.

By the time Mo manages to pin me to the bed, I'm panting and his arrogant smile has my erection throbbing against the material of my jeans.

"Babe, you need to lose that shirt. ASAP."

I tug him back down for another scorching kiss while I pull the shirt over his head. Hard muscle scraps against my hands, making every cell in my body weep with the need to worship that perfectly sculpted body.

Flipping us so his back is against the bed, I start kissing my way down those photoshopped abs, letting my hands roam beneath the waistband of his pants.

"I don't normally let guys be on top."

Mo kisses my neck, thrusting into my hand when I stroke him for the first time.

I grin, straddling his legs so he can't escape, "And here I had you pegged for a bottom."

He laughs, slipping his fingers into my own waistband, "Not in this lifetime, Montez."

"Pity. Guess I'll have to make-

My words come to a halt when Mo presses a finger against my hole. I gasp, feeling him circle the tight ring of muscle, teasing me with the pressure.

He smirks, making a show of licking his fingers, "Do us both a favour and put that mouth of yours to good use."

I have never stripped a man of his clothes faster.

Tossing the rest of Mo's clothes aside, I'm about to get my first taste of his raw masculinity when he grabs my head.

"Take off your clothes. I want you to come while my cock is down your throat."

Skin burning with fever, I release his member and make quick work of my clothes. He strokes himself as he watches me, the lust filling his expression the most beautiful thing I have ever seen. I crawl back on the bed, my body vibrating with need as I go down on the one man who was supposed to be untouchable.

Licking a path from base to tip, Mo lets out a moan as I swallow him down the back of my throat. My tongue presses on his slit when I suck back to the top and the grip on my hair tightens each time I swallow him back down.

"Fuck."

Mo thrusts into my mouth and I let my throat constrict around his cock in a way that I know feels amazing. He moans again, the sound triggering my own dick to twitch from the inattention. Mo notices immediately.

"What did I tell you to do?"

My hand doesn't need to be told twice. Within seconds I'm moaning around Mo's cock as I slide a hand up and down my length.

He grins, stroking my stretched jaw, "That's a good boy. Come for me."

My strokes get harder and faster as I take Mo back down my throat, my fist pumping twice as fast as I'm sucking. It doesn't take long until I'm ready to burst, and with every thrust and swallow, Mo's control starts to slip.

"Hurry up and come, Nico. I'm close."

He growls my name and that's what does me in.

I go flying over the edge while Mo watches with a satisfied grin. Never one for a solo finish, I give his balls a hard squeeze and he follows close behind. He explodes in my mouth and I swallow every last drop, savouring the saltiness coating my tongue.

Kissing my way back up his chest, I don't stop until I reach those wicked lips. Mo accepts his taste eagerly, kissing me back with just as much lust as before.

"Did I put my mouth to good use?"

I feel him smile against my lips as his finger strokes my cheek softly.

"We will need a few more tests before I can adequately answer that."

Chapter 17

Mo

He's gone.

My arm that was wrapped around Nico's warm body lies flat against the cold bed, the smell of his spicy cologne lingering on the pillow beside me. I roll onto my back, staring at the nondescript ceiling with a frown.

For the first time ever, my hookup didn't stay until morning. He didn't wait for me to make him breakfast or linger in hopes of another round. He just got up and left.

Just like I've always wanted.

I sit up in bed, the sheets tumbling down my naked body. My clothes are still on the ground where Nico tossed them last night, but otherwise, the hotel room looks exactly how it did the night before. As if he was never here.

Swinging my legs out of bed, I walk over to the bathroom and hop in the shower. Cold droplets pound against my back and I let out a sigh. My body feels satiated from the sexual escapades of last night, but something doesn't feel right.

I dunk my head under the freezing water, waiting for the feeling to fade.

Nico Montez has been and continues to be a pain in the ass, and last night was just a way to let off some steam. Waking up to an empty bed this morning should have been a pleasant surprise, not a disappointment.

Since when do hookups make me feel anything?

The thought has me feeling unsettled as I turn off the cold water. Grabbing a towel from the rack, I rub myself dry before pulling on the clothes I had laid out the night before. My body remains on autopilot, completing each step of my morning routine perfectly while my mind works to rationalize the unfamiliar emotions on hand.

Nico's always had a way of getting under my skin, so this isn't anything new. He probably knew that leaving without a trace would mess with my head more than if he stayed.

Pull yourself together, Maurice.

My father's voice rings in my ears, his familiar sneer staring back at me in the mirror. His cold gaze watches me run a comb through my hair, disappointment radiating through those cold, pale blue eyes.

I shake my head, Jonathan's eyes merging with my own. I got so used to my father's disappointment that eventually I started carrying it around as my own.

"Where's Cody?"

I look around for my friend, the sudden need for a friendly face hitting me unexpectedly.

Stella waves a hand, "He joined the boys on the bus. Wanted to reunite with the team."

Another pang hits my chest but I push it down and hold out a hand for the keys.

"I'm driving." My sister opens her mouth but I cut her off with a glare, "Unless you want to ride the bus with the team, I would choose your next words carefully."

She sighs, "It was worth a try."

A tinkling laugh steals my attention and I look at the two girls waiting by my Cadillac. The dark haired girl from the bleachers is holding her stomach, laughing at whatever story Lou is retelling.

"What's her name again?" I jerk my chin towards the girl and Stella smiles.

"That's Lacey, Wes' younger sister. She's an absolute doll."

"You say that about everyone."

Stella laughs, adjusting the pink backpack straps on her shoulders, "Not true! I only say that about the people I like. Lacey is a really sweet girl."

She pauses, giving me a sideways glance, "There is something off about her though."

"In what way?"

My sister hums, a telltale sign she's hunting for the right words to say.

"It's like there's something missing."

I fall silent, thinking about Nico's concern for her mental health. It's obvious he holds a lot of affection for the girl, and given his history with Wes, I would assume the three of them grew up together. It doesn't explain what led to Lacey trying to commit suicide but it does give me a glimpse into why Nico is so protective of her.

We don't say anything else as we approach the duo, both of us lost in thought about the beautiful girl with the broken past.

Lacey lets out another laugh, "Wesley is the world's worst cook. I should have warned you not to let him near the kitchen."

Lou smiles, "We just bought an air fryer for his dorm, so fingers crossed he doesn't burn the place down."

"Hello ladies. Ready to head back to Taber?"

Both girls turn to face me, Lou immediately blushing at my smile while Lacey gives me an assessing glance.

"Do you drive faster or slower than Stella?"

Familiar green eyes stare back at me, Lacey's resemblance to her older brother uncanny. She doesn't have Wes' signature dimples, but even without them, the Williams siblings could easily be mistaken for twins.

I tilt my head, "Depends on who you ask."

Stella tosses a braid over her shoulder with a grin, "If you ask anyone but Mo, the answer is me."

The girls laugh and I shake my head, walking over to open the back door for them. Lou gives me a quiet thanks and slips inside and Lacey follows suit.

I shut the door carefully behind them and turn to find Stella watching me with her hands on her hips.

"You know something I don't. Spill."

"There's nothing to tell."

Her eyes narrow, "Don't try and lie to me, Mo. I know you too well for that."

Sighing, I walk over and open the passenger door for my sister.

"It's not my story to tell."

Stella runs and jumps on my running boards, bringing her up to my chin.

"We'll discuss this later when we have less company."

Grabbing my shoulders, she pulls me in for a hug. The action takes me by surprise but it doesn't take long for her small arms to offer the comfort I didn't know I needed.

"Mom would have been so proud of you this weekend." Her voice cracks and it goes straight to my chest. "She would have been cheering louder than all of us combined."

I laugh softly, "Remember that terrible Tigers Mom t-shirt she always used to wear?"

"If they had a sister one, you already know I would wear it."

We release each other and I watch Stella's eyes start to glisten. A single tear falls onto her cheek but I make no move to wipe it away.

"Think it's time we hit the road."

My sister nods and the tear falls off her face like it was never there in the first place.

Nico

"CAP! Where have you been?"

Hunter jumps to his feet, running down the aisle to pull Cody into a bro hug. Our old captain laughs, patting his back before pulling away.

"Good to see you too, rookie." Catching sight of the buzz cut, Cody does a double take, "Where did the rest of your head go?"

Hunter grins, running his hand through the nonexistent strands, "The new missus likes the military look."

Wes pipes up, "Now that Hunter's an egg, you might not be the shortest guy on the team anymore!"

Cody laughs, flipping him off, "Low blow, rookie."

Hunter frowns, "Do I really look like an egg?"

I give him a loving pat on the back, "It's best if I don't answer that."

The bus rumbles to life, forcing everyone to take a seat as we lurch forward. I'm in the seat across from Wes, who is sitting directly behind Cody.

It's nostalgic, watching my best friend and our old captain catch up like they used to every practice last year. Ellsworth did his best to keep the favouritism to a minimum, but we all knew he had a soft spot for Wes.

"How is life on the other side?"

Cody grins, the tension he used to carry around nowhere to be seen.

"Amazing. Stella made me do stairs the other day and I still can't feel my legs."

Hunter coughs, "Whipped."

Cody ignores him and looks between Wes and me, "How are you liking being co-captains? I heard there's been some tension with the assistant coach."

Wes shoots me a glance but I turn and look out the window. Sneaking out of Mo's room this morning was surprisingly difficult. It took me forever to work up the nerve to slide away from his warm body, and even after my feet hit the carpet, I kept turning back to watch the rise and fall of his chest.

He looked so peaceful. So serene. I'd been half tempted to snap a picture just to have proof that Maurice O'Brien is human like the rest of us.

The silence pulls me back to the rattling of the school bus and I look around to find everyone staring at me.

"You feeling okay?" Wes peers at me with concern while Cody studies me from across the aisle.

Pasting a lazy grin on my face, I do my best to look normal, "Sorry I was just fantasizing about Hunter trying out for the Canadian forces. Would it be the sprints or the psyche test that disqualifies him?"

Laughter fills the bus and the normal chatter resumes. The grin slips from my face as I turn back to the window, my usual desire to join in on the raucous long gone.

I should have said goodbye. Or left a note.

A blonde fauxhawk slides into my peripheral and I turn to see Cody making himself comfortable in the seat in front of me. I sneak a quick glance across the aisle and find my co-captain deep in debate with one of the rookies.

Rubbing his jaw, Cody clears his throat awkwardly, "Stella heard a rumour that you might be into Mo. Given the fact I've never seen you so silent, I'm going to go on a whim here and guess it has something to do with him."

It's not really a question but I swallow my pride and nod.

He sighs, "The thing is, Mo has never been the relationship type. Not his freshman year and certainly not his senior year."

I open my mouth to tell him I'm the same, but no words come out. Somewhere between the start of our training camp and last night, that statement no longer rings true.

Once upon a time, I was the king of one-night stands and living my life with no regrets, but now I'm the guy who regrets treating Maurice like a one-night stand.

Catching my gaze, Cody continues, "Mo doesn't feel things like us. He doesn't wake up in the morning full of emotion and he doesn't associate flirting or sex with anything meaningful. He was raised to compartmentalize and when it becomes a choice between thinking or feeling, he will choose the first one every time."

A faint smile flicks past my lips, "Maurice is a heartbreaker. Got it."

Cody shakes his head, "That's true but not what I'm trying to say. Since the very first practice, you have managed to sneak under his armour and get a rise out of him. Besides his sister, I have never seen anyone trigger Mo enough to lash out. Until you."

I laugh, "My ability to irritate people is astounding."

He gives me a small smile, "Just be careful, Nico. The walls you're so desperate to climb over might be there for a reason."

"Hey Cap! The rookies want to hear how you took on Vector Vin this time last year."

Wes beckons him over and Cody slides out of the seat with a groan, "I swear to God if you break out the hospital pictures again..."

A smile tugs my lips as I watch him go, the captain's pep talk sizzling down to one gold nugget of information.

I have the power to make Maurice O'Brien feel.

Chapter 18

5 years ago...

Mo

I have to tell her.

My heart drops as I reach for my phone, scrolling through my contacts until I find my mother's name. My thumb hovers over the call button, panic already sinking in. Taking a deep breath, I mentally scold myself for being such a coward.

If anyone would understand the questions surrounding my sexuality, it would be the woman who raised me.

Right as I go to press the call button, an incoming call flashes across my screen. A smile breaks free, the tension easing from my body the moment I press accept.

"I was just about to call you."

My mother laughs, the familiar sound tugging at my chest, "Finally realized you miss me?"

"I miss having my laundry done."

She laughs again and more weight falls from my shoulders. My father may have raised me to be successful, but my mother raised me to be human.

"Besides being cheeky, how is my eldest son?"

"Fine. Grades are up and my lacrosse training is showing promise for this season."

The automatic response flies out of my mouth and she sucks in a breath.

"Is your father still asking for progress updates?"

I wince at her sharp tone, "No."

"Maurice Jonathan O'Brien. Did you just lie to your mother?"

I sigh, "The biweekly reports are to ensure I stay accountable. I can't take over the family business if my grades are simply average."

"I don't care about your grades and your father shouldn't either. University is a chance to discover who you are without any expectations or responsibility."

I walk into my dorm room, shut the door, and lean against it heavily.

"Just because I'm not in Vancouver doesn't mean the expectations go away. How are things back home, anyway?"

She falls silent and I can tell she's not happy about the change in conversation.

"Things are good here, although I think Stella misses you."

I smile, "A sentiment I'm sure she would deny. Are you still coming down for the tournament next weekend?"

My mother huffs, "What a ridiculous question. Your sister and I have already discussed what outfits to wear. The face paint is still in debate because it was so messy last time."

"The ridiculous question is why a mother and her teenage daughter would wear face paint in public."

She laughs, "Now we have to wear it."

Shaking my head with a smile, I walk over to the tiny desk pushed against the far wall and sit on the edge. Silence stretches between us and I feel the uncomfortable truth start to make its way to the surface.

"Mom, I think I might be-

"I'm taking your sister to New York."

My mouth snaps shut as my brain registers the shift in her tone.

"What?"

She sighs, "Your sister is not doing well. I didn't want to tell you before the big game next weekend but she's been struggling with school and that boyfriend of hers is causing unnecessary drama."

My jaw clenches, "I thought you said things were good."

"They are good, just not with Stella." She pauses as though sensing my darkening mood, "We are going to have a little get-away, buy some fabulous clothes, and things will be right as rain."

Protectiveness surges through me, "I can fly home."

"As much as I would love to see you, I have to say no. Stella and I are flying out tomorrow and you need to focus on this upcoming tournament. You don't want all that training and hard work to go to waste."

I bite my cheek, smothering the urge to argue, "Fine."

"I can't wait to see you next weekend." She sighs, "Stella isn't the only one who has missed you."

"I miss you too."

My mother blows me a kiss through the phone, "I better let you go. Take care of yourself and I'll see you next weekend. Love you."

"Love you too."

Hanging up, I shake my head and look at the black screen of my phone in disgust.

Jonathan was right. I'm not strong enough.

1 week later...

"Did you hear some of the guys are calling you Mighty Mo?" Brett grins, pulling his lacrosse jersey over his head, "Something about your popularity with the lacrosse bunnies."

Grabbing my helmet from the locker, I turn to him with a smirk, "And what do the guys call you?"

"Fuck you."

Brett grabs his water bottle and sprays me, making me jump back with a laugh. We have an hour to kill before warm-up starts and most of my teammates are buzzing with nerves. I'm feeling excited but in control, the perfect combination of adrenalin and anticipation flowing through my veins.

My ringtone goes off and I frown, reaching into my locker to grab my phone. I always silence it before games to ensure my distractions are kept to a minimum.

Reading the name flashing on my screen, I bite back a groan.

"Father, I can't talk right now." There's a heavy silence on the other end, and for the first time today, I feel my body start to tense.

"Father?"

Brett shoots me a questioning glance, but I turn away.

"You need to come home."

There's something off about Jonathan's voice, his usual commanding tone missing its usual bite. Unease pricks my skin as I exit the locker room, seeking privacy from the suspicious eyes of my teammates.

"I have a game in an hour."

Not that you would know that.

A twinge of annoyance seeps through my discomfort. For all his concern about my league status and academic records, when it comes to being a present father, Jonathan is severely lacking. If it weren't for the affection he showered over my mother, I would think he was incapable of loving at all.

"There's been an accident."

It takes a moment for the words to sink in, but once they do, panic floods my body. My mouth goes dry as a wave of nausea hits me, my knees almost buckling as I drop onto a nearby bench.

"Stella?" Fear builds with every beat of my heart, the pressure increasing until it feels like I'm about to explode.

"She's in Emergency."

My mind flashes to every worst case scenario but nothing prepares me for what my father says next.

"Your sister will be okay but your mother... she's dead."

By the time I make it to the Vancouver General Hospital, Brett has messaged me saying the Tigers won the game. I feel nothing as I read the message, my mind and body on autopilot as I turn off my phone. Life in Taber didn't press pause just because I'm rushing to a hospital to see what's left of my sister. It continues as it always has. Even though my favourite person in the world is no longer in it.

There's a part of me that doesn't believe my mother is dead. A part of me hopes that I'm rushing into the hospital to find both my mother and Stella waiting for me. It's a silly, irrational thought but it's the only one I've got.

Marching to the front desk, I hand the tired nurse my credentials.

"I'm looking for my sister, Stella O'Brien. Can you point me in the right direction?"

She takes a glance at my ID and points to the corridor to our right.

"First door on your left. Should be room 817."

"Thank you."

Resisting the urge to sprint in that direction, I walk as fast as possible to the designated door. Flinging it open, I'm almost knocked over by a nurse rushing through. The sight of her stained scrubs immediately puts a sour taste in my mouth.

Where the hell is my sister?

The corridor looks like a scene straight from a horror movie: doctors and nurses rushing past while bloodied and moaning patients are being wheeled into different rooms. Gritting my teeth, I make my way down the hall, scanning for the right room number. My father's cold, clipped tone catches my attention and I spot him barking into his cell phone outside the room at the very end. He looks exactly the same since the last time I saw him and relief crashes through me.

"Dad!"

Jonathan starts at my voice and quickly ends the call. My control slips and I finally let myself break into a run. I don't think before wrapping my arms around my father, his familiar build bringing a fleeting moment of peace.

"Tell me mom isn't really gone." My voice cracks and my shoulders start to shake as my control comes crashing down. Firm hands grip my shoulders and for a second I think he's going to hug me back.

"Maurice." Jonathan pushes me away and I stumble a couple of feet before looking at him in shock. His eyes narrow, their pale colour emptier than ever before.

"Pull yourself together. I did not raise my son to meltdown in public."

My spine immediately straightens but my hands continue to shake. Jonathan notices and curls his lips in disgust.

"Enough. Stop the dramatics and go take care of your sister. She needs you right now."

My brows pinch together as anger replaces the grief, "How can you be like this? Stella and I just lost our mother-

"And I lost my wife." Jonathan's eyes flash dangerously, "Don't think your loss is greater than mine, son. Your mother was mine long before you came into this world."

Despair wells up inside me, "It's not a competition! We just lost the heart of this family and you're acting like her death is something you can delegate. What if Stella needs you right now?"

What if I need you?

He shakes his head, "I can't deal with you right now. Go check on your sister while I deal with the lawyers."

Jonathan turns to go and I jump forward to grab his arm.

"Don't go. Please don't go."

Ripping his arm from my grasp, my father whirls around with a snarl, "I didn't teach you to beg, Maurice."

He hisses the words, each one sharpened to a point, "Grow up and be the man I raised you to be. Your mother thought you were strong enough to take over this family, so now it's time to prove it's true."

I flinch and take a step back. His words sink into the fleshy tissue of my conscience and I feel my body stiffen. My mother's soft voice and laughing eyes flash through my mind one last time before I lock them away, pushing the heartache into a box so I can focus on the problem at hand.

"Understood." I meet Jonathan's cold stare with one of my own and he gives me a nod before walking away. I watch his jacket disappear down the hall, my teeth clenching against the swell of emotion fighting its way back to the surface.

Are you strong enough to take my place?

I close my eyes, forcing myself to count to ten before walking into my sister's hospital room. Deep blue eyes, so like our mother's, meet mine and Stella promptly bursts into tears. Frowning against the lump rising in my throat, I swallow thickly and walk closer to the fragile frame shaking under her hospital gown.

"Mom's g-g-gone." Stella sobs, the wrecked noise piercing through my armour. Unable to speak, I make calming noises as I grab her hand, rubbing it softly.

She hiccups, squeezing my fingers painfully, "W-What are we going to do?"

Forcing myself not to look at the bloodied bandages peeking through the slit of her hospital gown, I meet her eyes.

"We're going to do what O'Briens do best. Meet the challenge head-on."

Stella continues to cry and with each tear that hits her cheek, I feel pieces of my freedom slip away. My priorities begin to re-formulate in my head, a numbness washing over me as the margin for error narrows to the point of extinction.

There is no space for imperfections and there is no time for mistakes. My sister needs a loving brother and my father needs the perfect son.

It doesn't matter what I need anymore.

Pressing a kiss on her forehead, I whisper a promise into Stella's matted hair, "We're going to get through this, Stel. You and me."

Her bottom lip trembles, "I'm scared, Mo."

My lips pull into the smallest smile as the weight on my shoulders multiplies by tenfold.

"That's what I'm here for."

Chapter 19

Present day...

Mo

I adjust my headset and try not to roll my eyes.

Steven is on another tangent, his data no more impressive than it was in the office. This is my first meeting back with the Vancouver team, and even though I'm attending remotely, it's no less painful than it was in person.

"Thus, given our predicament I think it would be best to review the entire fourth quarter." He peers into the camera as if the missing data is hidden inside.

Idiot.

Unmuting myself, I address the concern every financial advisor present is feeling.

"Have you had a chance to look at the CEO Update, Steven?"

He glares at a spot on his screen, "I don't have time to read the internal newsletters."

"You should make time. Last month's newsletter informed us that the blimp in our data was the result of a cyber-attack. Once IT resolves the issue, our data should realign itself with the rest of the report."

Leaning back in my seat, I wait for his response with a slow sip of water. I spot Cory's laughing face among the attendance gallery and resist the urge to smirk.

Steven shifts uncomfortably, "I see. In that case, I suppose we can proceed as normal."

"Perfect. Ensure you read all the internal newsletters moving forward." Taking off my headset, I log out of the meeting just in time to hear a knock at my door.

I frown, checking my phone for any guest alerts. Only residents have access to the upper floor so either a delivery guy got confused or one of my neighbours is stopping by for a favour.

Pushing back my chair, I walk out of my home office and open the door.

"Babe, I was thirty seconds from turning around and leaving. You gotta work on that recovery time."

Nico grins and something uncomfortable presses against my chest.

"Morning practice isn't until tomorrow. What do you want, Montez?"

He scans me from head to toe, those dark eyes undressing me every step of the way. A low whistle escapes his mouth.

"I want you out of those clothes. Why are you dressed like my perfect CEO fantasy?"

I raise a brow, "I just finished a meeting."

Nico leans to the side and peers into my apartment.

"You work from home?"

I step to the side, blocking his view, "At the moment I do."

He pulls a face, "Then why are you wearing pants?"

"Excuse me?"

"Your excused." Nico points to my dress pants, the dark material pressed to perfection, "Rule number one of working from home is to never wear pants. You put on a respectable top and rock your birthday suit below. It's the freedom of technology."

"That's ridiculous."

He shrugs, "Not as ridiculous as dressing up when no one will see you."

Irritation builds under my skin and I feel my nostrils flare. Waking up to an empty bed the other day left me in a foul mood and for some reason I'm still not back to normal.

I turn my attention back to the Latino taking up too much of my headspace.

"Why are you here, Montez?"

His smile falters, the arrogant confidence slipping for just a moment.

"I wanted to apologize for slipping out yesterday." I blink in surprise and Nico hurries to continue, "Not that I thought you were looking for a relationship, it's just I felt shitty leaving you like that so... yeah."

I pause, letting the words sink in. If any of my other hookups had pulled this stunt, I would have blocked their ass before they made it back to the lobby. But this feels different.

Nico is different.

"How did you make it past the elevators?"

He shrugs, "Eleanor needed help with her groceries so she signed me in."

I shake my head, "She loves the young ones."

"You're telling me. I'm pretty sure the old bitty coped a feel after we passed the second floor."

A laugh escapes me and Nico's face lights up. The uncomfortable feeling returns, building in my chest until I have to clear my throat and look away.

He shuffles nervously, "Anyways, I better get going. Just wanted to get it off my conscience."

"Right." Nico turns to leave but before he can take another step, I find myself speaking.

"I was just about to make lunch. If you wanted to stay."

He whips back around, that smug smile back on that ridiculous face, "What are you making?"

"Grilled chicken and kale caesar salad."

He pulls a face, following me through the doorway and into the kitchen, "That sounds disgusting."

I roll my eyes, "It's healthy."

"Still disgusting." Hopping up on my granite countertop, Nico takes a glance around my state-of-the-art-kitchen, "New plan: I make lunch and you can pick the music."

"Now we're playing music?"

He grins, "Babe, everything is better with music. Your disgusting lunch menu included."

I stop in my tracks when Nico hops off the counter and starts peeking in all my cupboards. He buzzes around my kitchen, the bright collared shirt hanging loosely over beige joggers. His hips sway to the music not yet playing and for a moment, it's like I'm back at my family home, watching my mother dance around the kitchen.

"Do you like spicy food?" Nico peeks over his shoulder and gives me a cheeky grin, "What am I saying? Of course you do."

Shaking my head, a smile hits my lips as I reach for my phone.

Nico

"Worst sex story. Go."

Maurice glances at me in amusement, "All my sex stories are good ones."

He takes a bite of the delicious curry I managed to whip up with his ultra-healthy food supply and smirks, "Obviously that's not the case for you."

I pout, "Don't be a party-pooper, Maurice. Everyone has a bad sex story."

"I don't."

"You do you just don't want to tell me." I gasp, using my hand to cover my mouth, "Was your first time traumatic?"

He chuckles, "It was fine. By the second round we had figured things out."

I take a scoop of the curry and chew it thoughtfully, "By we, do you mean a girl?"

He nods, "I was fourteen, she was sixteen."

"Scandalous." Taking a sip of my water, I notice Maurice looking at me curiously. I swallow slowly and mentally rejoice when his eyes drop to track the movement.

"When did you know you were gay?"

Pale blue eyes peer into mine and it's all I can do not to grab the nearest napkin and fan myself. Sitting this close to Maurice is doing something to me and I would be lying if I said I didn't like it.

"In second grade when I met Wes." His eyes widen in surprise and I laugh, "It's not what you think. I didn't fall in love with my best friend, although the dimples are super cute."

He lets out a low growl and I feel it all the way to my toes.

"Wes was my first real friend, he stuck up for me when some kid bullied me on the playground and then took me home when my parents were running late. I met his younger sister Lacey a few days later and I thought she was the most beautiful girl I had ever seen."

I smile wistfully, "I was convinced I was going to marry her. Every time Wes and I would hangout, I would make an excuse to see Lacey. Eventually I worked up the courage to ask if I could kiss her and when it finally happened..."

"It didn't feel right." Maurice finishes my sentence and I give him a nod.

"Exactly. I was sure there was something wrong with me, so I asked Wes if we could kiss so I could see what I was doing wrong. He was grossed out at first but eventually agreed. Long story short, I got my first boner and Wes ran away to rinse out his mouth with mouthwash."

Maurice looks at me with a frown, "That was surprisingly depressing."

I shrug, "Real life often is." '

My eyes run down the crisp dress shirt molded to that sculpted body and desire pumps through me. Leaning forward, I let my fingers trace the outline of the bicep closest to me.

Maurice tenses, his muscles flexing beneath my hand as I glide my digits up his arm and over his shoulder. The air thickens as our eyes meet, his cold irises flashing at me dangerously.

"Be careful, Montez. It will be harder to slip away when the sun is up."

My heart starts to pound as I let a smirk take over my face.

"Promise?"

He moves before I can think, hauling me into his lap and snagging my lips with his own. Rough hands grab my ass, pressing me tighter against him as I make quick work of that sexy dress shirt. Bare skin meets my hands just as he bites my lip and I gasp, hormones racing through me as his erection presses against my ass.

"That mouth of yours keeps getting you into trouble." Maurice breathes the words into my mouth and I swallow them whole.

"You didn't have a problem with my mouth last time."

Gripping his shoulders like I just found my new favourite climbing cage, I let out a shriek when he picks me up and starts walking us towards the bedroom.

I slap the firm muscle on his shoulder, "Babe, you're starting to emasculate me with all this carrying around."

Maurice smirks, "Do you want me to stop?"

"Hell no." Pulling his lips back to mine, I suck his tongue back into my mouth and don't say another word until Maurice is rolling on top of me.

He strips me quickly and thoroughly, making my skin break out in goosebumps from the fire burning in his eyes. I reach for his pants to help him match my state of undress but he bats away my hands.

I look at him, confused, as he pushes me back down on the bed.

"Not yet."

Planting his lips on my neck, Maurice makes a slow trail down my body, nipping and licking a brand new treasure trail. My dick throbs painfully as he draws near, that devilish mouth of his quickly becoming my new favourite sex toy. I hiss out a breath when he takes ahold of my length, stroking me gently before planting a kiss on the tip of my cock.

Maurice looks up at me from beneath dark lashes and the sight almost makes me come on the spot. He smirks, giving me one good lick from base to tip before sucking me in deep and making me forget my name.

My fingers weave through the silky strands of his perfect hair, the feeling of his wicked tongue against my dick pushing me to the edge far too quickly. I'm just about to finish when Maurice pulls back, popping my dick out of his mouth and flipping me over. My face lands in the pillow as he drags my hips in the air and bites my ass.

"I think this is your best position yet, Montez."

There's a wet smacking sound right before he presses a finger into me. I moan, pushing back against the burning sensation as Maurice hunts for my prostate. He slips another finger in and I start to shake.

"That's my good boy. Get yourself nice and ready for me." Pressing a kiss to my spine, Maurice withdrawals his fingers completely, leaving me achingly empty and harder than I've ever been in my life.

"Fuck me, Maurice." I'm panting against the bed, ass still in the air, "I need you to fuck me right now."

"Mm, I like it when you beg. Do it again."

"Fuck me-

Maurice presses his tongue against my rim and I lose it. Screaming his name, I come all over his expensive sheets until there's nothing left. Heart pounding and body shaking, I'm left a trembling heap, face down on his unbelievably soft comforter.

Panting like I just run a marathon, I roll onto my side and am immediately cocooned by a big, warm body. I sigh, snuggling into the protective shell and wishing with all my heart we could stay like this forever.

Chapter 20

Mo

Nico napped for twenty-seven minutes and thirty seconds.

I know because I watched every second pass on the clock while he was passed out in my arms. Pressing a kiss to his shoulder when he finally starts to stir, I let my hand wander down the smooth lines of Nico's stomach and stroke him gently.

He mumbles something in Spanish before pushing back against me, my erection just as painful as it was twenty-eight minutes ago.

"You up yet, Montez?" I growl into his ear, feeling him stiffen in my hand.

"Shh, I'm having the sexiest dream." He wiggles his ass, and a groan escapes my mouth. Nico chuckles, rolling on the bed so we're face-to-face.

"Is there a problem, Coach?"

"Keep talking and there will be."

He laughs and leans in to kiss me. His scruff rubs against my jaw as he tilts his head, coaxing my mouth open as I let his tongue touch mine. It's slow and sweet, and to my utmost surprise, I don't hate it.

My dick throbs painfully as Nico climbs on top of me, my dress pants completely tented as he sneaks his fingers under my underwear.

"Think we can take these off now."

He shimmies down the bed, pulling off my clothes in one swift motion. Before he can plant his lips on my cock, I grab him by the hair and haul him back up to my mouth. Our earlier sweetness turns into a distant memory as I ravish his lips like a wild animal.

Nico gives as much as I take, greedily running his hands along the hard lines of my body as I let my fingers wander back down to his ass. He immediately pushes back against them, moaning when one of my digits slip in.

My arousal spikes as he gasps and tilts his head back, exposing the long, tanned line of his neck when I press against his prostate.

"What are you doing to me?" His words turn into a moan when I slip another finger inside him.

"I'm doing what you've done to me since that first day." My words are harsh in his ear, the pressure in my chest building until I can't breathe, "Driving me fucking insane."

He grins, "If this is what hating me feels like, I should have hopped on the bandwagon."

Nico pushes me away, clumsily climbing over my body to yank open the nightstand next to the bed. Grabbing a condom and the lube bottle, he wastes no time in getting me wrapped and ready.

I grab his waist and flip us over so Nico is pinned against the bed. His legs wrap around my waist and I slide into position, the tight ring of muscle making me fight for control as I slowly ease into him.

"I don't make a habit of hating people." My breathing hitches as I bottom out, the pressure in my dick almost as intense as the one in my chest, "But you make it really fucking difficult to stay in control."

His nails scrape down my back as I start to move and the jolt of pain has my control unravelling faster than a thread. My hips drive into him with hard, punishing thrusts that make us both gasp for air.

"Don't stay in control then." Nico grips my ass and pushes me in deeper. His dark eyes meet mine right before he gives me a blinding smile, "Just let go."

I feel something break as my body takes over. My mind shuts off completely as I lose myself in the man beneath me, every sensation intensified to an almost painful degree.

"Fuck, Nico. I'm about to come."

Sweat trickles down my neck, my movements becoming more and more frenzied. Nico leans forward and licks the sweat right off my skin.

"Don't wait for me."

Capturing my lips, he kisses me right over the edge. My body shudders as the release hits, my hips pumping ferociously so Nico can ride the same high. He finishes with a cry, his ass clenching my dick so tight I almost come a second time.

Collapsing on the bed next to him, my chest heaves as I bring my breathing back down to normal. A hand snakes out to touch my stomach and without even looking, I can tell the smirk is back on Nico's face.

"So, on a scale of one to ten…"

I roll my eyes, fighting the smile trying to take over my face.

"How much do you still hate me?"

He nuzzles my neck, wrapping an arm around my sticky body. Normally, I'm the first one to shower after any sort of sexual activity, but for some reason, the warmth of Nico's body has me reconsidering that decision.

"Still a ten." He huffs out a laugh and I finally let the smile break free, "But keep this up and one of these days you might drop to a nine."

"You wound me."

I chuckle, letting my eyes drift close.

"In tenth grade, a girl got her period while I was eating her out. That's my worst sex story."

A stunned silence falls between us, both of us shocked by my honesty.

"Babe that's so… messy." Nico snorts, breaking the tension as his shoulders start to shake, "How did it taste?"

"You don't want to know."

He cracks up and the uneasiness gets replaced with something else. Something lighter.

"And let me guess. Even after your downtown liaison turned into a horror movie you kept going."

My shoulder lifts in a shrug, "I always finish what I start."

Wiping his eyes, Nico pats my cheek, "You are my role model."

"Doubt it."

He laughs, "When it comes to your prowess with women, no, you are not my role model. But everything else I admire."

I raise a brow, "This is coming from the man who said I have a stick up my ass."

"Technicalities. I admire how much you care about Stella. Few people in this world put other people's needs before their own, but I see you do that with your sister."

My breath hitches, "How could you possibly know that?"

He shrugs, using his fingers to tap a beat on my pec, "I'm observant. I grew up watching Wes be protective of Lacey and I see the same thing with you and Stella. You lost your mother a few years ago, right?"

I shift uncomfortably, feeling my barriers start to creep back up. Nico has already wiggled his way into my head, I don't need him touching what's left of my heart.

That part belongs to my mother.

"She was run off the road by a drunk driver." Sliding out of his embrace, I don't look at him as I tilt my head towards the bathroom.

"I should clean myself up. I'll see you at practice tomorrow morning."

He doesn't say another word as I leave the bedroom, and when I finally emerge from the shower half an hour later, he's gone. The empty walls of my bedroom stare back at me as I sit on the edge of the bed, waiting for the relief to hit me.

Except it never does.

Nico

Today's the day.

Sucking down air like it might go out of style, I force myself to knock on the door. Green hair hits my vision and I instinctively take a step back when Cecelia's terrifying gaze sweeps over me.

"What do you want?"

I fight the urge to flinch and paste a grimacing smile on my face, "Looking lovely today, CeCe. Is Lacey around?"

Her scowl cuts right through me, "That's a terrible nickname. Why would I keep tabs on my roommate?"

Choosing not to point out the fact they have an adjoining wall, I wave my white flag, "If you knew where Lacey was then I'm sure Wes would spend a lot more time talking to you."

Her eyes spark with interest and I know I've got her. She gives me a nod and steps aside, "He should come by more often."

I grin, slipping through the doorway before she can change her mind, "I'll be sure to relay the message. Thanks CeCe!"

Bolting for Lacey's dorm room, I throw myself inside and quickly lock the door. Lacey shoots me an amused glance from the tiny single bed, lowering the book in her hands.

"Cecelia?"

I nod, gasping for breath, "The scariest creature in all of Taber."

She laughs, moving over and making room for me on the bed. My feet dangle off the end as I join her, the heavy duty mattress topper softening the unforgiving Styrofoam pad underneath.

Tucking a strand of long, dark hair behind her ear, Lacey looks every bit the girl I fell in love with. The porcelain skin and green eyes are stunning even before you add the midnight-coloured hair and willowy frame.

"How are you doing, mi amor?"

I lean in and give her a kiss on her forehead. Lacey wrinkles her nose and gives me a sniff.

"That's not your cologne. What did you get up to last night?" She sniffs again and grins, "You were with Mo, weren't you? I remember that scent from the car ride home the other day."

I groan, dropping my head on her plush pillow, "Just call me out, why don't you."

She shrugs, "Not my fault you didn't shower before coming here. You should remember that for the future."

"Already noted." She nudges my shoulder and I sigh, "I was at his house this morning. We hooked up after the game this weekend and I wanted to apologize for leaving without a goodbye."

"Sounds like somebody has a crush." Lacey smiles, "And from the smell of things, I'd say the apology went over well."

"It did go well. A little too well."

And that's how, for the next twenty-minutes, I end up spilling all my assistant coach woes. Lacey listens patiently, absorbing my newfound romantic drama like a champ.

"So, he only got cold once the personal questions came up?"

I nod, "But he totally answered my worst sex story question without prompt!"

She grimaces, "Asking for someone's worst sex story and how their mother died are two very different things, Nico."

Shit. She's got a point.

"Damn it. And here I thought we were making progress."

Lacey smiles, leaning into my shoulder, "Don't be discouraged. It sounds like you've made more progress than anybody. I have to say it's nice to finally see you excited about a love interest."

My jaw drops, "Wow. There was no mention of love here. This is all about sex. Which happens to be exquisite. You know I don't do relationships."

"You never used to do more than one night either. Guess both you and Mo have both made progress."

I frown playfully, "And here I thought I would be the one giving you boy advice."

"That would require an interest on my part." She casts her eyes downward and pats her book, "That's what fictional men are for."

"You deserve a real man, mi amor. One that gives you the same hopeful feeling these books of yours do." I pick up the book and point at the cover, "There are definitely cowboys here in Taber. We just have to hit the right places."

"I'd rather read from the sidelines." Her smile slips, taking my heart with it, "I don't want to be hurt again."

The reason for my impromptu visit starts to burn a hole in my pocket and my heart kicks into overdrive. I swallow the nerves rising in my throat and grab the pill bottle that has been haunting me for the last seven days. Lacey's eyes go wide when she sees it.

"You found it! I've been looking for that everywhere." She takes it from my hand and hugs it to her chest. I stare, shell-shocked, as she beams in my direction.

"Where did you find it?" Her reaction has me at a complete loss for words, so it takes me a few moments to re-assemble this conversation in my brain.

"I found it at the bottom of your memory box on move-in day." She frowns but I continue, "I meant to bring it up sooner but then all this stuff with Maurice happened and I was a coward..."

"Why would you steal it?"

"Because I was worried you would try to take the pills again!" I blurt out the words, my biggest fear tumbling from my mouth, "I don't know why you kept the pills after you-

"Tried to commit suicide." She stares back at me sadly, the pain in her expression making me want to weep.

"I just didn't want to risk losing you again. Stealing the pill bottle was a stupid idea, but I just panicked when I saw it."

Hanging my head in defeat, I feel my tear ducts start to burn. Lacey's purple fingernails hit my line of vision and I watch her pop the lid open.

"Did you look inside?" Her voice is warm and soft and it somehow makes me want to cry more.

"Maurice suggested I look but I was too scared. I gave it one good shake and that was enough."

It doesn't take a genius to figure out what a rattling pill bottle means.

"Hold out your hand."

I frown, giving her a confused glance as I offer up my palm. Lacey dumps out the contents of the pill bottle and I stare at them in shock.

"Is this the friendship bracelet I made you?"

My hand trembles as I lift up the beaded bracelet, the mis-shaped letters spelling out *mi amor* staring back at me.

Lacey smiles sheepishly, "It's a trick my therapist taught me. My actions and my consequences affect the people I love and sometimes when times get hard, I need a reminder."

A tear slides down my cheek and she wipes it away with a sigh, "I realize now that trying to take my own life was selfish. It would have ruined you, it would have ruined Wesley, and it would have ruined my parents. This is a reminder that even when I hate the world, there will always be people in it that are worth living for."

"Awe Lace." I'm too choked up to say anything else, my tears soaking the sleeve of her hoodie as she pulls me close.

"I'm sorry, Nico. I never meant to hurt you." She sniffs, wrapping her arms tightly around me.

"I know you didn't, mi amor. I know you didn't."

I stroke her hair, letting the pain of our past drip away with every fallen tear. We hold onto each other until the last of it has passed and then I let my head drop onto her shoulder.

"I think I need another nap." My eyes are already starting to close when Lacey lets out a laugh.

"Shower first. Then nap." She finds my hand and squeezes it, "No offence but you can't pull off Mo's cologne."

"Ouch."

She lets out another laugh and my heart feels ten times lighter. Sliding off the single bed, I press one last kiss against her forehead.

"You know you can talk to me about anything, right? Good or bad, I'm always here for you."

She smiles, "I know. I love you, Nico."

"Back at cha, mi amor."

Chapter 21

Mo

He's doing it on purpose.

My eyes narrow as Nico bends over to touch his toes, his ass waving in the air like a fucking red flag. Until this practice, he was always the first one dissembling the nets, choosing to use cool down as clean up duty instead of actual recovery. Given Nico does whatever the hell he wants, I've never paid his post-practice routine much attention.

But now he's making it impossible not to pay attention.

I scowl as he steps back into a lunge, the bright red material of his shorts molding against his firm ass. The rest of the team is sitting on the ground, talking and stretching while Nico transitions into another pose that makes his shorts ride up another inch.

For fuck's sake.

Gritting my teeth, I tear my eyes away and watch Wes interact with the forward rookie. Out of all the first-years, Millard has improved the most. His skills are still far from impressive, but the effort he has shown on the field has been significant.

Someone claps their hands and I turn to see Nico finally standing upright.

"Great job today, team! Our next tournament is coming up quick and if we all want another tequila celebration, we better make it count."

A couple of the players cheer, the rest of them mustering up tired smiles. The first practice after a tournament is always the toughest, especially after away games.

Hunter pumps a fist in the air, "Go Tigers!"

"Go Tigers!" Everyone shouts back the chant before splitting off and heading for the showers. Nico lingers behind, his usual swagger back in place when he throws me a smug grin.

"Let me guess. It's unprofessional to talk about the consumption of alcohol with my players."

I close the distance between us with five long strides.

"Are you hunting for criticism?"

His eyes flick between mine, "Considering that seems to be your only form of feedback, yeah I guess I am."

I frown, "I provide constructive feedback. Whether that's positive or negative depends on the player."

"Babe, it's been over a month and I don't think you've told a single player well done."

"Not true."

"Name one."

I open my mouth then close it. Frustration burns through me, the familiar weight of disappointment sinking down on my shoulders.

Nico tilts his head, "Thought so."

Fuck.

"Millard has done well. His passing needs some serious work but the improvement is there." I bite out the words, cursing myself for giving in.

"Did you tell him that?"

"No." I level him with a glare, "I did not."

He taps his nose, "See? You are incapable of providing positive feedback. And I know the reason why."

"Please, enlighten me."

Ignoring my mocking tone, Nico takes a step closer. My eyes flick to the dark scruff lining his jaw, those smug lips sending an unwanted jolt of lust racing through me.

"You're scared, Maurice. You're scared that if you drop the hard-ass persona it will show that you are weak. That you are soft." He pauses, "You put up these barriers that no one can climb over but at the end of the day, the only person you are blocking is yourself."

"Is that right?" My teeth snap together as my blood starts to boil, indignation crashing through me.

Nico grins, "You know I'm right. That's why you want to punch me in the face right now. Nothing hurts like the ugly truth."

"Ugly truth? You want me to speak the ugly truth?" Staring him down, I lean in until we're only inches apart, "My father didn't raise me to hand out positive feedback, he raised me to get results. You perform well or you don't perform at all."

I pull back and shake my head, "The sooner these players realize that life doesn't hand out rewards, the better. You have to earn every position and fight every day to keep it."

"I'm sorry, Maurice."

"I don't... what?"

My brows pinch together as I stare back at him, the sympathy spilling from his expression bringing me to a halt. Giving me a small smile, Nico reaches up and uses his thumb to smooth out the crease between my brows.

And for some unknown reason, I let him.

"You must be so tired of fighting."

I blink as his words wash over me. The unfamiliar ache returns as Nico looks at me, the warmth in his gaze triggering an onslaught of grief I thought I had buried four years ago.

"You can't get tired if you don't stop."

And that's the truth.

When you don't have time to breathe, it's impossible to realize how suffocating your life has become until after the pressure has passed. Pushing myself to the limit day-in, day-out is what has kept me going since my mother was laid to rest, and I don't see that changing anytime soon.

Nico purses his lips, "That's how you run yourself into the ground."

"Maybe."

"Babe, we've got to work on this communication thing. It's supposed to go both ways."

I raise a brow, grateful for the pivot in conversation, "You make it sound like we are in a relationship. Catching feelings already, Montez?"

He grins, "Hell nah. I'm just using you for your body."

A chuckle escapes my lips and I don't bother trying to hide it. Nico is so far buried under my skin by this point he's an infectious disease that won't stop spreading.

"But while we're on the topic..." A gleam brightens those dark eyes, "Give me your number. That way we can facilitate booty calls and work on your communication skills all at the same time."

I smirk, "So no more unannounced house calls?"

"Now that I know what you wear to your virtual meetings, I make no promises." Nico winks, "Your dress-up might be weird as fuck but at least I'll be the one undressing you."

I roll my eyes, "Most people attend meetings in work clothes."

"Not virtual ones. Ask anyone."

Nico flashes me a grin before turning and running off the field. I watch him go, my level of annoyance nowhere near as high as it should be. In fact, the only frustration burning through me is from the tent rapidly growing in my pants as I watch those tight red shorts disappear from view.

Forget infectious disease, Nico Montez is a fucking tumour.

Nico

"Hear me out."

"No." Wes shakes his head, lifting his hands in the air, "Absolutely not."

"You don't even know what I was going to ask you!"

"I don't need to know what it is to know it's a bad idea." He shifts his chair closer to Trip as if her proximity might save him, "Consider me out."

My jaw drops, "You're supposed to be my best friend!"

"I am your best friend. That's why I can refuse whatever concoction you've come up with."

Trip gives him a pointed look and Wes visibly melts, "Fine. Tell me about this terrible plan of yours and then I'll decide."

I grin, "Knew you would come around."

"Ooh, plan making? I want in."

Platinum blonde hair flashes past our table as Stella plops herself down in an open chair. Trip immediately brightens, abandoning her boyfriend to give her roommate a quick side hug.

"I thought you and Cody were leaving today."

Stella pulls a face, "We were supposed to but Ellsworth has an interview this afternoon, so we've bumped the trip to next weekend."

Wes leans forward, "What's the interview for?"

Stella opens her mouth but I clear my throat, "Excuse me, but can we get back to my plan now?"

Stella waves a hand for me to continue.

"Thank you. As I was about to say, we need a theme for the next team party. Stella, the *Teen Wolf* theme last year was genius, so we need to bring the same energy this time around."

Trip smiles, "That was such a fun one."

Stella snorts, "You and Wes almost got kicked out of the club for public indecency."

Wes clasps his hands together, "It should not be a crime to show your love to the world. Amen."

Stella scoffs at him, "Sharing love and having sex in a dingy nightclub booth are two very different things."

Trip blushes, "We didn't have sex in a booth. We were just..."

"Mixing body paint to enhance our visual display." Wes shakes his head solemnly, "It was all in the name of art."

"You were displaying a lot more than-

"Okay!" Interrupting Stella, I clap my hands for everyone's attention, "Now that we've embarrassed Trip and confirmed Wes is an exhibitionist, let's get back to the matter at hand."

I pull out my phone and tap the sacred app that is Pinterest.

"Here is the list I've come up with but we need to narrow it down. Is everybody ready?"

Nods go around the table and I feel a swell of pride. Look at me being a leader.

"We've got Fireball Fiesta, Tequila Togas..." I continue down my admirably long list, the hours spent assembling this particular vision board well worth the GPA drop.

"What's ABC?" Trip blurts out the question and I look at her in surprise.

"You've never been to an ABC party?"

Trip shakes her head and Stella reaches over to pat her hand, "This one is new to the party scene."

Trip wrinkles her nose, "Does everyone wear a letter?"

I burst out laughing and Wes bites back a grin. Trip glances between us, confusion written across her face.

"Am I missing something?"

Wes pops out his dimples, softening the blow, "It's an acronym. ABC stands for Anything But Clothes."

"That sounds... horrible."

Stella laughs, "It is horrible but that's the point."

"So, everyone just shows up naked?" She swallows, "Is that legal?"

I grin, "If there was a nude party in Taber, you already know I would be there. Sadly, this one is tame and most people end up wearing sheets or garbage bags taped together."

Trip grimaces, "This keeps getting worse. Why would anyone want to wear a garbage bag? That would be so sweaty."

I look to Wes for help but he's already on the ball.

"Don't overthink it, Gorgeous. It's basically a fun game to see how creative people can get with their outfits."

Trip blushes and takes his hand, giving it a squeeze.

"Got it."

He smiles back at her, and for a moment, I wonder what it would feel like to have someone look at me that way.

To have Maurice look at me that way.

Mildly disgusted with my myself, I shake the rose coloured glasses from my love-infested brain and address the table.

"It's settled then. We're throwing an ABC party so Trip can get the full experience."

Stella squeals and claps her hands, "I already have the perfect outfit for us, Lou!"

Trip pales and looks to Wes for help. He shrugs, giving her another puppy dog smile that has my heart aching.

I cough, interrupting the cuteness overload, "Where should we host it?"

"We could rent out BA$$ again."

I nod, "Brilliant. I'll reach out to my friend."

Stella grins, "Maybe this time Wes can keep it in his pants."

He throws her wink, "Where's the fun in that?"

Stella laughs and Trip rolls her eyes. The girls fall into conversation and Wes looks at me with a dimpled smile.

"This was one of your tamer ideas. I was expecting much worse."

I shrug, "What can I say? I've been brushing up on my responsible leader skills."

He gasps, covering his mouth, "Are you, like, a captain or something?"

"Like totally."

Wes snorts, his gaze straying back to Trip.

"But I was thinking..."

"Oh no."

"We should invite Maurice to the next party."

Wes sighs, "This was the bad idea I was worried about."

"How is it a bad idea? I'm being inclusive!"

He crosses his arms, giving me the look that says I'm being stupid.

"Be serious, Nico. Can you honestly picture Mo agreeing to attend an ABC party? Let's not forget the fact he despises us."

I frown, "Despise is a strong word."

"It's an accurate one." Wes runs a hand over his face, "I just don't want you getting hurt, Nico. No one likes rejection but as someone who has never experienced it..."

I sigh, "It would be catastrophic to my ego. I get it."

"What are you guys talking about?" Stella pipes in, leaning eagerly across the table. Her petite nose and pink lips are such a contrast to Maurice's masculine features that it makes me wonder which parent each of the siblings took after.

Wes smirks, "Nico wanted to invite Mo to the ABC party."

Screw best friends. This man is my new mortal enemy.

Stella tilts her head at me, "You want Mo to come to the party?"

I flap my hands, hoping to steer their attention away from my rising embarrassment.

"Why is this such a big deal? Coaches come to parties all the time."

Trip frowns, "Do they?"

"Forget I said anything."

Grabbing my backpack off the ground, I push back my chair and get ready for a quick getaway. I've never felt flustered talking about a guy before, but somehow this conversation has turned me into a blushing pre-teen girl.

Time to abort mission.

"I think that's a great idea." Stella's excited voice halts my escape route, my body hovering above my chair as her big blue eyes meet mine, "Mo needs to get out more. All he does is work, workout, and fool around."

I mean, the man does all three really well.

Accepting my fate, I sit my ass back down, "Wes is right though, there is no way Maurice would agree to attend. He's a seriously hot stick in the mud."

Stella hums, twisting a long strand of hair around her finger, "Gross but you aren't wrong. Leave my brother to me, I'll think on it and work my magic."

Wes draws a cross on his chest, "That man is in my prayers."

Trip laughs but I shudder in agreement. If there's one thing the O'Brien siblings have in common, it's no matter the cost, they always achieve their goals.

Chapter 22

Mo

You've got to be kidding me.

"It stands for-

"I know what it stands for."

It's been years since I attended an ABC party and from what I can remember, most of the night was spent getting flashed by my teammates. The only thing that makes a drunk group of lacrosse players worse is throwing in a juvenile game of no clothes.

"So, you'll come?" Stella beams at me, her hands clasped tightly together.

"No."

"But Mo-

"I said no." I lean back in my chair and give her a look that means the subject is closed. She frowns, stabbing her fork in my direction.

"I know for a fact you used to be fun. What changed?"

The question almost has me laughing. I wouldn't know where to even start.

"I grew up."

She sighs, "Grow back down then. You need to let loose and live a little."

My mind flashes to Nico and a smirk tugs my lips, "I live plenty."

"Hookups don't count as living."

I raise a brow, "Most people would say hookups are equivalent to letting loose."

Stella narrows her eyes, "Letting off some steam with whatever lacrosse bunny is nearby is not the same as enjoying life. When was the last time you did something just because you wanted to?"

I take a sip of my whiskey, letting the burn chase away the truth of her words.

"What is this really about? You've never cared about my presence at parties before."

My sister takes a bite of her salad, suddenly avoiding my gaze, "I just want to make sure you're making the most of your time here at Taber."

"Bullshit."

She glares at me, "I hate when you do that."

"Call you out for lying?"

"No. Make everything more difficult." Stella huffs, dropping her fork onto her plate, "Is it wrong to want to party with my older brother?"

"It is when you're planning something. I know you too well, dear sister."

She grins, "What if I'm planning something for your benefit?"

"Stella…"

"Fine." She gives me the stink eye, "Nico wanted you to come to this party and I promised I would make it happen."

I tilt my head, "Was that so difficult?"

"You're the worst."

"Thank you."

Finally satisfied, I feel the tension ebb from my body as my mind wanders to the goalie in question. It's unusual for Nico to not just ask me point blank to come to the party, God knows that man has no filter whatsoever.

"So will you come?" Stella looks at me pleadingly, "Nico will be so disappointed."

"No."

Her face falls and a twinge of guilt hits my gut.

"But I'll do my best to make an appearance." Her face immediately brightens, and I hurry to continue, "No promises, though."

"A quick appearance is all it will take." I frown at my sister's choice of words but she's already on to the next topic before I can question it.

STELLA: Are you on your way yet??

I roll my eyes at the text message before grabbing my keys and heading out the door. It's decently early for a Saturday night, only 11 PM, but my sister hasn't stopped blowing up my phone since this afternoon.

I have no idea what Stella is planning, but I do know it won't be anything good. The only good thing about this situation is that I don't have to wear some ridiculous costume made from random items lying around my apartment. Anything But Clothes is easily the worst party theme anyone can choose and I will gladly sit this one out as a stranger just passing through.

It takes less than ten minutes for me to arrive at Taber's one and only nightclub, BA$$. I can feel the music pounding through the pavement the second I step outside and despite my earlier resistance, excitement leaks through my veins as the music grows louder.

I pull out my phone, sending my sister a quick *I'm here* text and open a new conversation with Nico. He's probably three sheets to the wind by now, but I quickly fire off a message to him anyways.

ME: Heard you wanted me to come tonight.

Within seconds, typing bubbles appear.

NICO: The night is still young but I'll do my best ;)

A grin hits my face, my thumbs flying over the keyboard before I have a chance to think.

ME: Promise?

NICO: Don't go stealing my lines, mi amor.

The smile drops from my face just as my sister comes barreling around the corner.

"You made it!" Her small body latches onto mine and I force my thoughts away from Nico's response.

"I told you I would."

I go to wrap my arms around her but the amount of exposed skin has me pulling back with a grimace.

"Where is the rest of your costume?"

"This is my costume!" Stella strikes a pose and I let out a groan. Her chest and ass are barely covered by thinly wrapped caution tape, the edges of her scar almost completely on display.

"You're going to get arrested."

"That's what I told her." Cody wraps an arm around her, casually covering up her scarred side with his hand. She smiles up at him, leaning into the embrace as I try to look anywhere but the yellow tape barely covering my little sister's body.

"And I told Ellsworth he'll just have to fight off the cops for me." Stella laughs, shamelessly raking her nails down Cody's bare chest. I shake my head, glancing at the towel modestly covering his lower half. Knowing my old teammate, he's probably wearing underwear under the towel as an insurance policy.

Sadly, I can't say the same for my sister.

"Cap! I need you at the pong table."

Wes' voice captures my attention and I turn to see the co-captain wearing nothing but a green swim ring around his lower half. He's waving Cody over to a table set up in the corner, dragging my attention to the other players mingling nearby. The standard uniform of bedsheets and tapped garbage bags meet my eyes as I do a scan of the crowd, but the lean edges of Nico's body is nowhere to be found.

"Want to join us? Cody could use the support." Stella smiles, nodding over to the beer pong table.

I shake my head, the humid air already starting to suffocate me, "I'll make my rounds then head out."

"Loser." Grabbing Cody's hand, she blows me a kiss and follows him into the crowd. I shake my head, doing my best to erase the image of Stella's nonexistent costume from my mind.

The pounding beat of the music thunders through my veins, the desire to get out on the dance floor almost as strong as the desire to leave. Freshmen in various stages of undress stumble and grind against each other on the raised platform, the usual black lights shining down on the gyrating mass.

I make a beeline for the bar in the far corner, sliding easily through the rowdy line-up to place my order. My hands drum the counter impatiently, my eyes still scanning the crowd for the only person who wanted me here tonight.

My phone buzzes just as I throw cash on the counter, and a quick glance at my screen has the beginnings of a smile taking over my face.

NICO: You were supposed to wear anything BUT clothes.

ME: Must have missed the memo.

NICO: Rule breaker except when he's the one making the rules. Should have known.

ME: ABC is just a suggestion, not a rule.

I lift my head, ignoring the girls looking in my direction, and do another scan of the crowd. If Nico can see my attire he must be somewhere nearby.

ME: Where are you?

I'm impatiently waiting his response when one of the girls sidles up next to me. Tossing her long, auburn hair over her shoulder, I get a direct shot of her cleavage popping from a Captain Crunch cereal box.

Classy.

"The problem with these establishments is the boys who come here are just that. Boys." She smiles, twirling a strand of red hair as she leans in closer, "But I've just found my solution."

"And what's that?" I let my gaze drift over her shoulder, the semi-impressive rack not enough to stop me from searching for Nico.

"A man. You're the first one to walk through that door tonight." Her eyes glint, and I fight the urge to smirk.

"Appreciate the compliment but I'm afraid my interest is already taken."

Her smile doesn't so much as falter, "By who?"

"By me."

Nico

Cue the mic drop.

The look on the redhead's face when we make eye contact is one I will cherish for the rest of my life. Part shock, part disgust, it perfectly sums up how my evening had been going thus far.

That is to say, subpar until my man rolled in.

She gives me a quick assessment, flicking that luscious hair over a pale shoulder, "Didn't have the famous Mighty Mo pegged for a fag, but the more you know."

That. Bitch.

My gasp is loud enough to be heard over the music but before I can launch into an offensive attack, Maurice steps in.

"I prefer the term bisexual, but I'm sure that word is above your reading level."

He smiles, those perfect teeth making me want to melt to the floor, "Use that derogatory term on me or anyone else again, and I will personally see to it that the nudes you love to send are leaked onto the web. Any hopes of future employment will disintegrate and I will be sure not to tip you the next time I see you at the gas station. Do I make myself clear?"

The girl bares her teeth, "Prick."

Maurice nods, "Better but your language needs some work. Now, if you'll excuse us."

He takes my arm and leads me away from the seething woman. We don't stop walking until we hit a booth in the far corner and laughter explodes from my body.

"Babe, the look on her face!" Wiping my eyes, I lean against the edge of the table, "That was fucking brilliant."

He raises a brow, a smirk tugging at his lips, "Entertained, Montez?"

"Quality entertainment. I would pay top dollar to replay that scene one more time." My laughter dies down as a terrifying thought occurs to me.

"Shit, Maurice. I totally outed you." Mind racing, I push off the table and start to pace, "We can still undo this. I can say it was a misunderstanding with a jealous ex-

"Montez."

I stop my rambling and turn to see him watching me with amusement, "I don't care what people think. I spoke the truth and there's no changing that."

"But-

"But nothing. You didn't force my hand, so take a deep breath and calm down." Stepping forward, he drops his hands to my shoulders, "I never do anything I don't want to do. If I didn't want to say something, I wouldn't have. Got it?"

I nod, sucking in a breath and letting it out. Maurice watches me closely, rubbing soothing circles on my shoulders that has my heart melting and my dick stirring.

"How did you know she sends nudes?"

He shrugs, "Her tits were out and she knew my name. Didn't take much to make an educated guess."

I burst out laughing, "The fact you delivered that with a straight face makes you my new favourite person."

Something flashes across his face before he smirks, trailing his fingers down my shoulders to the foil-wrapped edges of my costume.

"You wore this for me."

It's not a question but a statement.

One I plead guilty to.

I shake my head, "I wore this for my other assistant coach who hates my guts but can't keep his hands off me."

"Is that right."

Maurice takes a step closer, flicking the blue wrapper of one of the many condoms taped to my body. I am a walking, talking, condom vending machine and it's got to be the best investment I've ever made in my life.

I nod, feeling my blood thicken as the distance closes between us, "You've probably heard of him, once upon a time he was sort of a big deal at Taber University. Went by the name Tiny But Mighty."

His smirk breaks into a full-blown grin and it takes every ounce of self-control not to rip off a condom and put it to good use in the closest bathroom stall. I've only had two drinks over the last six hours but if a cop registered me a sobriety test right now there's no way in hell I would pass.

Because looking at Maurice O'Brien, I've never felt more intoxicated in my life.

"Tiny is a first for me." He squints at the closest condom, the one I painfully taped to my left nipple, "But at least you got the condom size right."

I choke out a laugh, "The cashier gave me the most disbelieving look when I checked those out this afternoon."

"You didn't want to use self-checkout?"

"Hell no, I wanted to show off these extra-large condoms."

He laughs and the rumbling sound goes straight to my dick. Every fibre of my being is screaming at me to close the gap between us and kiss him but the raucous cheer of my teammates has me hesitating.

It's one thing for Maurice to label himself as bisexual to a total stranger, it's another thing for us to kiss in front of my teammates. Although rumours will spread about the newfound label, there will be no evidence tying us together.

But if we kiss... suddenly everything becomes real.

And I'm not sure I'm ready for that.

Taking a step back, I drop my gaze to the black t-shirt stretched tight across Maurice's broad chest. My body immediately mourns the newfound distance between us, the confusion and desire swirling through my mind making me sway uneasily on my feet.

Maurice frowns, "How much have you had to drink?"

"Can't remember." I lie, choosing the safe route as Maurice glances around the club, tension seeping back into his features.

"We should get you home. Do you want me to find Wes?"

I shake my head, "I'll send him a text."

Pulling out my phone, I type an inappropriate number of eggplant emojis and hit send.

"Lead the way, Tiny."

Chapter 23

Mo

It's the worst case of déjà vu.

The Cadillac's engine rumbles beneath us as we idle outside of Nico's residence building, neither of us saying a word as I wait for Nico to get out of my vehicle.

Except this time, I don't want him to go.

My grip on the steering wheel tightens as another minute of silence ticks by, the tension between us thickening until my skin feels like it's on fire.

Clearing my throat, I fight to maintain my composure, "We've arrived."

Nico nods, his dark eyes boring into mine. It feels like we're having a silent power struggle, each of us waiting for the other to make a move. Normally I would break the barrier and invite him back to my place except now I'm in a precarious position. I don't know how much Nico has had to drink and as his coach, I should see to it that he gets home safely.

Not fuck his brains out.

Gritting my teeth, I break our stare and look out the windshield. My dick has been rock hard since we left the club and it's not making this situation any easier.

Why the fuck did he have to drink so much?

Frustrated with my lack of self-control, I'm just about to snap when Nico finally breaks the silence.

"Walk me to the door?"

I nod and guide us into a nearby visitor lot. Turning off the engine, I follow Nico into the night as he leads me to the entrance of his residence building. I don't say a word when he swipes his access card and the light flashes green. The tension between us builds as he casts those dark eyes over me, the lingering glance at my zipper not going unnoticed.

"Your pants seem tighter than usual, Maurice. Anything I can help with?"

"Nothing that won't get me arrested. Get inside and get sober. Then we'll talk." Tamping down the flames coating my skin, I turn to leave but Nico grabs my arm.

"Come inside with me." His hand trails down my arm and disappears into the front pocket of my jeans. His fingers brush against my aching cock and I hiss out a breath.

"You're drunk."

"Am I?" Nico grins, withdrawing his hand, "One cooler and one shot is not what I call a heavy Saturday night, mi amor."

My chest tightens at the slip of the nickname. The first time it happened, I brushed the text message off as a simple drunk miscommunication. But now Nico is looking at me like...

No. Absolutely not.

"In any case, if I was really that drunk, I wouldn't have been able to do this."

A set of keys dangle in front of my face and it takes me a second to recognize them as my own.

Son of a bitch.

Nico smirks, "Might be tough to make it back home without these."

I hold out my hand, "You have five seconds to hand those over. Five."

He tosses them to his other hand, holding them in front of my face like bait. I smirk, tilting my head without making a move to grab my keys.

"Four."

"Babe, the countdown is a little condescending but I'm kind of into it." Nico shimmies on the spot, creating his own impromptu dance to whatever music is playing in his head.

"Three." My lips pull into a grin as he starts to inch towards the open door.

"You really don't handle authority well, do you?"

"Two."

"Fine. You can have them." He tosses me the keys before bolting through the open door. A laugh escapes me as I sprint after him, shoving the key ring back in my pocket as we go barreling down the narrow hall of the residence building.

It doesn't take me long to close the distance between us, Nico's inability to stop laughing has him wheezing before he makes it to the end of the hall. Grabbing his waist as I round the corner, I lift him into the air and slam his back against a nearby door. He groans from the impact, but I don't give him a chance to speak before capturing his lips with mine.

His fingers tangle in my hair, pulling me closer as he wraps his legs around my waist. Sharp foil edges bite my fingers as I run my hands down his torso, the ridiculous condoms he tapped all over himself acting as a protective shield.

"Is this your room?" I breath the question into Nico's mouth as I press harder against him, my erection throbbing painfully against the zipper of my jeans. He mumbles unintelligently against my mouth, his nails raking down the back of my neck.

"Montez. I need an answer."

Leaning back to give him thinking space, I chuckle at the dazed look on his face. If he wasn't drunk before, he sure looks it now.

He gives me a lazy grin, "One more floor to go."

Locking his legs more securely around my waist, I lift him off the door and start carrying him towards the elevator down the hall. He purrs, folding himself more tightly around me as I walk us into an open elevator. I press the button for the second floor, but before we can pick up where we left off, a girl walks into the elevator.

"CeCe! How have you been?" Nico shifts in my arms to give her a bright smile. The girl crosses her arms, giving us a thorough once-over.

"What do you want?"

Nico gasps, "Since when do I have to want something to be considerate?"

A pierced eyebrow goes up, "You don't like me."

"I don't *not* like you."

I snort, catching the girl's attention. She jerks her head towards me.

"Who's your new playmate?"

Nico groans under his breath before giving her a bright smile, "This is my assistant coach. You can call him Tiny."

I roll my eyes and the girl gives me a smile, "I like this one."

Nico's jaw drops, "You just met him!"

"So?" She flicks a piece of green hair over her shoulder before giving me a sly smile, "You're hot."

"Thank you."

Nico slaps my shoulder, "Don't encourage her. She's already gunning for Wes."

The elevator lets out a screech as it comes to a stop at Nico's floor, and CeCe throws me a salute.

"When you get tired of his dramatics, hit me up." She exits the elevator, leaving Nico staring after her, mouth hanging open.

"Can you believe she called me dramatic?" He scoffs, "As if dying your hair green isn't a dramatic act for attention."

I chuckle, feeling another condom wrapper cut through my shirt, "Says the man wearing condoms-

"For the sake of a good party."

-refusing to walk through his own residence building." My brow raises, "Shall I continue?"

He grins, those dark eyes shining as he plants his lips back on mine.

"Shut up and get us to my room."

Nico

What type of idiot uses double-sided tape to stick condoms all over their body?

Me. The idiot would be me.

"That hurts!" I shriek and slap Maurice's hands away as he rips the third condom off my body. Why the hell did I think putting double-sided tape on my nipples was a good idea?

"You should have thought of that before choosing tonight's theme." A smirk tugs his lips as he reaches for another foil wrapper. I flinch, waiting for the rip that hurts a thousand times worse than waxing.

Maurice sighs and drops his hand away without inflecting any more red marks on my body.

"Contrary to popular belief, I don't want to hurt you. But we just need..." His eyes light up and I see the lightbulb flash above his head, "Come with me."

He grabs my hand, pulling me towards the tiny closet that is my dorm's bathroom. Maurice flicks on the lights, blinding us in an unflattering yellow hue that makes me cringe.

"Babe, this is the worst place for mirror selfies. Trust me, Wes and I have tested that theory too many times."

He rolls his eyes, "Your generation's obsession with selfies is ridiculous."

"My generation? We're basically the same age."

Maurice opens the grimy shower door and turns on the hot water. Steam starts to fill the tight space almost immediately, making my skin tingle with the humidity.

"I'm a good four years older than you." He smirks, crossing those delicious arms over that equally delicious chest, "Which explains a lot."

My face splits into a grin, "I've always been a sucker for older men. How old are you, anyway?"

"Twenty-four." Maurice nods towards the running water, "Get in."

"So bossy." Leaving the shower door open, I step under the hot water, "Aren't you going to ask how old I am?"

I close my eyes as the spray hits my face, the feeling of Maurice's eyes on me heating my skin more than the water ever could.

"I know how old you are."

Blinking water out of my eyes, I look at him with a smirk, "Been stalking my varsity profile?"

"Educated guess."

Heat fills his eyes as they follow the water trailing down my body, the hot water helping to loosen the tape's hold. I start peeling the condom wrappers off me, exposing more skin with each one.

Running my hands down my naked, condom-free body, I meet his eyes as my fingers tease the tip of my hard cock.

"Tell me, Maurice, how old am I?"

A smirk plays on his lips as he pushes off the bathroom counter, the predatory glint in his eyes making my fist pump faster.

"Twenty." Reaching out, he replaces my hand with his own, "And I'll tell you something else."

Pressing his thumb against my slit, I let out a moan. He grins, using the running water to increase the friction, "By the end of the night you won't remember your name never mind how old you are."

"Deal."

Grabbing his shirt, I haul Maurice into the tight shower stall with me. His head knocks the shower head, sending water everywhere as I press my wet body against him. He doesn't waste a second, using his arms to trap me against the tiled wall before dragging my leg over his hip and grinding into me.

I moan again, feeling his erection press against me through his soaked clothes. Gripping the ends of his t-shirt, I peel it off his body and latch onto the closest nipple I can find. He hisses out a breath as I tease the pink bud, the sting of my teeth making his hips thrust against me.

"Fuck, Nico."

The sound of my name on his lips has a smile painting my face as I hop to the next nipple. I continue my torture, switching between gentle sucking and not-so-gentle biting when Maurice snaps and hauls us both out of the shower.

"Get your lube. Now."

I go running out of the bathroom, slipping and sliding to my dorm room so I can yank open my nightstand and grab the lube bottle. By the time I make it back to the bathroom, the shower has been turned off and Maurice is waiting for me in all his naked glory.

My mouth waters as I take in the sight of him, the water glistening off his body and slicked back hair making him the sexiest thing I have ever seen.

If God created each of us, he sure took his sweet time with Maurice O'Brien.

"Get over here." The second I'm within reach, he hauls me against him, stealing the bottle from my hands and stealing my breath with his lips. My hand wanders down to stroke both of us together, the sensation paired with Maurice's hands kneading my ass cheeks making me harder than I would have thought possible.

I gasp when a lube-covered finger circles my hole, the tip of his finger mercilessly teasing me.

"Babe, keep that up and I'm not going to last much longer."

He releases my mouth with a grin, watching my reaction when he sinks the entire digit into me. I moan, pushing back shamelessly as he slips another finger in. Maurice leans forwards and plants a kiss on my neck, the softness of the action a complete contrast to the punishing thrusts of his fingers.

He pulls back and looks at me, eyes blazing, "Turn around."

Turning so my back is to him, I meet his gaze in the foggy bathroom mirror and smirk, "Better?"

A growl rips from his throat, "Grab the counter."

The sound of foil ripping is the only warning I get before he bends me over and pushes the tip of his dick inside me. I groan as he sinks in, the burning sensation making my muscles clench around him.

He hisses out a breath, "Fuck. You're so tight."

We both groan when he bottoms out, our eyes locking in the mirror as Maurice starts pumping his hips. Wet hair falls across his forehead as his thrusts turn savage, my grip on the counter the only thing keeping me from falling over.

My hand wanders down to my dick, increasing the pleasure strumming through me with a few good strokes. He watches me in the mirror, slowing his rhythm to match the pace of my hand. It's blissful torture as I watch the gorgeous man take control of my body, my strokes and his thrusts increasing in synch until we both reach the finish line.

I scream his name as I fall over the edge and the grin that crosses his face right before he comes is one I will remember until the day I die.

Chapter 24

Mo

I take one look at Nico's single bed and shake my head.

"Not happening."

He tilts his head, squinting at the mattress as if that might turn it into a double.

"It would be a tight fit but we could make it work."

I cross my arms, "I barely fit on that bed during my freshman year. There's no way I would fit on it now, never mind the two of us."

"I could sleep on top of you?" My brow goes up and Nico sighs, "Fine. I won't make you sleep on a single bed, as fun as that would be."

"Fun is not the word I would use for it."

He sticks out his tongue, "Party pooper."

I roll my eyes and walk towards the collage of pictures stuck to his closet door. Discarded clothes cover the floor in front of the closet, and the sight of the rumpled silk shirts on the floor has me frowning.

"I know my room is a mess." Coming up beside me, Nico kicks the pile of clothes into the corner, "Not all of us are neat freaks, you know."

I shake my head, my gaze stuck on the torn shirt sticking out of the pile, "It's not the mess."

"Is it the smell? It can get musty in here."

My throat tightens unexpectedly as I look from the pile of clothes to the man trying to pry open the dorm's pathetic window.

"I was just thinking about the night I found you." I clear my throat, struggling to contain the sudden surge of emotions, "In the parking lot."

Nico's smile falters, "Oh that."

He turns and starts rummaging through his drawers, being careful to look anywhere but my face.

"Lost my favourite top that night. But hey, at least the bruises are gone now."

I close the distance between us, hesitating only a second before wrapping my arms around him. He crumples against me almost immediately, the shake in his shoulders putting a tightness in my chest that wasn't there before.

"It was such a good colour, you know? Bold and bright." His voices cracks and I pull him tighter against me. My skin grows damp as Nico's tears start to fall, his muffled sobs making me feel weaker than the day I found my sister in the hospital.

Back then, I had a plan of action.

Here, I have nothing.

Swallowing thickly, I let my hands run through his hair the way my mother used to, wishing for the first time I had inherited her knack for providing comfort.

"I should have killed them. The men who did this to you."

He chokes on a watery laugh, "I would have had to drain my savings to bail you out. Then I would be shirtless and homeless."

"You've never had a problem going shirtless before."

Nico lets out another laugh before pulling away, "Got to show off this impressive physique somehow."

Before I can think about what I'm doing, I reach out and wipe the tears off his cheeks. He blinks in surprise but before he can open his mouth, I go ahead and open mine.

"You don't need a shirt to be bold and bright, Nico. You do that all on your own." Forcing the weight of emotion off my chest, I nod towards the sad single bed, "Now, what are we going to do about that mattress?"

His face lights up, chasing away the tightness in my chest, "I've got an idea."

"Ta-da!"

Nico grins, motioning towards makeshift queen size mattress assembled on his bedroom floor. Two-thirds of his creation stand at the same four-inch height thanks to the mattress topper from his bed and the spare one he had stashed away, while the other one-third of the bed sits at least two inches lower, the Styrofoam pad pulled off Nico's dorm bed looking even more depressing lying on the floor.

I cross my arms, leaning against the doorframe, "Not sure this is any better."

"What do you mean? I've made us a fortress!" Nico grins and throws his duvet over the crude bed, the green material not quite big enough to reach all the corners.

"It's on the floor."

He waves his hand, dropping onto the mattress with a wince, "Don't get so caught up on the details, Maurice. I've solved the single bed problem."

I nudge the edge of the bed with my toe, "You realize I have a California King back at my apartment, right?"

"Babe, we're way past that stage." Nico crawls under the duvet, the mattress toppers groaning loud enough to make me think he bought them from the clearance rack.

Patting the space next to him, he gives me a reassuring grin, "It's more uncomfortable than you think. Come join."

"You really sold it."

"It's what I do best. Hurry up and turn off the lights, I'm getting tired over here." He throws me a wink, snuggling down under the green duvet, "I always sleep better with a body pillow."

Rolling my eyes, I hit the lights and carefully navigate my way over to where Nico's shadowed form is waiting. The Styrofoam pad squeaks as my weight sinks down on it and the ridiculousness of the situation makes me shake my head.

"Stop being judgmental and get your sexy ass over here."

A hand slaps the bed a few feet from me and I sigh, "I can't believe you talked me into this."

Crawling under the covers next to Nico, I can see his smug smile even in the darkened room.

"You love it." His arm snakes around my stomach as I lie beside him, the lingering smell of his cologne filling the space between us.

"You have a strange idea of the things I love." Threading my arm underneath his pillow, I roll onto my side so we're face-to-face. My free hand trails down his bare torso, his quick inhale putting a smile on my face.

"What do you love, Maurice?" The whites of his eyes glow as they rake over my face, "Besides hating me."

I fall silent, thinking over the question. For once, Nico stays quiet, not pushing for an answer but giving me room to think.

"I love dancing." My mother's smile flashes behind my eyes, "It was the one thing my sister and I always had in common."

Nico grins, "Now that I can concur. Give me a Spanish bass and a little rhythm and I'm done for the evening. Died and gone to heaven."

A chuckle escapes me, "You would be a fan of Spanish music."

"Babe, you're talking to a Latino. Salsa is in my blood." He shimmies next to me and I let out a laugh.

"You would love *Lifestyle*. They always have a Spanish section during the night."

"Oh my God. You've been to *Lifestyle*?!" The excitement in his voice buries its way under my skin and I can't fight the grin taking over my face.

"It is the only gay nightclub within driving distance."

"We have to go! Together, I mean." Snapping his mouth shut, Nico's eyes widen as his words sink in, "What I meant to say was-

"Are you asking me on a date, Montez?" I smirk, letting my fingers trickle down his smooth skin, "I thought you were just using me for my body."

He shivers against my touch, "I was. I am. This is a strictly physical transaction, right?"

"So many questions." My fingers continue their path downwards, enjoying the way his body reacts to my touch, "So little answers."

He falls silent, an internal battle raging out right in front of me.

"Would you want to go to *Lifestyle* with me?" Minty breath hits my face as Nico blurts out the words, the sudden rush giving away his nerves, "Like on a date."

I contemplate dragging out the response time just to torture him, but one look at Nico's eager face has me shooting down the idea immediately.

"Sure."

"That's it? All I get is *sure?*"

His head flops back against the pillow as he blows out a breath, "I shouldn't have given Wes such a hard time last year. That was fucking terrifying."

"I'll make a note to be more enthusiastic next time."

He snorts, "Screw that. Next time you're gonna be the one asking."

Nico

Mistakes were made.

Struggling to sit up, my back screams at me for last night's stupid sleeping arrangements. The two mattresses I'm balanced on start to separate and my ass falls through the crack with a loud thud. I glance over at the man sleeping next to me and find a pair of blue eyes laughing at me.

"Shut up."

"I didn't say anything."

I shoot him a glare, my morning attitude mildly improving when Maurice stretches his arms above his head and I catch a glimpse of the abs running down his stomach.

If I'm ever in need of a cheese grater, I know who to turn to.

"Babe, your face says it all." I wave a hand in his general direction which only serves to make his smirk grow bigger.

"I'm not the one who insisted on sleeping on the floor."

"Watch it, Maurice. I'm not above kicking your ass out."

A perfectly thick eyebrow raises, "I'd like to see you try."

Letting out a growl, I jump on top of him, the soft material of my duvet the only thing separating our naked bodies as I try to pin him to the floor. We wrestle for less than thirty seconds before Maurice flips me on my back and knocks the breath out of my lungs with a full-blown grin.

"We need to work on your technique, Montez."

I squirm under his bodyweight, the sharp point of his erection capturing my full attention. I let my body go slack and the second Maurice loosens his grip, I slip out from his grasp and use the element of surprise to hook my leg around his waist and reverse our positions.

"You shouldn't underestimate me, Coach. I've got a few more moves to show you." I wiggle my eyebrows and he rolls his eyes.

"You need to work on your-

"NICO!"

Wes' voice fills the dorm and I look at Maurice in panic.

"What should we do?" I half whisper, half-yell the question as my best friend's loud entry gets closer to my bedroom door.

He taps my thigh currently locking him in place, "For starters, you could let me up before I have to throw you across the room."

My jaw drops, "You could do that?"

He smirks, "You aren't what I consider to be heavy."

"NICO!"

A bang hits my door and I jump off Maurice, lunging for the pair of black briefs lying on my floor. Hauling them over my legs, I stumble over the corner of our makeshift bed, and nearly fly headfirst into the door. Maurice snorts and I blindly flip him the bird before opening my door.

"Hey man! How was your night?" A bright-eyed Wes grins at me, his sparkling eyes and chipper mood unmatched for this early in the morning.

"Great! How was your night?"

Something in my face must give me away because Wes narrows his eyes suspiciously.

"Your acting weird. What's going on?" His eyes flick from me to the doorway I'm trying to block and suddenly he gives me a dimpled grin, "Code red?"

God bless my childhood friend but he makes the worst assumptions.

I let out an awkward laugh, hoping like hell Maurice has suddenly gone deaf in the last five minutes.

"Nope. Not a code red. I'm just feeling off this morning."

"No worries, man. I got you." Wes throws me a wink and my heart starts to sink. Clearing his throat, my roommate gives me a shit-eating grin before pulling out the worst French accent known to man.

"What do you mean there's another monsieur in your room? I thought we agreed to be exclusive?" He wails the last part, putting a hand over his heart like it might burst from his chest. Covering my face, I let out a groan.

"Please, l'amour, don't do this! I need you."

Pretending to weep, Wes gives me a thumbs up before taking my hands and falling to his knees. Normally, this would be when my one night stand makes a hasty retreat from my dorm, and after a ten-minute window, we would head down to get breakfast like nothing ever happened.

Naturally, that's not the case here.

I tug at Wes hands, trying to get him off the ground, "Not a code red. You can stop now."

"Don't stop on my behalf. That was just getting entertaining." The door swings open and we both turn to see Maurice standing in my doorway wearing nothing but a smirk.

"Nice accent there, Williams."

Wes scrambles to his feet, his shell-shocked gaze swinging from me to our very naked assistant coach.

"You didn't."

I raise my hands, "I can explain."

Maurice clears his throat, "If you'll excuse me, I left my clothes in the bathroom."

Wes shakes his head, "Right. Of course."

Awkwardly shuffling to the side, I give Maurice's firm ass an appreciative glance as he walks by, ignoring the hole my friend is burning into the side of my head.

"You're unbelievable."

"Can you just let me explain?"

A toilet flushes from our bathroom and I wince. Wes crosses his arms and glares at me while we wait for the hunky lacrosse legend to finish up his morning routine. After what feels like forever, Maurice finally emerges in his clothes from the night before, looking every bit the sexpot he did the first time around.

He gives us both a nod before slipping out the front door, leaving me to deal with my less than happy roommate.

Wes opens his mouth but I beat him to the chase, "Can we get breakfast first?"

He sighs, "Yeah but you're buying."

"Just to make sure I've got this straight: Mighty Mo, the assistant coach who hates your guts, has been your bedmate for the last few weeks?" Wes takes a bite of his pancakes, chewing thoughtfully, "And now you're going on a date with him?"

"I mean, it hasn't been a consistent few weeks... but yeah, that's pretty much it."

I dig into my breakfast sandwich without a trace of fear. Unlike the ape with the D-name, Maurice is a man who understands the importance of manscaping.

Something I will never take for granted again.

Wes grabs the maple syrup and adds a healthy amount to the pool his pancakes are already sitting in.

"Do you like him?"

He glances up at me, concern written across his face. I squirm in my seat, not because I don't have an answer but because the answer came to me instantly.

"You know me, Wes. I don't do more than one night."

He sighs, looking down to ensure his next bite is completely drenched in syrup. Wes is a lot of things, but a sugar freak is at the top of the list.

"Guess that's all I need to know."

I take another bite of my sandwich, letting the silence grow between us until I work up the courage to break it.

"Are you upset that he's your lacrosse idol or because he's our assistant coach?"

Wes drops his fork and leans back in his seat, "I'm upset because you didn't tell me. When I was struggling with all that stuff with Trip first semester, do you know who I turned to?"

Guilt hits my stomach as he gives me a pointed look, "You. The guy who is supposed to be my brother."

"Awe, mi amor."

He turns away, "Don't mi amor me right now, Nico. I'm still mad at you."

"Can I at least thank you for executing the best code red that dorm has ever seen?" His lips start to twitch and I know I've got him.

"We might have to make a trip to Quebec just to break out that accent again."

Wes turns back to me with a grin, the usual sparkle back in his gaze, "It was one of my best performances, wasn't it?"

"Babe, if I had an Oscar, I would be handing it over right now."

Both dimples pop out as Wes throws his head back and laughs, causing the other café patrons to look our way. I grin, reaching across the table to take his hand.

"I'm sorry I didn't tell you, Wes. I was scared you would brush it off as another one of my inconvenient hookups."

"Your hookups aren't inconvenient."

"No, but this one is. It puts you in a tough position as the team's captain." I release his hand with a squeeze, bringing my attention back to the half-eaten sandwich on my plate.

"But you like him?"

I sigh, "Too much."

He shrugs, picking up his fork, "Then it's not inconvenient in the slightest. Do what makes you happy, Nico, and we'll make it work."

"Don't you mean, do *who* makes me happy?"

Wes groans and tosses his napkin at my face. I dodge at the last second, successfully ranking us as the most disruptive customers of the day.

I toss the napkin back at him, laughing, "You have to admit, I was quick with that one."

He grins, "Not as quick as I was predicting Mo was your type."

Damn it. He's got me there.

Chapter 25

Mo

One punch.

That's all it would take to knock Wes right on his ass. We both know it and yet he still corners me in the locker room after our morning practice.

It's admirable in the most pathetic way possible.

"Hey Mo, do you have a minute?" Wes runs a hand through his sweat-soaked hair, the tension in his posture a dead giveaway, "Just want to talk about the other morning."

Closing my locker, I keep my expression carefully neutral as I give the co-captain my undivided attention.

"Go ahead."

He gulps down a breath, "Right. So, about the thing with you and Nico..." Wes sighs, shaking his head, "I'm no good at this. You're an older brother, right?"

"Stella is my younger sister, yes."

He nods as if my confirmation was some much needed ammunition, "So you know what it's like to look out for someone. To have their best interest at heart even when it doesn't align with your own."

It's easy to see where this conversation is going, but I stay silent, letting him continue.

"What I'm trying to say here is Nico is like a brother to me. There's no point in threatening you bodily harm because we both know that wouldn't end well for me."

I huff out a laugh and he grins, "And I can't afford to break the money-maker. So, the moral of the story is be transparent about your intentions and I won't have to get my ass kicked in his honour. Deal?"

I tilt my head in acknowledgement, "Deal."

He turns to leave but I open my mouth before he can make it to the door.

"You did well during the passing drill today." Wincing, I force the rest of the words out, "Demonstrated excellent leadership skills. I was impressed."

Wes whips around, excitement radiating from his every pore, "Really?! Which drill do you think was the best? I thought the last one..."

He trails off, catching my frown.

"Ah, what I meant to say was thank you."

I grimace, wanting this conversation to end as quickly as possible, "See you next practice, Captain."

Wes gives me one last beaming smile before turning and walking out of the locker room. Taking an internal assessment, I wait for the disappointment to hit me, for the panic of a newfound weakness to descend.

But it never does.

You put up these barriers no one can climb over but at the end of the day, the only person you're blocking is yourself.

The memory of Nico's confrontation floods my mind, and I can't help but think maybe there was more truth in his argument than I gave him credit for.

I'm supposed to be on my way home for the weekly office meeting, but the moment I spot Cody's blonde fauxhawk weaving through the crowd, I adjust my path to intercept him.

"Ellsworth!"

He turns at my voice and gives me a grin, "Hey, Mo. Didn't realize you'd still be on campus at this hour."

I sneak a quick glance at my watch and throw away any intention of making it to my meeting on time. Steven will have to entertain everyone with his latest misinterpretation of our financial data until I arrive.

"I'm not usually, but one of your captains needed to have a word with me after practice." I nod towards the textbooks piled in his arms, "On your way to class?"

Cody nods, "My next class is in the science building if you're up for the walk."

"Lead the way."

He takes us through Taber's courtyard as a shortcut, the crisp fall air and fallen leaves leaving no doubt that winter is just around the corner. There are a couple students studying together on the benches lining the stone walkway, their easy laughter and chit chat reminding me of my own freshman year before the accident.

"Was it Nico?" Cody glances at me, casually clocking my reaction.

"To what are you referring to?"

"The conversation that kept you overtime." He grins, "Unless there's something else you want to tell me."

I feel my defences creep up as I turn my attention back to the scenery around us. Until last weekend, I had never acknowledged the bisexual label out loud. Once I discovered my appetite for both sexes, it became a fact that was internally known rather than stated.

Frankly, it was something I never felt the need or desire to share. It was the one part of my life that was completely my own until I met Nico Montez.

And then he fucked it all up.

"It was Wes, actually. He wanted to talk to me about my relationship with Montez." I glance at Cody to gauge his reaction. Not a flicker of surprise crosses his features.

"Fair enough. Are you still enjoying coaching the team?"

My shoulders lift in an easy shrug, "It's a nice break from the board meetings. Has the potential to be rewarding if the players continue their improvement."

Cody lets out a whistle, "Improvement? I don't think I've ever heard you speak so highly of your teammates, O'Brien."

I frown, "Don't get ahead of yourself. These guys have a long way to go before anything impressive happens."

He smiles, "And there's the O'Brien mentality. Always striving for a goal that will never standstill long enough to be attained."

My frown deepens as the truth of his words sink in.

There has never been a time when I've been truly satisfied with my performance, when I've walked away from a tournament without a list of things to improve on. It was the way my father raised me but I hadn't realized it had crossed over into my coaching as well.

Clearing my throat, I voice the question suddenly burning the tip of my tongue.

"Did I provide positive feedback back when I was captain?" Meeting his gaze, I force out the second, more important part of the question, "When I was your mentor?"

Cody's brown eyes flick between mine, his silence an answer in itself. I swallow thickly, turning away from my friend before he can see the disgust in my eyes.

I've become my father.

"I wouldn't say you provided me with positive feedback." Cody speaks slowly, his considerate tone breaking through my dark thoughts, "But you were the role model both me and the team needed. Never settling for average, you were the reason the Tigers became undefeated champions. Because you weren't afraid to push for more."

He shrugs, "Maybe some validation would have been nice, but at the end of the day, it was your drive and commitment to the team that got the results. And that was enough for me."

A laugh escapes me, "I knew there was a reason you were my favourite. You always know the right thing to say."

He grins, shifting the books in his arms, "I was your favourite because I was the only player who didn't complain about the extra time in the weight room."

"That too."

Cody chuckles just as we arrive to the science building. The beige structure looks identical to all the other buildings on campus, except for the faded science sign hanging above the main entrance.

"Seriously though, don't get in your head with all this coaching stuff. You're a natural leader, Mo, and nothing like your father."

Pulling the science door open, I shoot him a look, "Who said anything about my father?"

Cody grins, "Your face did. Oh, and good luck with Nico. I think you'll need it."

I give him the middle finger and he laughs, bounding through the door before I can let it swing shut on his ass.

Nico

"Maybe I'll just go naked."

Lacey puts her hands on her hips, "You are not showing up to your first date in your birthday suit."

"Why not?" I throw another shirt over my head and onto the growing pile on my floor, "It's better than any of my other options."

She gives me a pointed look, "The reasons are endless. It leaves a bad first impression-

"Already checked that one off."

-you wouldn't be allowed inside the club. If you *were* allowed inside you would catch some sort of disease-

"A STI sounds pretty good right about now."

-and your dick would shrivel up from the cold and be nothing to brag about." Lacey purses her lips and stares me down, "Do you want me to continue?"

I sigh, "The last one got me."

"Then it's settled. You're wearing clothes like a normal person." She turns and starts sorting through my closet, leaving me with no choice in the matter.

"Since when is being normal my custom?"

Lacey pulls out a black crop top and holds it out for my inspection, "Since when do you go on dates?"

"Touché." I shake my head, rejecting yet another of my signature club outfits, "Nothing too scandalous. I don't want Maurice thinking I'm gay."

She bursts out laughing, "Pretty sure he's already figured that one out."

I groan, "No, not gay as in homosexual, I mean gay as in flamboyant. He's about as straight as a gay man can be and I don't want to scare him off with my wilder tendencies."

"Nico, the man has already seen your code red charade. If that doesn't have him running, showing a little skin certainly won't."

Tucking a strand of hair behind her ear, Lacey gives me a shy smile, "Besides, that's what makes you special."

"Wearing outrageous tops?"

She shakes her head, "Your ability to be yourself in any situation. The guy I know wouldn't care what his date thinks of his outfit because *he* would already know it looks amazing."

This girl is too smart for her own good.

"Awe, mi amor. Bring it in."

Pulling her in for a hug, I breathe in her floral scent and relish the fact we are back living in the same town. Having to talk to Lacey through video calls and text messages last year was harder than I had anticipated.

Long distance friendships are not for the win.

A knock on my door interrupts our moment, the familiar squeal of excitement telling me exactly who is waiting on the other side. Lacey tilts her head to look at me, resting her chin on my chest as she gives me a grin.

"Do you want to let her in or should I?"

I wince, "You go. I need to hide damaging evidence."

She snorts, "I'm pretty sure Stella has seen condoms before."

"Not when they're being used by her brother, she hasn't."

Shooing her towards the door, I start running around my room, tossing clothes back into one main pile on my floor and throwing all the spare condoms and lube bottles into my nightstand.

I've just shut my fun drawer when Maurice's younger sister comes barging in.

"I've got a special delivery!" Strutting into my bedroom like she owns the place, Stella gives me a blinding smile and hands over a plain paper bag.

"You didn't have to get me anything."

I take the bag without hesitation, my love of gifts immediately overtaking the need to scan my room for more condoms.

"It's not from me. Hurry up so I can see what's inside!" She claps her hands and I look at Lacey with a frown.

"If you didn't get this for me then who..." My voice dies when I spot an elegant white card sitting inside.

Try not to get this one dirty -Maurice

My jaw drops as I read and re-read the handwritten note, the perfect calligraphy making me want to have it framed so I can put it up on my wall.

"What is it? Mo refused to let me see it." Stella creeps closer, trying to peer past the tissue paper. Lacey joins, taking the card from my hand and flipping it over.

"It looks like the type of card that comes with flower bouquets. Or something equally expensive." She looks at Stella, "Where did he say he bought it?"

"He didn't say. He just handed me the bag and said to have it delivered today by 7 PM." Stella gestures impatiently at the bag in my hand, "Can you open it already?"

I gulp, trying to calm my racing heart, "This is a lot to take in."

Lacey smiles and passes back the card, "Open the gift before you overthink. Stella might die of anticipation if you don't."

"I almost went into cardiac arrest on the way here." Stella grins, flicking her platinum braid over her shoulder, "It took all my self-control not to peek."

Lacey looks at her admirably, "I would have looked for sure."

"It was close. I almost broke waiting at the door."

The girls break into laughter while I pull apart the tissue paper with shaking hands. Bright red material assaults my vision as I unveil the gift, the silky material of the dress shirt one thousand times softer than any of the shirts I've invested in over the years.

"Oh, Nico." Covering her mouth, Lacey looks at me with glassy eyes, "He found the one you lost."

I can only nod, the emotions clogging my throat as I carefully switch out my pre-date loungewear for this masterpiece. The impossibly soft material strokes my skin as I adjust the collar around my neck and undo the top two buttons.

Maurice bought me a shirt.

Maurice bought me *the* shirt.

Struggling to catch my breath, I give the girls a spin, showing off my new top from every angle. Stella lets out a hoot and Lacey shakes her head with a smile. Something sharp stabs my side, and with a frown, I pull out the price tag

And scream.

"What's wrong?" Lacey races forward, reaching for the tag but Stella snatches it away before she can see how many zeros are attached to this shirt.

"You weren't supposed to see that." She huffs, "Mo always forgets to take off the price tag. It's such a bad habit."

"Why would he pay that much for a shirt?!"

The question comes out as a shriek, my eyes still glued to the price tag in Stella's hands, "That's not normal."

Lacey snorts, "Didn't you just say normal wasn't your custom?"

I open my mouth but Stella beats me to the punch, "Mo wouldn't have looked at the price tag before buying this – and trust me when I say this is not the most he has spent on a shirt."

Holy shit.

I've found the hottest sugar daddy in Canada.

Stella waves a hand, "The important thing here is the gesture of a gift. I can't remember the last time Mo did something spontaneous let alone something spontaneous for someone else."

Meeting my eyes, she suddenly drops the smile, "If you break my brother's heart, I will cut you into pieces and bury them at my family's estate. My father could easily hire a hitman but I would rather have the pleasure of killing you myself. Understood?"

And to think Maurice is the O'Brien everyone fears.

I give her a weak thumbs up while Lacey watches the interaction with wide eyes. Stella's sparkling smile soon returns and she leans forward to give my hand a quick squeeze.

"So glad we got that out of the way. Have so much fun tonight!"

She bounces from the room like an evil fairy and I only let out a breath when I hear the dorm door open and close.

"I think that went well." Lacey bursts out laughing while I stare at her with my jaw on the floor.

"What just happened?"

Wiping her eyes, Lacey walks over and pops the third button of my top open.

"You just got the best first date present ever. But moving forward, just make sure you stay on your sister-in-law's good side. Even Cecelia wouldn't stand a chance against that one."

"Amen."

I heave out a breath, unable to tear my gaze away from my reflection in the mirror, "At least Maurice helped me figure out tonight's outfit theme."

Lacey tilts her head, assessing the new fit.

"Red and ready to shred?"

My face splits into a grin, "Bold and bright."

Chapter 26

Mo

He wore the shirt.

I watch Nico fix his hair one last time before hopping out of his car. The shirt I picked out for him fits better than I expected, the bright red material cutting close to the edges of his frame but maintaining enough shape to give him room to breathe. The crevice of his tan chest peeks out from the three buttons undone and I have to bite back a grin when I see the gold chain glittering against his neck.

"You clean up well, Montez." I tilt my head, letting my eyes roam down the fitted black dress pants, "I should have asked you out sooner."

He snorts, "Babe, we both know I did all the asking."

Pushing off the side of my apartment building, I close the distance between us with two long strides. Nico's pupils dilate as he scans me from head to toe, his gaze lingering on the dark grey material of my own dress shirt.

I smirk, "Keep looking at me like that and we won't make it to the club."

He licks his lips, "That would be such a shame."

Putting my hand on his waist, my mouth brushes his cheek as I speak softly in his ear, "Don't forget who wanted to go on this date. We could have spent the night in bed."

Nico shivers against me, his fingers teasing the waistband of my pants.

"It was a mistake. Let's call it quits while we're ahead." He leans in for a kiss but I pull away with a raised brow.

"Don't think you can handle being my date for the night?"

He grips the front of my shirt and pulls me closer, "I can barely handle being on the same lacrosse field with you. Seeing you and not being able to touch you is torture enough without the seduction of Latin music thrown in."

"It's a good thing you're my date then." His dark eyes flick to mine and I grin, "Tonight you can see and touch."

Nico's smile falters as he steps out of the embrace, "But what if someone sees? The last time I claimed you as my man, it didn't go over so well."

I frown, "We're going to a gay club. That's not going to be a problem tonight."

"But that's the problem. What if we weren't going to a gay club?" Nico backs away, running a hand through his hair,

"Would we find a couple of girls to dance with until we could sneak off together?"

His question hangs in the air as silence falls between us. Nico scruffs the pavement with his dress shoes, his emotional state derailing faster than our plans.

"Say something."

I sigh, "I don't know what you want me to say."

He throws his hands up in the air, "Anything. Say anything, Maurice."

"I don't know, okay? I don't know what dating would look like for us."

"It would look like nothing because there would be no dating. Don't you get it?" Nico barks out a bitter laugh, "This was a ridiculous idea. I don't know why I thought we could go out like a normal couple."

"You need to calm down."

He whirls around, eyes blazing, "No, you need to not be calm for once. If we go on this date, it will only add to the messy pile of emotions I already have for you. One date will turn into more until suddenly we've adopted a mini golden doodle but can't walk it together because it wouldn't be socially acceptable."

"Are you listening to yourself? This was supposed to be a fun night out, not an opportunity for you to analyze the homophobic mindset of small towns." I take a step towards him but Nico shakes his head and backs away.

"I'm in too deep. I can't do this." He squeezes his eyes shut and holds up a hand to stop me from coming any closer, "I'm sorry, Maurice."

Panic wells up inside me but I shut it down before it can make an appearance.

"Montez. Listen to me." I blow out a breath, waiting for him to meet my gaze, "Taber is a small, agriculture town. You knew coming here that things would be different. But think about the things we could do in a big city-

"But would it really be any different?" Nico's eyes scan mine, his lips pulled down, "It's not the small town. It's you. The great Mighty Mo has a reputation to uphold, and it spans a lot further than whatever this could be."

"I don't care about a fucking reputation." My teeth snap together, barely keeping the rest of that sentence from falling out.

He rubs a hand along the scruff on his jaw and sighs, "Be honest. Would you ever feel comfortable introducing me as your boyfriend? Bringing me home to meet the family?"

I fall silent and he shakes his head, "That's what I thought."

"It's complicated."

"Not from where I'm standing." Nico turns and starts walking back to his car.

"Montez, wait."

He keeps walking and I let out a curse.

"I just need some time to figure things out... Nico!"

His headlights sweep over me as he turns the engine and punches the gas before I have the chance to take a breath. The screech of his tires fills the night air as his rust bucket of a car goes flying by me, a flash of red the last thing I see before he pulls out of the parking lot.

I stand on the sidewalk long after his taillights disappear, wondering how the hell my night went from a promising date to a complete train wreck.

I care about you.

The unspoken words float through my mind, mocking my cowardliness as I turn and walk back inside my apartment building.

Alone.

I blink as my name is called, the crackling static shooting through my headset.

"Maurice, you still with us?" Steven peers into the camera as if his virtual proximity will recapture my attention. I catch my father's frown through his video screen, the silent chastise snapping me back to present.

Focus, goddamn it.

I clear my throat, making a point to adjust my headset, "My computer froze for a moment there but I understood your request clearly. I will have the updated report to you by the end of the day."

"Oh." Steven blinks, no doubt surprised by the lack of an argument, "That would be much appreciated, Maurice. Thank you."

I give him a nod before muting my mic and tuning out the rest of the meeting. The moment the meeting is dismissed my work chat pings with an incoming message.

COREY: How you holding up, big man? You seem distracted.

I almost let out a laugh. Last night, I spent five hours staring at my bedroom ceiling, replaying the conversation with Nico on repeat until I cracked and hauled my ass out of bed at 4 AM to hit the gym. The endorphins did nothing to help my situation and thanks to my sleepless night I've had a skull-splitting headache all morning.

The last 12 hours have been hell and the only thing my coworker can say is I seem distracted. I should be happy that my self-preservation is somewhat back intact but the only thing I feel is empty.

Alone.

ME: Just had a rough night. Things are fine.

Typing bubbles appear then disappear. I sigh, closing the chat box and re-focusing on my emails. Five minutes later another ping goes off.

COREY: If there's one thing my wife has taught me, it's that no one is fine if they use the word fine. Anything I can help with?

I blink in surprise before typing out a response.

ME: You have a wife?

COREY: Going on five years now. I popped the question after graduation so now she's stuck with me.

COREY: But back to your own wife problem...

I crack a smile, thinking of how Nico would react to someone referring to him as my wife. I can't imagine that one going over well.

Would you ever feel comfortable introducing me as your boyfriend? Bringing me home to meet the family?

My smile slips and all too soon I'm back thinking of last night and all the mistakes that went with it. The problem with people and relationships is they are a lot harder to accumulate data from. It's one of the main reasons I've avoided them up until now.

Well, that and no one sparked my interest for longer than one night.

Typing out a response, there's a knock on my door just as I press send.

ME: Thanks for the support but I'll figure it out.

COREY: You always do.

Pushing back my chair, I walk over to check the peephole of my front door.

"Is there a reason you're intruding on my day off?" My voice comes out perfectly calm, successfully masking my volatile emotions as I open the door and stare at the one co-captain I did not want to see today.

Wes gives me a tight smile, awkwardly holding out the shopping bag I gave to my sister a few hours ago.

"Can I come in? Nico asked me to return this."

"No."

He winces, eyes flicking from my face to the blocked doorway, "No I can't come in or no I can't return this?"

I cross my arms, my expression leaving no room for argument, "Both."

"Fair enough." Wes gently places the bag on the ground, "I would have kept the shirt for myself but it's really not my colour. The red does nothing for my eyes, the trick for me is to wear cool undertones like blue or-

"What are you doing here?" I cut him off with a pointed glare, "I've got actual work to do so I would appreciate it if you made this quick."

He sighs, running a hand through his dark hair, "Nico's leaving."

My stomach drops, "What?"

Wes throws up his hands, a quick smile breaking across his features, "That came out wrong. Nico is heading home for the week. Said he wanted to catch up with the family before lacrosse training gets too intense. He'll be back next Monday."

Catch up with his family? I call bullshit.

Nico is running away.

Swallowing the urge to smash something against the wall, I tilt my head, assessing the captain in my doorway.

"And you felt the need to tell me that because..."

"You make him happy." Wes sighs, taking a step back to lean against the wall, "For the first time, I saw my best friend want

a future that wasn't waking up drunk next to a stranger every weekend."

I give him a disbelieving look, "I was explicitly told last night that dating was not in the cards."

Wes groans, "Come on, Mo, you know Nico! When push comes to shove, he always takes the easy way out. You know it, I know it, even Nico knows it – that's why he had his little meltdown last night. He was scared that if you guys actually start dating, it would be his heart on the line, not yours."

"That's ridiculous."

"That's Nico." He shakes his head, "It's partly my fault. I've been telling him to stay away since the first day you arrived and now he's starting to understand why."

I think back to Nico's reaction last night, the way he couldn't get past the impossibility of a future together. He was so caught up in what we couldn't be that he forgot to look at what we already were.

My scowl deepens as I consider the new data at hand, "So he's looking for reassurance. Validation that his feelings are reciprocated."

"I mean, you aren't exactly an open book. I'd personally label you as a high-security vault with lasers and security dogs." Wes grins, popping out a dimple and I look at him dubiously.

"Words of affirmation and opening up. Those are my two options?"

He shrugs, "I'm sure there are plenty of other routes you could take, but in my opinion, those would be your best bets of winning him back."

I frown, "He was never mine to begin with."

"And yet he ended up being yours to lose." Wes scoops the bag off the floor and turns to me with a grin, "See you tomorrow at practice!"

He sings to himself all the way down the hallway, a terrible rendition of a Disney soundtrack that has me quickly slamming my door shut. Mulling over our conversation, I head back to my work computer and pull up the financial spreadsheet I promised Steven.

What the hell am I doing?

Taking a deep breath, I close the document and pull up a new one. Saving it to my personal drive, I ignore the weight of my deadlines and start planning for my future.

Nico

Nothing screams heartbreak like hightailing it home.

"I'm not sure one week is going to change anything, Nico." Lacey bites her lip, tugging at the ends of her hoodie, "Maybe you guys should just talk it out now."

I shake my head vehemently, "You didn't see his face when I drove off. The best thing I can do right now is let the emotions cool off for a bit."

She sighs, "You've already made up your mind."

"It's for the best, Lace." Swallowing hard, I pull her in for one last hug before turning and heading out the door.

"Give Mrs. Montez my love!"

I peel out of the residence parking lot like a man possessed for the second time today, cranking the tunes all the way to where my family awaits. The open road doesn't soothe the ache in my chest like I thought it would, but I don't ease off the gas pedal until I pull onto the patchy driveway of my family home.

The Montez household sits on the edge of a different small town, and truth be told, it's nothing to write home about. The shutters need replacing, the bungalow needs a new coat of paint, and I'm pretty sure there are more weeds than flowers growing in our garden, but at the end of the day, it's home.

"Carlos, can you get the door?" My mom's shriek has my face breaking into a smile before I make it up the stairs.

"What are you talking about? No one has knocked."

She scoffs, "Don't ask questions, just do as I say."

"Woman, questions are the only thing you leave me with most days." The bickering continues as I draw near, the volume increasing with every verbal spar thrown in the ring.

"Don't you remember the last time I told you to do something and you refused? We ended up eating chicken curry without the chicken because someone decided we already had some at home."

"That only happened because someone complained we were spending too much on groceries."

I clear my throat, not bothering to knock, "Your one and only son has returned!"

A gasp sounds from inside, "Nico?!"

The sound of running feet draws near and I brace myself for impact. The door swings open to reveal both of my parents standing on the other side, their wide smiles as familiar as my own.

"What are you doing home, my boy?" Tilting her head, my mom's beaming smile slips into a concerned frown, "Where is Wesley?"

This is what happens when you are best friends with someone for over a decade. You become attached at the hip to the point where your parents can tell something is wrong simply by showing up unchaperoned.

I give her a weak smile, "He needed to stay and help out with the team."

My dad squints in my direction, "But you didn't have to stay?"

"Well, no, I ah…" My voice cracks and I have to snap my mouth shut to keep from sobbing.

"Oh, mi amor." Wrapping her small arms around me, my mom pulls me into the house and flicks a finger at my father.

"Make yourself useful and go warm up some cookies."

Breathing in the comforting scent of my childhood, I look at my mom with a wry smile.

"Since when do you make cookies?'

My dad grunts, heading for the kitchen, "Lucia's been trying new recipes all month. I've been eating shit for three weeks."

"Your father does not appreciate my culinary skills." She huffs and leads me into the living room. As the biggest room in the house, you would think our family would maximize the space like most people do.

Nope. Not the Montez family.

We like clutter, so half of the living room is covered with bits and pieces from every monumental life stage I've ever had. It's sweet, seeing the emphasis my parents put on every occasion but it really doesn't leave a lot of room for sitting space.

Shifting a pile of newspaper clippings from the couch, she gets me settled before making space for herself. A Taber University article floats to the ground, the smiling faces of last year's lacrosse team staring back at me.

I sigh, bending to pick it up and placing it back on its respective pile. The shot was taken after the Tigers won last year's championship tournament, back when Cody was captain and Wes and I were just a couple of rookies. Wes has his arms around me in the picture, his face breaking into a wide grin as he lifts my laughing ass in the air.

A wave of nostalgia hits me as I look at our smiling faces. I wish I could go back to when the only question in my life was figuring out which stranger to take home for the weekend.

Back before Maurice O'Brien entered my life.

My mom takes my chin in her hands, forcing my gaze to meet hers, "Tell me what's wrong."

The couch dips beside me as my dad reappears with a plate of cookies in his hand. He passes it to me, shaking his head sagely, "Eat with caution."

"Carlos!" She reaches around me and gives him a slap upside the head, "Keep it up and you'll be making your own dinners from now on."

He scoffs, "As if you would ever let me in the kitchen."

She clucks her tongue in disapproval and turns to me with a smile, "Ignore your father. He doesn't understand his place in this family."

I let out a small laugh, the ache in my chest refusing to let me do much else. My mom frowns, reaching out to smooth the frown line between my brows.

"Tell us what's wrong, Nico."

My dad grabs my hand and gives it a reassuring squeeze. My throat tightens at the simple display of love and support, the one thing I was never without growing up in this house.

Taking a deep breath, I push the words out.

"I fell in love."

And then I burst into tears.

Chapter 27

Mo

"What do you think?"

Stella sighs, taking a sip of her protein shake, "I think you should have come to me sooner."

I raise my brow, "So you could invite me to another ABC party?"

She points her drink at me threateningly, "Don't get snappy with me, brother. My matchmaking skills were in top performance that night."

"I barely saw you at that party."

She smirks, "And yet somehow Nico knew exactly where to find you."

I groan, already regretting my decision to consult Stella about my plans.

"You're insufferable."

She grins, "I know."

I shake my head, ready to end this conversation when Stella speaks up.

"There's only a couple of unpredictable variables with this plan." She holds up two fingers, counting one off, "Nico being the first. We really don't know where his head is at or how he will react."

She taps the second finger with a grimace, "And the second one being-

"Jonathan." I breathe out my father's name, wishing it didn't trigger a familiar bout of anxiety.

She nods, "Jonathan."

I give her a pointed look, "Those are the only two variables in this situation."

"Well then, let's hope you figure out the best solution to appease both." Stella grins, wiggling her eyebrows at me, "How was that for corporate jargon?"

I shake my head with a laugh, "Father would be proud."

She tilts her head, twirling the straw of her drink mindlessly, "He's not the one I want to make proud."

"Oh?"

My sister smiles, "You are."

Warmth fills my chest as I look at the young woman sitting across from me. We've come so far since that terrible day at the hospital, since the day my title as older brother became something else completely.

Since the day we both became something else completely.

I stare at her, noticing the way her cropped shirt lets the edges of her scar peak through. It might have been Stella's skin that was ruined, but it didn't stop me from staying up at night, trying to think of a way to bring back her confidence. It took a long time for me to come up with a solution, and even once I did, it didn't turn out the way I expected.

The memory washes over me, but for once, I don't try and fight it.

Pain hits my gut as I meet my sister's gaze in the mirror. Her dark blue eyes, normally so full of life, seemed dull as she turned to look at the scar cutting through her left side. It was a hideous scar, running from the waist band of her leggings and branching off into a spiderweb of angry scar tissue that disappeared beneath her sports bra.

Stella had finally finished physiotherapy and had been hitting the gym as if her life depended on it. The new, lean lines of muscle made her body a work of art but I could see in her eyes that it wasn't enough.

"It will fade over time." I say the words with as much confidence as possible, wishing them to be true. Stella blinks, turning from the mirror to look at me.

"It will never be the same."

I nod slowly, both of us well aware that her torso will never be what it once was. Just like our family, Stella's side will always be marked with a permanent, ugly reminder of the accident that took our mother's life.

And stole the rest of our father as well.

"I could take you to get a tattoo." She blinks at my words, the tiniest flicker of emotion lighting up her eyes.

"You would do that?"

I nod, *"If it would make you feel better, absolutely. Find an artist you like, who has the ability to work with unusual skin patterns, and I'll take you."*

"Deal."

Not two weeks later, my sister came bounding into my room with a studio in mind. We drove for three hours to find the nondescript tattoo studio Stella had found online. There wasn't a moment of hesitancy in my sister's step as we walked inside and made a beeline for the counter. I didn't question her decision to go into the back alone, I simply signed the guardian form and waited until she was done.

Stella didn't say a word when we started the drive back, she just stared out the window, murmuring along to mom's favourite playlist.

When we finally made it home, I turned to her with a tight smile, *"Can I see it?"*

She didn't say anything, she just pulled up her shirt. My breath caught when the scar reappeared – it's twisted red lines just as grotesque as before. Stella twisted so I can see her other side and I stared at it with a frown.

"I thought you were going to cover up the scar."

She gives me a sad smile, *"So did I. But once I was there, I knew I couldn't erase what had happened with a basic floral design."*

I swallow, my gaze tracing the bolded letters, "You picked a good word."

"It felt fitting." She let her shirt fall back down, covering up the damage no therapy or tattoo could ever repair, "Father raised us to take accountability, so this is me accepting what's left."

I pictured the strong print Stella had picked. It was just as permanent as her scar, but this one would serve to fuel her.

Blinking back to the present, I swallow the sudden lump in my throat.

"You have always made me proud."

Stella smiles, her cheeks flushing with the faintest streak of pink, "You make me proud too, Mo. And I know mom would have been as well."

My throat tightens as a wave of grief threatens to breach the surface. My lips start to pull down and my brows pinch together, but I force myself to breathe through it.

"She would have loved to see us now."

Stella sighs, her glistening eyes reflecting all the emotions I refuse to express myself, "Do you think Jonathan would be different? If mom was still alive?"

I swallow thickly, thinking about the last time our father looked truly happy.

"I don't know, Stel. And I'm afraid we never will."

Nico

When I came out as gay, do you know what my mom said?

Love is love, Nico. It doesn't matter who the love is for.

There wasn't a moment of hesitation. There wasn't a single blink of surprise. It was simply a moment full of acceptance, support, and love.

When I told her my sob story of falling in love, do you know what my mom said?

"You're a stupid boy, Nico." She slaps my head, giving me a glare that is neither acceptive nor supportive.

My dad hums in agreement, his comforting hand leaving mine, "You can't expect to be lucky enough to fall in love and keep it. When you find someone worth fighting for, that's when the real challenge begins. You don't just turn and run like a fool."

And to think I drove all this way for some familial love.

My jaw drops, "You're supposed to be on my side! Team Montez till the end."

My mother clucks her tongue, stealing a cookie from the plate in front of me, "How can we be Team Montez when you are clearly in the wrong?"

Well then.

Shaking my head, I'm about to launch into another indignant rant when my father stands up and takes my mom's hand. I watch, stupefied, as he pulls her into his arms and they start swaying together in the middle of our crowded living room.

Planting a kiss on his lips, my mom tosses me a knowing smile over her shoulder.

"You can't be in love if you refuse to let your heart be taken by someone else. It doesn't work that way."

She lets out a laugh as her husband twirls her, their twenty-plus years of marriage never once diminishing the affection they have for one another.

If my parents weren't so damn cute, this would be sickening to watch.

"Your mother was a difficult one to catch. I had to surrender both my dignity and pride to ask for her hand in marriage." My dad grins when he gets a whack on the shoulder, "But it was worth it. The biggest risk leads to the biggest reward."

I sigh, leaning back against the couch with tired eyes, "What type of reward could be worth the humiliation of rejection?"

She scoffs, "Have we taught you nothing?"

"Is that a rhetorical question?"

Carlos smirks, giving his wife a pat on the ass before turning his attention back to me, "It's only a rhetorical question if you don't know the answer."

Coming home was a terrible idea.

I fling myself down on the couch, giving them both the evil eye, "You are no help whatsoever."

My mom sighs, untangling herself from my dad and returning to my side. The couch dips as she sits down next to me, her soothing fingers running through my hair.

"The answer is love, Nico. To love and to be loved is the greatest reward a person can receive."

I frown, wrapping my arms around her waist, "But how do you know if they love you back?"

She clucks her tongue, "You don't. That's why it's a risk."

Talk about shooting your shot blind.

My mom cups my face, her dark eyes twinkling down at me, "Part of the fall is not knowing the outcome. But if you don't take the leap, you will never know if Maurice was the one for you."

Blowing out a breath, I close my eyes. I picture every stolen moment we've had together these last few weeks and arrive at one stomach-plummeting conclusion.

That ridiculously handsome resting bitch face somehow became the one thing I looked forward to seeing every day.

Damn you, Maurice.

"You've got to ask yourself, is he worth it?" Her voice floats over me, her soft hands in my hair making me drowsy, "Would you rather risk your heart or lose the potential of something great?"

I open my mouth but she puts a finger against my lips, "You don't need to tell me. Just make sure you tell yourself."

ME: I'm out of town for the week but maybe we could talk when I get back??

I groan, deleting the message before hitting send.

ME: I'm sorry for the other night. I shouldn't have run away the way I did. Forgive me?

Gag. Delete.

ME: I fucked up our first date but any chance we could jump straight to a second?

Have I always been this awkward or is this a new development?

I groan, tossing my phone on my childhood bed just as a notification pings. Leaving my pride at the door, I eagerly grab my phone, pulling up my messages.

WES: Why do I keep getting notifications saying you're typing? We've talked about your misuse of this conversation thread.

Disappointment hits me as I register the name.

ME: Sorry not sorry. I was practicing what I was going to send to Maurice.

WES: ...

WES: Well, what did you send?

I wince, typing out my confession.

ME: I haven't sent anything.

WES: Dude. Just send the message. Trip keeps giving me dirty looks because my phone keeps going off in class.

ME: I thought you and Trip didn't have any classes together this semester??

WES: Who said it was my class?

I snort, picturing the snark Wes is getting for interrupting another one of Trip's classes. The man just can't stay away. It's seriously pathetic.

Though speaking of being pathetic...

ME: How have practices been without me?

WES: Are you asking about practice or do you want to know how Mo has been?

Busted.

ME: The second please.

Biting my lip, I watch the typing bubbles appear and disappear. Minutes start to tick by, so I switch to my vision board on Pinterest and add a few more photos to my latest collection. The incoming ping finally sounds and I jump back over, eagerly anticipating the essay Wes no doubt spent the last ten minutes writing.

WES: Come back and ask him yourself.

That bastard.

My thumbs fly over the keyboard, spamming the cruel man I insist on calling my best friend.

ME: That's it??

ME: That's all you're giving me??

ME: Wtf were you doing before sending me that shit response?

WES: I got distracted.

Please. Like we all don't know what that's code for.

ME: You're unbelievable.

WES: Trip just said the exact same thing ;)

Chapter 28

Mo

The team feels off without Nico.

You can always count on morning practices being subdued energy-wise, but usually by the time the team hits the sports performance room for afternoon weight training, most of the guys have perked up. And yet, without one of the co-captains, even the lift sessions seem to be lacking the Tigers usual spunk.

Wes has done a remarkable job of stepping up to fulfill the entirety of the captain role with Nico missing, but without the wise-cracking goalie, the team dynamic just feels off.

"Two more." I lift my brow, watching Preston slowly push the barbell above his chest. A hint of a tremor goes through his arms, but I ignore it.

"One more."

The rookie grunts, his face turning an alarming shade of purple as he raises the bar again. I watch him reach the top, his arms trembling in earnest when I finally let him re-stack it.

"Shit, Coach. That was brutal." Preston pants the words and lets his arms flop over the sides of the bench. I smirk, glancing at the weight stacked on either end of the barbell.

"The only way to hit a personal best is to push yourself. Well done, rookie."

The freshman's mouth drops open as he stares up at me, "Are you feeling okay, Mo?"

Grabbing the plates off the end, I can't help but glance around for the arrogant smirk that has been grating my nerves since day one. Nico's inability to stay quiet irritates the hell out of me, but now that his incessant flirting is gone, the performance room feels much too quiet.

"I'm fine, why?"

I catch a couple of the other players glancing around the room as well. Wes is in the far corner spotting Millard on the squat rack while the rest of the players murmur quietly amongst themselves. It feels like everyone is waiting for Nico to walk through the door with his smug grin and swagger to bring the energy back.

Preston sits up on the bench, rubbing his neck sheepishly, "Ah, it's nothing really..."

"But?" Resisting the urge to roll my eyes, I return my attention to the tomato-faced freshman.

"It's just that you've been handing out praise, Coach." He clears his throat, nervously meeting my gaze, "And until this week, that was something we all dreamed about."

"Excuse me?" I tilt my head, studying the rookie closely. He flinches, a red flush creeping up the side of his neck.

"Well, maybe it was less of a *we* thing and more of a *me* thing. It's just... you left a legacy at Taber and we just want to make you proud." Preston gulps, dropping his eyes, "That probably sounds dumb, but most of us didn't think we'd make it onto the varsity team. Especially once we found out Mighty Mo was going to be the assistant coach."

Guilt needles my stomach as I stare at the blushing rookie, his beetroot face only adding to the regret taking over me. I've never had a problem getting results but somewhere along the way my method of attaining those goals became cold and impersonal.

Until Nico, I only ever thought about strategies and maximizing efficiency.

But now I'm starting to care.

Clearing my throat, I cast a glance around the room and note the quiet determination of the players around me. All of the boys this season have shown nothing but commitment and dedication at each and every practice. Based on skillset alone, most of them wouldn't make it onto the field to play, but when individual effort is taken into consideration, they all deserve to wear a Taber Tigers jersey.

"Go get the rest of the team." Gritting my teeth, I give Preston a nod, "I would like to say a few words to everyone."

He jumps to his feet and rushes off. Within minutes, the team has clustered around the centre of the performance room, sweat-soaked bodies and weary faces looking at me curiously. Wes breaks through the wall of lacrosse players, approaching me with his usual dimpled smile.

"Should I be concerned you called for a team meeting?" He lowers his voice, coming to a stop beside me, "If this is about the other day…"

"It's not." I roll my eyes, "But thank you for the reminder."

"Hey, anytime." Wes grins and claps his hands together, "Alright everyone, listen up! Coach Mo would like to say a few words so unless you want to run sprints for the last ten minutes of practice, I recommend giving him your utmost attention."

I shoot a glance at the co-captain, "Didn't have you pegged for a sprint hater, Wes."

He throws me a wink, "I'm not. But they are."

Shaking my head, I tamp down a laugh and step forward. The quiet chatter immediately falls silent, Wes' threat and my presence intimidating enough for the players to press pause on their conversations. I clear my throat, wishing I didn't suddenly feel uncomfortable. Most people would rather crawl out of their skin than make a public speech, but for me, it's the words I'm about to say that have me uncharacteristically nervous.

Making eye contact with Preston, who looks significantly less red than he did five minutes ago, I feel my resolve solidify when he gives me a weak smile.

"It has come to my attention that my constructive criticism is often just that. Criticism." I pause, moving my gaze from one player to another, "I helped the Tigers become provincial champions five years ago and we continued that winning streak until we achieved the label of undefeated."

Cheers go round the group but they quickly fade when they see my frown, "Until this year, the only thing I cared about was bringing home the championship banner. I didn't care how many bridges I had to burn, how much criticism I had to deliver, I did what needed to be done to achieve the results."

The performance room falls deathly quiet, anxious faces staring back at me. My eyes rake through the crowd, fruitlessly searching for the one person who isn't in attendance.

"But thanks to your co-captains, I've come to realize that you can achieve results and have fun. You can hand out praise and not impair a player's ability to achieve their personal best."

I turn to Wes, who is watching me with wide eyes, "Consider this my official apology, Captain. I have knocked you and your partner since day one but now I see that it was my perspective that was skewed, not your leadership techniques."

Taking a deep breath, I turn back to face the crowd, "Delivering praise does not come easily to me, but you have my word that moving forward, I will do my best to provide positive feedback in addition to constructive criticism."

I pause, meeting Preston's gaze with a slight smile, "Well, only when it's deserved of course."

Wes lets out a hoot, "That last shot was meant for you, Hunter."

I laugh with the rest of the team, the energy and camaraderie seeping back into the room as tired teammates laugh and jostle with one another. Any sense of discomfort dissipates as I cast my eyes over their smiling faces.

"It has been a privilege coaching this team. Keep up the good work and we may bring home another championship banner this year."

The team breaks into cheers and a few of the players whistle their approval. My chest feels lighter as I step back and let Wes have the spotlight, my father's ever-present disappointment lifting from my shoulders as I watch my players disperse among the performance room.

My players. My team.

My lips pull into a smile as a newfound sense of freedom descends. For the first time in a long time, I know what path the future holds.

I know what path I *want* the future to hold.

All that's left to do is lean forward and take it.

"If I'd known you were that good at public speaking, I would have offered up my captain title after the first practice." Wes shakes his head, eyes crinkling at the corners, "That was incredible."

I grin, "It's all about preparation, Williams. You should try it sometime."

The co-captain's smile widens as his eyes drift over my shoulder.

"That's the beauty of life, Mo." Wes winks at me before throwing a wave to someone over my shoulder, "There are some things in life you can't prepare for."

I don't get a second to think about his comment before someone else speaks up.

"And here I thought your corporate persona was all suit and no talk." Dark eyes and days' worth of scruff steps into view as Nico flashes me his signature smirk.

"Hey babe. Long time no see."

Nico

He's fucking pissed.

My confidence starts to falter as Maurice glowers at me, his clenched jaw and stiff posture making me think that wasn't my best entrance.

Risking life and limb, I take a step closer, "Did you miss me?"

Maurice raises a brow, the unimpressed look on his face identical to the one he gave me on that first day.

"That's how you want to play this?"

Wes coughs, interrupting our moment, "And that's my cue to leave. Glad to have you back, Nico."

He gives me a quick pat on the back before turning and following the rest of the team out of the performance room.

And leaving me to face an angry O'Brien alone.

I swallow, gathering my courage as I take another step closer. Maurice narrows his eyes but remains silent as I close the distance between us. A hopeful part of me thinks this is him offering an olive branch, but the other, more realistic part is screaming at me to run before the predator makes his move.

He crosses his arms and the physical barrier does not go unnoticed.

"I thought you weren't coming back until next week."

I give him a tight smile, "So did I."

Maurice falls silent and I use the opportunity to study him. Looking sexier than ever, it's not an exaggeration to say he looks like he belongs in a sportswear commercial. Maurice looks exactly the way I left him: arrogant, handsome, and completely unwrinkled.

It's a little annoying to be honest.

"Aren't you going to ask why I came back early?" I breathe out the words, my nerves suddenly jumping into overdrive.

"No." Maurice stares back at me, unblinking, "You didn't tell me you were leaving so why would I care that you came back?"

Ouch.

I clear my throat, "It's been established that I'm a chicken shit-

"I prefer the term coward."

-but the reason I left ended up being the same reason I came back early." I pause, searching his gaze for some sort of emotion, "You."

There.

The tiniest flicker of emotion crosses Maurice's face before the neutral mask slides back in place. I was expecting to see surprise, maybe even disappointment in those gorgeous blue eyes, but it ended up being the worst one of all. Hurt.

A wave of sorrow hits me, regret filling my veins for my stupid decision to run away, for not sending that text, and most importantly, for hurting the man I love.

Swallowing the fear of rejection, I ditch the rehearsal speech I practiced the entire drive back and speak from the heart.

"You're too fucking perfect." I blurt out the words, adding another regret to the growing list, "At least that's what I used to think."

Maurice scowls, "You ran away because I'm put together?"

"Yes. No. Kind of." I grimace, silently vowing to never free verse again, "You're an idol, Maurice. A legend who has more threesomes under his belt than most B-list celebrities."

His lips twitch, "Are you calling me the B team?"

"Hell no, and that's my point. You are the hottest, most confident, put together person I've ever known and that's intimidating as fuck, do you know why?"

I'm on a roll now, so I don't give him a chance to answer, "Because it makes you seem untouchable. Inhuman. Too sexy to be anything but on the cover of a magazine."

I blow out a breath, "But then I got to know you. I saw the cracks beneath the armour, the motion sickness behind every offer to drive. You aren't the emotionless robot people paint you out to be, you're just a regular guy with ridiculously good genetics and a defence mechanism that keeps people at a distance."

Maurice frowns, and without thinking, I bridge the space between us to smooth out the crease. His body stiffens against my touch.

Throwing my heart on the line, I take one last breath and lay out the barren truth.

"I ran away because I was scared you wouldn't fight for me. That one day you would wake up and realize the inconvenience of having a gay partner wouldn't be worth the effort."

My voice cracks right at the end, so I snap my mouth shut and try not to fall over from the emotional purge I just went through.

Maurice tilts his head, his expression carefully blank as he mulls over my words. I drop my thumb from his forehead, searching his face for anything that might give me a glimpse of what's going through his head right now.

Nothing. He's giving me nothing.

I scuff the toe of my sneaker on the ground, jamming my hands into the pockets of my jeans to stop the nervous fidgeting. I'm dying to break the tension with an inappropriate comment but I hold back, giving him space to think.

So, I wait.

And wait.

And wait some more.

Truthfully, it's only been two minutes since I cut off the emotional onslaught, but every second feels like eternity as I wait for Maurice's response.

He clears his throat and I swear my heart stops on the spot.

"Which magazine would you feature me on?"

Maurice grins, a wide, heart-stopping smile that reaches his eyes and that's all it takes for me to burst out laughing. My knees buckle with relief and if it weren't for his strong arms reaching out to stabilize me, I would be a puddle on the floor.

"Babe, I would put you on them all."

He chuckles, "Well said, Montez."

I sigh, soaking up the rare moment of him looking carefree and happy. Most people would snap a picture to frame this shot, but I prefer knowing this moment will only ever exist between us.

Right here, right now.

Maurice shakes his head and just like that, the moment vanishes with his smile.

"Why would you think I wouldn't fight for you?" He gives me a pointed look, "I've never once shown discomfort at the thought or reality of being with a man."

I flap a hand, "You get too focused on the data, Maurice. Of course you haven't given me any red flags, if you had I would have dipped a long time ago."

He glares at me but I shrug it off, "I don't run on logic like you do-

"No shit."

-so, at the end of the day my insecurities came from a place in here." I tap my chest, "When I ran away, I wasn't thinking. I was feeling."

Maurice closes his eyes with a sigh, "Wes told me you were searching for validation and reassurance from me."

My best friend is a dead man.

"And he was right. I haven't been open and although I haven't done anything to be of concern, I haven't confirmed anything either."

My mouth drops open, the sincerity in his tone making me want to pinch myself.

He opens his eyes, "My mother died in a car accident five years ago. Stella was in the car and they were driven off the road by a drunk driver."

He swallows, "The morning after my sister got discharged from the hospital, my father woke us up at 4:30AM and took us to the gym. Stella wasn't cleared to do anything beyond her physio exercises but that didn't matter. Jonathan kept us there for hours, telling us that the only way to change yourself is to challenge yourself."

I stare at him in shock, horrified that anyone would put their children through that, never mind after losing a loved one.

"That routine went on for two weeks until I had to come back to school and finish the semester. By then, my priorities and perspective of the world had flipped upside down with only one thing staying the same. My father's expectations."

He lets out an empty laugh, "You said I was too perfect? Let me reassure you, Nico, perfection was always the one thing I could never attain."

Blinking back tears, I step forward and wrap my arms around him. His strong frame melds against mine, the hard edges of his muscles cutting into me as the barriers between us start to fall.

"Perfection is an illusion, mi amor. Keep chasing it and nothing will ever be enough."

He smiles against my neck, "Losing me with the Spanish there, Montez."

"You'll get used to it."

Maurice sighs against me, his broad shoulders collapsing against mine.

"You remind me a lot of her, you know."

I let my hand trail down his back, offering the comfort he should have received a long time ago.

"Who?"

"My mother."

My hand stills and I pull back to look at him, "I can't tell if that's a compliment or not."

He smirks, "Well you certainly don't have her class. But you have her uncanny tendency to make me throw logic out the window and do stupid shit like sleep on a makeshift bed on the ground."

I burst out laughing, "You had so much fun that night, admit it."

"My back still hasn't recovered."

"Old man."

He rolls his eyes, "The point is, I heard what you said the other night and this is me trying to make it right."

"By comparing me to your dead mother?"

He glares but I catch his lips twitching, "I forgot how infuriating you are. I'm starting to think asking you to be my boyfriend was a bad idea."

My brain screeches to a halt.

"You want me to be your boyfriend?!" I shriek the last word as adrenalin, excitement, and a little bit of fear pumps through my body.

He shrugs, "Unless you'd prefer to be called something else."

I hold up a hand, trying to stop reality from crashing down, "Pause. Rewind. Do you understand what you're saying?"

A brow goes up, "I'm saying what I should have said the last time you felt insecure in our relationship."

Somebody call an ambulance because this boy needs a heart doctor.

I gnaw my lip, the lingering doubt rearing its ugly head, "You realize the implications of dating a man, right? Especially in a conservative small town, people are going to talk and they won't have nice things to say."

I pause with an aching heart, "And if this works out, we will never be able to have kids."

Maurice tilts his head, "There's a lot of ways to have kids. And if I remember correctly, we were going to be dog co-parents after you move-in."

Any trace of fear slips away as my face breaks into a grin.

"You want me to move-in?"

He chuckles, "Eventually. If our next few dates make it past the parking lot."

Before he has the chance to say anything else, I grab the front of his shirt and haul him against me, finally planting my lips back where they belong.

On his.

Chapter 29

Mo

All that's left is part two of my plan.

Nico derailed the first part with his impromptu visit, something I didn't appreciate at the time but an inconvenience he more than made up for later that day and the week that followed it. I've never been in a relationship before, but Nico and I are going on ten days now and I'm not sure my chest has ever felt lighter.

He's still annoying as hell but now, strangely enough, it's our futile arguments on and off the lacrosse field that I look forward to the most.

We agreed to wait until the end of the semester to reassess our living situation and ensure my coaching contract with Taber University gets approved for an extension before we announce our relationship to the team.

Personally, I couldn't care less what the other players think, but Nico felt like it might look inappropriate if the coach and the captain are sleeping together. Not that everyone hasn't figured it out already.

My boyfriend is many things, but subtle is not one of them.

I smile, thinking about the last rendezvous we had in the locker room after today's morning practice. I don't think I'll ever get tired of hearing Nico scream my name.

The soft bump of the aircraft jolts me out of my thoughts as the Vancouver runway comes into view. The long stretch of asphalt is lit up against the dark night sky, the late hour of my arrival shining back at me in the familiar glow of the city skyline.

Despite my confidence in my plan, nerves hit me the second the driver drops me off outside the O'Brien mansion. The immaculate landscaping alongside our front entrance does nothing to calm the anxiety suddenly pounding through my bloodstream.

I've been a top competitor for years and yet nothing compares to the apprehension I feel walking down the maze of hallways to my father's office. Stained glass doors mark Jonathan's sanctuary as the plush carpet of the hallway turns into glistening hardwood. With a deep inhale, I push the doors open and confront the familiar sight of Jonathan signing papers at his massive, custom-made desk that proudly sits before the famous Vancouver skyline.

"You shouldn't be here."

My father doesn't bother looking up from the papers on his desk, the rigid outline of his silhouette growing with the passing sunset. Most people would pause their work to admire the view splayed out in front of them, but not my father.

He doesn't spare me or the sunset a glance as he turns to his computer.

I clear my throat, "I needed to talk to you."

"Then you should have booked an appointment." Pausing his work, Jonathan frowns at me, "You know I hate surprises."

That's not what mother used to say.

I bite back the words just in time for him to look at his computer, "I can schedule you in for half an hour at noon tomorrow. Don't be late."

My spine stiffens, "I need to talk to you now."

"Quit being a nuisance, Maurice. I'm working." He scowls at the computer, the prominent frown line the same one I've seen in the mirror too many times.

"It's 10 PM."

Jonathan lifts a brow, "And yet you were able to contact Johnson and get him to fly you out here. Guess working through the night is not such a rare occurrence after all."

My teeth grind together at his condescending tone, "He's my uncle."

"But still on my payroll." He shoots me a pointed look, "Don't make me ask again, Maurice."

"I want to extend my part-time contract."

That gets his attention.

Pushing the papers on his desk to the side, Jonathan leans back in his chair, displeasure etching through his features. Silence spans between us, my father assessing me from his position at his desk while I remain standing in the doorway.

It's poetic, really, looking at the ten feet of space separating us. In all the years that has passed since my mother died, Jonathan has yet to put in the effort to bridge the gap between us.

When it comes to my father's priorities, work always comes first.

He tilts his head and the remnant rays of the sunset catch the silver streaks in his hair. The stretch of grey seems to have doubled in the last five years.

"Who is she?"

I frown, "I'm sorry?"

"Who. Is. She." Dragging out the words, Jonathan pierces me with his stare, "The only reason you would want to extend your contract is because someone changed your mind."

I exhale slowly, "My decision is not made on behalf of someone else. I've come to realize coaching lacrosse is something I enjoy and I would like the opportunity to explore it further."

He drums his fingers on the desk, his cold gaze never leaving mine, "But there is someone."

"Yes." I hold his gaze and push out the rest, "His name is Nico."

I see the moment my words sink in. Like a vintage jukebox, every thought shuffles across my father's face, his stoic expression ripping apart at the seams.

"I knew this would happen." Jonathan hisses out a breath, "Your mother insisted you were just having a bit of fun at that gay club but I should have stopped that nonsense back in your freshman year."

I blink, my world tilting on its axis, "You knew about *Lifestyle*?"

"Of course I knew." His fist slams on the desk, "Who do you think reviews your credit card statements, Maurice? Did you really think I would let the future head of this company out of my sight?"

He opens a drawer and throws a thick envelope on the desk.

"I know everything, Maurice. There is nothing and no one you've done that I don't know about." Jonathan lets out a bitter laugh, "I blame the club. Until then, you only ever fucked girls."

I flinch, my mind whirling from the newfound information. My father knew about my sexuality all along. My *mother* knew and convinced him to let me explore.

My racing thoughts get caught off by Jonathan rounding the desk and closing the distance between us. His strong build, identical to my own, stalks across the hardwood and comes to a stop in front of me. I've got a couple inches on him, but that has never impeded his ability to look down on me.

"Listen to me." His eyes narrow into slits, the expensive sleeves of his suit within touching distance, "You will come back to MacNeil Incorporated like we planned and you will terminate this ridiculous fling. The only reason I'm not cutting you off right now is because you have an appetite for both sexes, so we can chalk this up to a simple misguided phase."

Matching his glare with one of my own, I hold my ground, "You would disown me for being homosexual?"

He scoffs, "Don't play the pride card with me, Maurice. This isn't about public image, this is about me not wanting a freak for a son. To think I wasted hours teaching you the nature of being a man when all along you were just looking for someone to bend over-

The punch sends him stumbling back, blood spurting from his nose. I calmly shake out my hand, my jaw clenched hard enough to break teeth.

"Talk about me or my partner like that again and I will spread the word that our CEO has a problem supporting diversity." I step forward, savouring the sight of blood staining my father's suit, "And as for the rest of your homophobic tangent, do us both a favour and grow up. You are down to one child now, so if you ostracize Stella the way you did with me, there will be no one left to carry your empire."

I pause, watching my father wipe his bleeding nose with the back of his hand. It was heartbreaking, seeing the dark sky illuminate the man who only had money left to give.

"Stella asked me what our family would be like, if Charlotte was still alive."

The mention of my mother's name has Jonathan's composure crumbling faster than my respect for him.

Swallowing the lump in my throat, I press on, "I didn't have an answer for her then but I do now."

My father blinks at me, his emotionless façade ripping at the seams.

"We would be just as broken because she would have hated the man you have become."

And with that, I turn and walk out the door.

Leaving my father to fall to pieces alone.

Chapter 30

1 week later...

Mo

Stella doesn't bother holding back her shriek.

"I knew it! I *knew* this was going to happen."

Cody chuckles from beside her, "I'm just glad I won't have to hypothesize about your sex life anymore."

Stella slaps his chest, "Don't pretend you weren't as equally invested. You were cheering for Nico just as much as I was."

I watch the couple go back and forth, their familiar bickering putting a smile on my face as I take a sip of my whiskey. Even before Cody and Stella got together, they always found something to argue about.

I used to find it sickening to watch.

Now I find it endearing.

Clearing my throat, I break the current showdown with a question that's been lingering at the back of my mind for a while.

"How did you pick Nico as my partner if you didn't know I was into men?"

Cody grins and leans back in his chair, looking at my sister. Stella quickly drops her gaze to her nails and studies them intently.

"I figured it out during winter break."

I narrow my eyes, "That's funny because I don't remember bringing a guy home for you to meet."

Stella hums, tapping her fingers on the table, "How strange."

Cody barks out a laugh and earns himself a glare. I tilt my head, refusing to look away until my sister meets my eyes.

"Fine. I looked through your messages and saw the names of your hookups. Most of which were male."

I blink, "How did you get into my contacts?"

She grins, "My facial recognition is programmed into your phone."

Cody shakes his head and takes a sip of his beer, unsuccessfully hiding his smirk behind the glass. Ignoring my friend, I slide my hand across the table.

"Give me your phone."

Stella groans, "But Mo-

"Phone. Now." I hold out my hand, waiting for her to pass it along, "If you have access to my phone, I get access to yours. It's only fair."

"Fine." She pulls out a sparkling pink case and places it in my outstretched hand, "But the only thing you're going to find are all the nudes I send to Ellsworth."

Cody chokes on his drink and I swivel my head to look at him.

"Are you kidding me right now?"

Stella reaches over and pats my arm, "Don't worry, this is an equal partnership. Cody sends me just as many."

Jesus Christ.

Cody finally catches his breath and gives me a weak smile, "I don't save them."

I cross my arms, "Like that makes it any better."

Stella gasps, looking at her boyfriend, "You don't save them? I put a lot of effort into taking those pictures."

Cody rubs his neck, looking anywhere but my darkening expression, "Let's talk about this later, Stel."

She shakes her head with a huff, "And to think I saved all of yours. What does a girl have to do around here to have a man keep her nudes?'

"Did someone say nudes? Count me in."

Nico plops himself down in the chair next to me and despite the current topic of conversation, my lips pull into a smile. I've noticed this has become a tendency whenever Nico is around.

Smiling. Laughing. Feeling less on edge.

The strangest thing of all is I still feel like myself. All my core values have remained the same, most of my priorities have as well, the only difference is the face that looks back at me in the mirror each morning is no longer my father's.

It's my own.

Nico throws his backpack on the ground, steals my drink, and shifts closer to Stella. All without saying a single word to me.

"Whose nudes are we talking about?"

She sighs, "Mine. And Cody's."

"Ooh, I would love to see what the captain is packing under there." Nico throws me a wink and I do my best to burn a hole through the side of his head, "See if it compares to my own lacrosse player."

Cody pales beside me and I grimace, "Enough. Phones away and let's have a normal conversation that doesn't include nudity."

Nico pouts, "Buzz kill."

Stella nods in agreement, "That sums Mo up well."

Throwing me a lifeline, Cody turns to me with a wry smile, "How's the job hunting going?"

I shrug, "It's going. I've applied to a few remote positions in Vancouver and reached out to a few connections, so there shouldn't be a problem finding something that fits with my coaching schedule."

Nico pipes up, "He heard back from three different companies but the salary they offered him was too low."

Stella smiles, "He knows his worth."

I smile back at her, understanding flowing between us. Jonathan may have fallen short in his role as a father, but when it comes to being successful in business, he certainly gave us the tools to standout.

"Have you heard from him?" My sister tilts her head, watching my reaction carefully, "Since you last spoke."

I shake my head, automatically glancing at my phone. Ever since I walked out of Jonathan's office, I've been waiting for my letter of termination to make its way into my inbox, but so far there's been nothing.

Truthfully, I don't know how to feel about the situation. My father may have crossed a line but he's still my father. I no longer view him as a role model, but he's still the man my mother once loved. And as pathetic as it sounds, that fact alone makes me think I could forgive him.

"I've heard nothing yet."

Stella sighs, "You will. It just might not be what you expect."

Before I can answer, Nico lets out a groan, "Babe, why do you insist on drinking this shit? It's tequila or cocktails. There's no in-between."

I give him a pointed look, "You could always buy your own drink."

He perks up, "Round of tequila everyone?"

Cody frowns, glancing at the clock on the wall, "It's 1 PM on a Sunday."

"So?" Nico nudges me, his dark eyes twinkling, "There's no time limit when we're celebrating."

Stella brightens, "I'm in."

I look at her in shock, "Are you sure?"

She takes Cody's hand, giving him a small smile before turning to face me.

"I've been working my way up to this. Last week, I had one of those slushy drinks."

Nico lets out a hoot and snags the attention of our waiter, "In that case, what are we waiting for? Tequila for the table, please."

My chest starts to ache as I watch my baby sister take her first shot of alcohol since the accident. Her hand never leaves Cody's as she takes a hesitant sip before pulling a face and tossing it back. Cody whispers something in her ear that has a smile replacing the grimace and I feel something inside me break.

Stella doesn't need me anymore.

Feeling like my chest is collapsing in on itself, I excuse myself from the table and hastily make my way to the bathroom. My breathing grows ragged as I yank open the door, and my knees give out the moment it shuts behind me.

I collapse to the ground, struggling to catch a breath as my throat thickens to the point of suffocation.

What the hell is happening to me?

I squeeze my eyes shut, trying to push the emotions back down, but its no use. My control cracks then shatters as unwanted emotions break past the surface, the years of repression ripping apart my barriers like a man starved. My hands start to shake as I gasp for air, the pressure in my chest building until all I can hear is the angry thud of my heart.

My chest caves inward as the wave of grief crashes down on me and a broken sound escapes my throat. The foreign noise echoes around the empty bathroom and it takes me a moment to recognize what's going on.

I'm crying.

For the first time in twelve years.

"Mi amor? Are you alright?"

I jerk back against the door, forcing it shut with my body-weight. My vision refuses to clear as more tears stream down my face.

"Not now, Montez."

There's something wrong with my voice, something missing, but I don't have time to decipher it before another wave of sorrow hits me. I hunch over as sobs overtake my body and the next thing I know, the blurry outline of Nico's jeans step into view.

I jerk away, turning my head so he can't see the streaks marking my cheeks.

"Get out."

Instead of answering, Nico sits down beside me. He shifts around, knocking our shoulders together as he makes himself comfortable and a bolt of anger goes through my system.

"I told you to leave." Refusing to look in his direction, my teeth snap together, "Get the fuck out."

I refocus on my breathing, the age-old trick that has kept me in control all these years. The trick gets thrown out the window as every memory I've ever had with my mother flashes through my mind like a time capsule, her carefree laughter ringing in my ears as I try and fail to get a reign on my body.

"I've never been good at following instructions." A warm arm wraps around my shoulders, pulling my shaking body closer. He presses a kiss on my neck, whispering softly in my ear.

"Let me in, Maurice. Let me take care of you."

Shaking my head, my heart starts to ache as I fight to hold on. My mother's face flashes behind my eyes, her colourful dress twirling in front of twelve-year-old me as her voice echoes through my mind.

Stop thinking, Mo. Just feel.

Squeezing my eyes shut, I finally let go.

Falling against Nico, I stop fighting and let the tears flow freely. Pitiful sounds escape my mouth but Nico accepts them all, murmuring to me in Spanish until the pressure in my chest softens and slowly disappears.

My body sags as the emotions drain out, Nico's soothing touch the only thing that's keeping me from melting to the floor.

"Feel any better?" Running his fingers through my hair, Nico plants another kiss on my neck, "This is the first time I've seen you look less than a ten."

A watery laugh escapes me, "I hate you."

"It is always good to know whether or not you're an ugly crier. And you, my gorgeous boyfriend, most certainly fall into the second category."

I huff another laugh, letting the warmth of his embrace chase away the remaining shakes. Once I'm somewhat certain there won't be another episode, I push myself up to sitting and clear my throat.

"Thank you. For not leaving."

Nico smiles and reaches over to smooth out the crease between my brows.

"For you, Maurice, I will always stay." He tilts his head, dark eyes studying me intently, "It was Stella drinking the alcohol, wasn't it?"

I sigh, giving him a resigned nod, "Watching her take that shot felt like she was letting go of the past. It felt like she was letting go of mom. Like she was leaving us behind."

"Awe Maurice."

I shake my head, falling back against the door, "It's ridiculous because I am genuinely happy Stella has moved on. I couldn't be happier that she's making a new life for herself, one where she can leave the consequences of her past in the past."

"But now you're wondering where does that leave you."

"Exactly. She's got Cody, Lou, an entire support system that doesn't include me." I frown as I repeat the thought that triggered this meltdown in the first place, "Stella doesn't need me anymore."

Nico taps my nose, "You're only looking at half the data, Maurice. Even though it might look and feel different, your sister will always need you."

"How do you know?"

He smiles, "Because that's what it means to be family. Stella might not rely on you the way she did after the accident but that's a good thing. You don't have to be her caretaker and protector anymore. You can finally be the one role you were meant to be. Her brother."

We fall silent, staring at each other on the bathroom floor of Taber's only sports bar. My skin starts to itch from my dried tears but I don't make a move to wash it off.

Feeling back on steady ground, I take a calming breath and nod, "You're right."

"Am I ever wrong?"

I roll my eyes and haul myself off the ground. My ringtone bursts to life just as Nico climbs to his feet and he shoots me a horrified look.

"Babe, not to ruin a sentimental moment but why are you still using the basic ringtone that comes with the phone?"

I raise a brow, pulling my phone out of my pocket, "Why would I waste time choosing a different one?"

"There are so many things wrong with that answer. The first being you're a sad, old man." I shoot him a glare but Nico blows it off with a smirk, "Good thing you have a hot young stud who can change it for you tonight."

"You're ridiculous."

"You love it."

Ignoring him, I glance down at my phone and freeze when I see the name of the caller. My stomach drops as I press accept and mentally steel myself for an unpleasant conversation.

"Father."

"Maurice." There's a beat of silence and I hear papers shuffling in the background, "I called to let you know your contract for an extension has been approved."

I blink once, twice, thinking maybe I misheard him. Nico widens his eyes at me, the question in his eyes the same one that's running through my head.

"What changed your mind?"

Jonathan sighs, "It would be inconvenient for all those years of training to go to waste."

Holding back a disappointed sigh, I give Nico the smallest shake of my head.

"I see."

My father clears his throat, his discomfort echoing down the line, "Along with your contract approval, I've decided to accept this new... relationship of yours. It's what Charlotte would have wanted."

Nico gives me a thumbs up and I roll my eyes.

"The gesture is appreciated, father." I pause, scanning my boyfriend's face for the answer I'm looking for, "But the thing is, I don't want to work for you anymore."

A slow smile spreads across Nico's face and it's all the motivation I need to keep going, "Consider this my official resignation. I'll send the paperwork this evening."

There's a brief silence before a harsh voice returns, "Think about what you're saying, Maurice. You're throwing away a remarkable income as well as a promising future."

"No Jonathan. I'm throwing away the future you laid out for me. If you want to be a part of my life, it will have to be as my father and not my employer."

Angry words fly down the line but I press end before they have a chance to register. Tucking my phone back in my pocket, I turn to see Nico grinning at me.

"Babe, that was fucking hot. How do you feel right now?"

I stare back at him, my face breaking into a wide smile.

"I'm finally free."

Nico

Lacey leans closer, her lips pursed in concentration.

"Stop moving."

"I'm not moving!"

She lifts a delicate brow, "How can you not be moving if you're speaking?"

I huff, falling silent and letting her finish my eyeliner. For someone who rarely wears makeup, Lacey has the hand of an artist when it comes to application.

She pulls away, squinting at my eyelids so I give her a flutter.

"How do I look?"

Lacey lets out a laugh before putting away her weapon of choice.

"You tell me."

I jump off her bed, racing to the bathroom to check out my girl's artistry. Letting out a hoot, I'm in the middle of rejoicing when the toilet flushes and a very unimpressed Cecelia comes walking out of the stall behind me.

"Why are you always here?"

I give her a beaming grin, my raised spirits no match for the negative aura of the evil roommate.

"Because I love seeing you, CeCe."

She rolls her eyes, pushing past me to wash her hands. I step to the side, doing my best to radiate friendly vibes as she stares me down in the mirror.

"Your eyes look good." Giving me a half-smile, she points to my jaw, "But your facial hair could use some work."

Ignoring the temptation to check the mirror, I let my grin grow wider, "Was that a compliment I just heard? CeCe, I think we're starting to become friends."

Another eye roll.

"You talk too much."

And with that final comment, she turns and stomps back to her room, leaving me to double check my beard to make sure it didn't suddenly become patchy.

The wicked witch of the dormitory was lying through her teeth because I look hella good tonight.

At my request, Lacey kept the eyeliner as minimal as possible, leaving on just enough to make my eyes look darker than usual. I'm not sure how Maurice is going to react when he sees the slight addition but I figure we will cross that bridge when we get there.

"You look perfect." Lacey smiles at me from the doorway, her baggy hoodie hanging off her lanky frame. She would make an incredible ballerina if it weren't for the fact she didn't have an athletic bone in her body.

"Thank you, mi amor. It's perfect." I run over and scoop her up in a hug, "You're perfect."

Lacey laughs, squeezing me back, "Just try to remember when the doubts creep in, communicate with him. Don't have a meltdown on the sidewalk and run away again."

Well said.

"You got it." Pressing a kiss against her forehead, I give her one last grin before grabbing my wallet and heading for the door.

"Have a good second first date!"

"Red looks good on you."

Maurice does a scan of my body over the hood of his car, his arms resting atop the Cadillac. My dick presses against the zipper of my dress pants as I take in the casual dominance of his relaxed position.

As if reading my thoughts, Maurice pushes off the massive vehicle and walks around to greet me properly. My mouth goes dry as I take in the shoulders outlined through the fitted material, the pale blue colour of the shirt a perfect match for those devastating eyes.

Letting my hands brush over the silky material of my own shirt, my lips pull into a grin, "An admirer got me this."

He comes to a stop in front of me, an amused smile painting his lips, "Is that the same admirer you tried to return it to?"

"Maybe." I step forward, soaking in the view, "Or maybe it's from a different admirer."

A brow goes up, "I'd hate to see what the other guy looks like."

I burst out laughing, barely catching my breath before Maurice steps forward and captures my lips with his. His tongue traces the seam of my lips and I open them, letting him claim every piece of me. Sucking on his bottom lip, I'm about to shove my hands down his pants when Maurice pulls away with a scowl.

"Stop distracting me. We're going on a date tonight."

I grin, my hands cupping his ass, "Somebody is feeling out of control."

"Give me two minutes and I'll show you out of control."

Giving his ass one last squeeze, I plant another kiss on his lips before pulling away, "You've got tinted windows. We'll make up some time on the road."

Maurice reaches up and grabs my chin, tilting his head in study, "Are you wearing makeup?"

I gulp, sending up a prayer that the dark sky and my scruff will be enough to hide the flush suddenly spreading over my cheeks.

"I wanted to do something different tonight."

He stares at me silently, the expression on his face unreadable. I sigh, feeling oddly disappointed, "I can take it off."

He frowns, catching my arm before I can turn away.

"Why would you do that? It looks good."

"Really?"

"You know how I feel about repeating myself." Maurice smirks, reaching up to touch the corner of my eye, "But yes, it looks good. It will make your eyes pop when you're sucking me off on the drive to the club."

I huff out a nervous laugh, "So you don't think it's too... gay?"

"Did you not hear a word I just said?"

He lets out an exasperated sigh, "Just because I'm bisexual doesn't mean you have to lean into your masculine tendencies. I'm not with you because you're a guy, Nico. I'm with you because you're the only person I can't stand being around almost as much as I can't stand being without."

And there goes my heart.

My face splits into a grin, "Does this mean you don't hate me anymore?"

"I wouldn't go that far." Maurice grins, officially engraving his name on the memory box marked forever, "But I'll let you in on a secret, Montez."

My cheeks start to ache from all this smiling but I soldier on, feeling stupidly in love and certain about who I want to spend the rest of my mornings arguing with.

"Do tell."

His smile widens, mirroring my own.

"I wouldn't want to hate anyone else."

Epilogue

2 weeks later...

Lacey

"Is Mojo not the cutest name for a dog?"

Nico shifts in his seat to look at me, the massive backseat of Mo's Cadillac giving me more than enough legroom to stretch out comfortably. My latest romance novel lies open on my lap, the explicit sex scene staring at me from the ink on the page.

Mo shakes his head from the driver's seat, "We are not naming our dog Mojo."

"But you admit we're adopting a dog?"

I look up and survey the scene with a wry smile. Nico's endless taunts are something I've gotten used to after years of shared childhood experience. His boyfriend, on the other hand, still doesn't seem to have a handle on the wild card that is my closest friend.

Mo rolls his eyes, his profile just as handsome through the side mirror. Nico has always gone for confident, athletic jocks who are considered to be universally attractive. Our joke used to be Nico likes his men big and mean whereas I like mine lean and pretty.

"No."

Nico turns and winks at me, "Are you sure?"

"Yes."

I laugh and catch Mo's amused gaze in the side mirror. He's loosened up a lot since I first met him, the stiff exterior and forced charm eventually giving way to genuine thoughtfulness. I can see how some people might find Taber's lacrosse legend intimidating, if not downright rude, but I can also see the caring person underneath. The one that Nico feel in love with.

If there's one thing life has taught me, it's to always look beyond the surface.

Glancing back at the graphic scene splayed out in front of me, I let out a sigh. The heroine just finished her second orgasm and the couple haven't even gotten to the actual sex part yet.

Unease creeps over me as my eyes skim the first moment of entry, the moment when the man enters the woman, and I have to shut the book before the discomfort gives way to darker, more sinister thoughts.

It's pathetic, really. I've been reading romance novels since I was thirteen years-old and I still can't get past the sex scenes. At first it was because I felt awkward reading them, the typical young girl reading things she shouldn't be, but now it's for an entirely different reason.

"You ready for today, mi amor?"

Nico glances at me with concern, something that has become a routine between us every time it's his turn to drop me off at therapy. If it were up to my brother, he alone would do all the driving, but after spending the first week of university dodging *are you okay?* questions, I knew I had to put my foot down.

Wesley means well but there's only so much sibling protection I can handle.

"I'm ready to grow and take on my next adventure." I quote the words with a smile, thinking about the sunshine tissues my therapist hands out.

Nico grimaces from the passenger seat, "Babe, you sound like a bad car commercial."

I smile, looking out the window as the passing prairies gradually turns into the dainty shops of Silverwood. Known as Taber University's biggest lacrosse rival, the town is a half hour drive east of Taber and the closest place with a certified therapist.

Truthfully, the town is a lot cuter than Taber, the little mom and pop shops a welcome change from the sad country bar and gas station our university town offers. I haven't had the chance to explore the town much, given the school rivalry and the tight carpooling scheduling I'm on, but one of these days I would love to explore Silverwood and discover what hidden gems are buried here.

The car rumbles to a stop outside the nondescript white building that takes up two hours of my week, every week. Unbuckling my seat belt, I lean forward to give Nico a peck on the cheek.

"I'll see you in a little bit."

Nico studies me intently, the same way he always does before these sessions. I give him a reassuring smile and get out of the car.

Sometimes I wish my life wasn't so routine. That people weren't always walking on eggshells around me. It feels like I'm stuck in this limbo where I'm not the girl I once was but not quite brave enough to be the girl I want to be.

So I stay the broken girl.

The one who tried to commit suicide after her boyfriend dumped her.

Releasing another sigh, I follow the pathway to the front door like I always do. I ring the doorbell upon arrival and turn to admire the bellflowers creeping along the edge of the property. The purple, star-like shape holds a simple beauty that makes me want to steal a piece and transplant it for my collection back home.

Maybe next week I'll work up the nerve.

As I turn back to the door, a flash of yellow catches my eye. Abandoning my position by the door, I creep closer to the row of flowers, trying to pinpoint the location of the anomaly. It takes me a few minutes to find it, the tip of a yellow cloth sticking out from a pile of stones hidden beneath the mass of green leaves.

Heart pounding with excitement, I carefully extract the thin piece of material, watching it unfold in front of me.

Happiness is not by chance but by choice.

My excitement starts to fade as I read the sunshine tissue, the familiar black script screaming at me from the bright material. Someone must have lost it on their way out.

I hold the tissue up to the sky, comparing the bright rays to the artificial colouring of my therapist's signature tissues. I squint against the sun, trying to pinpoint exactly what drew the tissue's inspiration when I see it.

The black text bleeding through.

Bringing the tissue back down to eye-level, I peer at the material, but the black text is nowhere to be found. I frown, flipping the material over and let out a gasp of surprise.

But what if that choice doesn't belong to you?

The handwriting is so beautiful, it takes me a moment to look past the calligraphy and actually read the words.

"Lacey! Are you there?"

Karen's voice rings out from the doorway, jolting me from my thoughts. Snagging a pen from my bag, I quickly scribble a response before tucking the tissue back where I found it.

"Coming!" Giving the yellow material one last glance, I feel excitement seep into my body as I follow Karen inside the building.

My therapist gives me a warm smile, her floral dress swishing around her ankles as she leads me to the living room where we conduct these sessions.

"You seem to be in a cheerful mood today, Lacey. Any exciting news?"

I smile, settling myself down on the beige couch just like I do every week.

"This may sound silly, but I think I found myself a new friend."

Karen grabs her notepad from the table, giving me an understanding look, "That is far from silly, my dear. Where did you meet this friend?"

"Well, I haven't actually met her yet, but I have a feeling we are going to be the best of friends."

"Oh." Karen blinks, confusion crossing her face before a warm smile takes its place, "In that case, I wish you all the best with this friendship. Now, tell me how you've been feeling since the last time I saw you."

Normally, this is the part that brings me down. The mundane routine of working through my every thought, dream, and aspiration so Karen can have a look into my psyche. But today, I answer her questions happily because an abnormal thought races through my mind.

Someone else might understand what it's like to be the broken girl.

Skylar

The tissue isn't how I left it.

The perfectly folded corners stick out like a sore thumb from the pinched space between the rocks, a place I started leaving my thoughts on tissues just for the hell of it.

It started as a joke. A way to speak my mind without the fear that my brother's reputation might tarnish it. But somewhere along the way it became my solace. A safe space for me to give voice to the dark thoughts bouncing inside my head.

Each week I leave a question to Karen's tissues and each week I replace it with a new one.

Except for today.

Unfolding the yellow material, hastily scrawled letters scream back at me, the dainty scripture making me think it's from a girl.

Then maybe it's time to make the choice your own again.

I tilt my head, studying the words. I've never considered the possibility that someone might read my thoughts.

Let alone respond to them.

Pulling out the pen clipped to my sketch book, I copy the last two lines of our conversation onto the newest tissue, adding a new line beneath.

Who took the choice from you?

I fold up the note, placing it back between the rocks just as a small figure comes walking up the trail. The girl stops to look at me, the defiance in her posture identical to that of her older brother.

"Vin." Stella gives me a stiff nod, the connotation of my last name echoing loud and clear, "Nice day for therapy, hey?"

There's a challenge in her voice, an unspoken rivalry that descends from our universities to our respective siblings, both of them well-known in the lacrosse circuit.

She's the younger sister of Taber's champion.

I'm the younger brother of Silverwood's bully.

Pulling up the hood of my Sabers hoodie, I give her a shrug, "Something like that."

Her stare burns into my back as I turn to leave, shoving my hands deep into the pockets of my sweater with the mystery girl's message clutched tightly in my hand.

Acknowledgements

If Stella and Cody were my easiest couple to write, Nico and Mo were my toughest. These two characters fought me every step of the writing process, detouring from every plan I made and creating their own story. There were a few moments when I didn't think we would make it to the end – Maurice, Nico, and my sanity – but here we are, at the finish line and somewhat intact.

I am so grateful for the support system I have around me, and this book was no different. I will do my best to include everyone, but if I miss your name, you have my apologies.

Mom – thank you for picking up on the breadcrumbs in my debut and nearly giving me a heart attack when you secretly read my book and casually dropped "so does Nico recognize Mo from the gay club" in a conversation. I hope this one was worth the wait. Love you.

Dad – thank you for reading your first romance novel as my debut. If you managed to make it through the second book and this one, we should probably both go to therapy. Love you.

Mara – the girl who has been with me since I said I wanted to write a book back in the hot tub after our conditioning swim. I asked you to hold me accountable through email updates and you have gone above and beyond for over a year now. Thank you for everything.

Gen – thank you for helping me celebrate this milestone with a late-night trip to Marble Slab. It was the first time I've celebrated a completed manuscript and you helped to make it a night I'll never forget. Thank you.

Katie – You not only binged my debut novel in two days, but you also read my second one in a matter of hours. I'm still salty about the auto deposit situation, but I truly appreciate the enthusiasm and support. Thank you.

Angel – I don't know where to begin. Thank you for being my biggest fan, the never-ending enthusiasm and support, and for ranking as one of my top favourite people to catch-up with. You've helped me believe writing is something I should continue to pursue, and that is something I will be forever grateful for. Thank you.

Christine – You promote my books every chance you get and always make sure to tell me your favourite moments of the book (re: talking about the IBTA's bathroom scene on the plane ride of the trip we don't talk about). Thank you for being a tremendous friend and for always choosing laughter over tears whenever we are together.

Grace – Thank you for letting my books turn you into a reader and an expressive one at that. Your enthusiasm and excitement about my books are some of my favourite parts about writing.

Taylor – You bought my debut as a Christmas gift for your friends and read my second book in the freaking Bahamas. Thank you for the unbelievable support and companionship these last few years. Cheers to figuring out our lives post graduation.

Elizabeth – The girl who is never on her phone until I send you a ridiculous message about completing another manuscript. You were the first person to send the celebration text for my debut and my series finale, and that felt pretty perfect. Thank you for always picking up your phone when it counts.

Granny – You send your love and support through text messages, bitmojis, pocket pals, and special tokens throughout the year. Love you to the moon and back.

Grandma W – You take my books around the world with you and I absolutely adore seeing the photos you send. My words are officially more well-traveled than I am and it is my favourite thing ever. Love you.

A huge thank you goes to the bookstagram community and the loyal followers who send me messages and tag me in reviews. Your enthusiasm and support has meant the world, and I will be forever grateful that you decided to take a chance on an indie author. Thank you with every piece of my heart.

To anyone who picked up this book and made it to the end. I hope Nico and Mo's story offered the escape you were looking for.

And lastly, celebrity shoutout to Sarah J. Mass who gave me a new obsession with ACOMAF. Thank you for creating the most delightful high lord.